Praise for

baby, you're a rich man

"From the first page, Christopher Bundy's *Baby, You're A Rich Man* drew me seductively into its world and never let go. This engrossing novel is filled with the spark of adventure and a hero whose relatable pains are rendered with striking originality. Mark your calendars, make room on your bookshelf: *Baby, You're A Rich Man* is worth your time."

—Laura van den Berg, author of *What the World Will Look Like When All the Water Leaves Us*

"*Baby, You're a Rich Man* is part picaresque, part noir, part tale of a (not so) innocent abroad, part send-up of the ridiculousness of made-for-TV consumer culture. Kent Richman's fall and rise and fall and rise is as weird and unlikely as his childhood infamy and his adult fame, and Christopher Bundy's masterstroke is to make of that weirdness a heartfelt novel for the new century, a novel in which everything and anything is possible: love, loss, and maybe even redemption.

—Josh Russell, author of *A True History of the Captivation, Transport to Strange Lands, & Deliverance of Hannah Gutentag*

baby, you're a rich man

a novel

christopher bundy

with illustrations by max currie

baby, you're
a rich man

a novel

christopher bundy

with illustrations by max currie

ISBN 10: 1-936196-09-3
ISBN 13: 978-1-936196-09-8
LCCN: 2001012345

Illustrations by Max Currie

C&R Press
812 Westwood Ave.
Suite D
Chattanooga, TN 37405

www.crpress.org

For Dad

But heh I'm big in Japan I'm big in Japan I'm big in Japan
Heh ho they love the way I do it
Heh ho there's really nothing to it
—Tom Waits

PART ONE

THERE'S REALLY NOTHING TO IT

From *Star-Gazer.com*

RI-CHU-MAN-SAN! BACK IN JAPAN: LIVING IN CAPSULE HOTEL

An intrepid *Star-Gazer.com* iCU reporter captured John Lennon look-a-like Kent Richman, also known as *RI-CHU-MAN-SAN!* and formerly of the Tokyo-produced game show *The Strange Bonanza*, inside a bar—in the country! Looking good, *RI-CHU-MAN-SAN!*

Following the fallout of a love triangle turned vicious, Kent Richman vanished from the celebrity spotlight. iCU reports from *Star-Gazer* global correspondents placed the American playboy at various times in Katmandu, Singapore, and on an island in the Gulf of Thailand. Recent reports, confirmed by the photo above, reveal that *RI-CHU-MAN-SAN!* has returned to Japan. Alone—sans Kumi. Boo-hoo, *RI-CHU-MAN-SAN!*

Will *RI-CHU-MAN-SAN!* return to television? Will he once again fill his seat on the front row of *The Strange Bonanza?* A former co-star of Richman's, who preferred not to give his name, tells *Star-Gazer* he saw Richman in a bar with an unidentified woman. According to the former co-star, the couple appeared "pretty cozy, like newlyweds." When the former co-star attempted to speak with Richman, he was snubbed. Richman left the bar with the woman. "She was dressed like a hostess. But I didn't care. I just wanted to find out how he was doing, you know, ask about Kumi. He acted like we never knew each other."

And that brings up the questions all of our readers want to know: Has the ill fated pair finally gone their separate ways? Could Kumi ultimately not forgive Kent for cheating on her? Will the Ozman Incident haunt the pair forever? And has Kumi finally found someone to treat her right?

And—what really happened in the Crystal Palace Condominiums on September 15th? If you know or know someone who knows, send us an email. Even better, send us a photo or a video. This story is not done yet.

Look for more iCU reports here from our global correspondents as we pursue the truth behind former TV personality *RI-CHU-MAN-SAN!*'s return to Tokyo.

To send your iCU reports visit: www.Star-Gazer.com/iCU.html and click on the iCU! link.

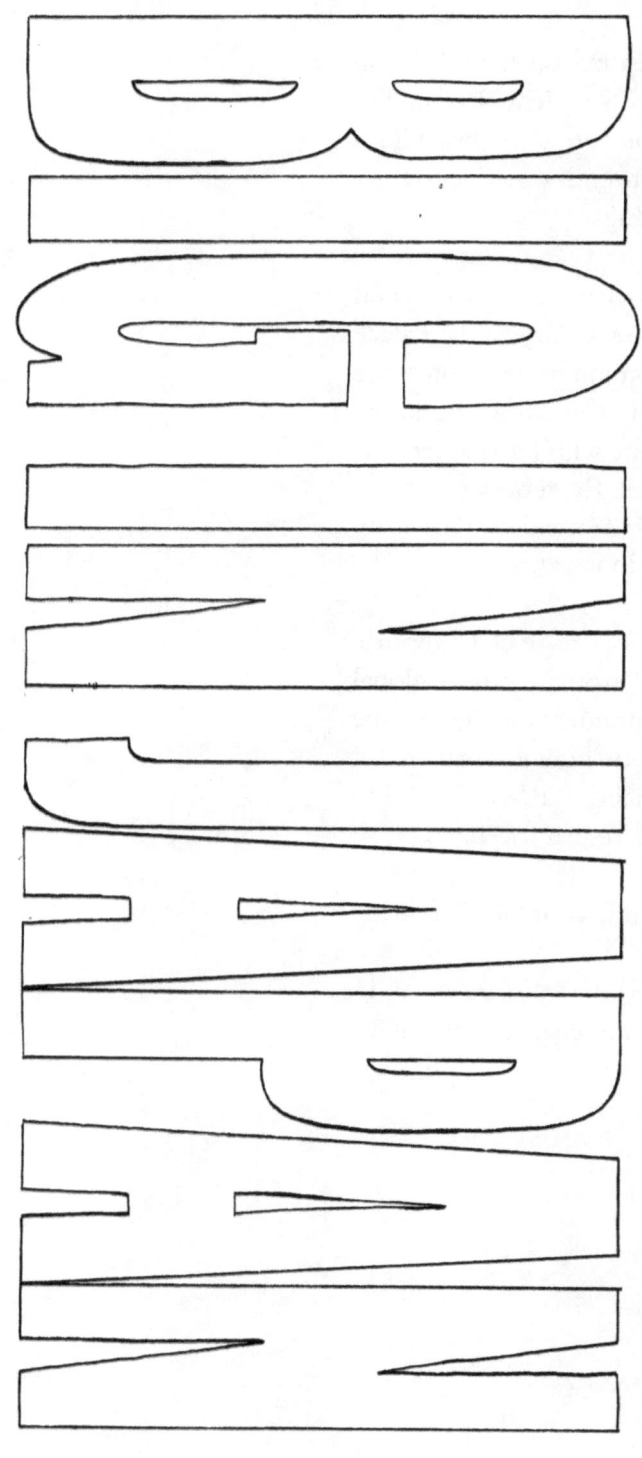

CHAPTER ONE

—

BIG IN JAPAN

The sign out front read *Making the Best of a Small Space,* which Kent had done for almost three months. His narrow capsule offered just enough headroom for a six-footer to sit up and read when he felt like it, though he hardly did anything but watch the television built into the ceiling and sleep when he was inside. He could never fully unfold his legs. What few possessions he owned were stored in a hockey bag in one of the lockers on the first floor. The walk-in closet in his Shibuya apartment had been bigger than the combined spaces Kent now occupied, full of blue, gray, brown and black, where just looking at the suits had left him high, a soft carpet underneath, the smell of clothes: new and pressed. Halogen lights shone upon polished leather, black and brown shoes on and on along a rack running the length of the closet. Some three dozen shirts waited in rotation, a variety of colors, each wrapped in clear plastic. Pants followed in shades of dark and light next to silk ties, colorful emblems of his success. Kent would lie on the carpeted floor to gaze up at the parallel rows of suits—he enjoyed dressing in the fine fabrics of successful men so much that he'd reluctantly shed the second skin each day. Then Kumi, his wife, ex-wife—he still wasn't sure, there was no divorce—had sold or given away almost everything he owned before leaving him.

And when she left him, Kent escaped to Thailand for his great getting away. He kept the smoking jacket Kumi gave him their first Christmas together, now worse for wear, Kumi's Saint Christopher medallion, and a tattered copy of Salman Rushdie's *Midnight's Children*, a book he'd been trying to finish for years because he said it was his favorite novel when a reporter from *Tokyo Journal* interviewed him for a piece called "The Next Kent"—he thought it sounded smart. Kent also had mementos from the hit television variety show that had once called him a "major talent," *The Strange Bonanza*: his dressing room star, a bottle of *Kent! The Cologne for Rich Men*, and a bottle of limited edition *Kame no O sake* from Wataribun given to him by Beat Takeshi. And there was the urn he'd been lugging around for over five years.

When he was deported from Thailand for an expired visa and proximity to a dead body, Kent returned to Japan—where else would he go? But his career was in tatters. He picked up occasional print ad work, mostly for English cram schools, and voiceover work for a video game company, and even handed out cologne samples (not *Kent!*) in a Takashimaya department store. But the Japanese gave him a wide eye and a wide berth every time, certain they recognized him but not sure why. And nobody would give him an acting gig. *Dasai*, they said, he was uncool now. People who used to send Kent swag bags and VIP memberships just so he might consider their project, product, or club pulled a curtain over those days. Returning to the States was never an option, not after what he'd done. There was little for him there anyway.

baby, you're a rich man

Kent's agent, Renzo Royama, told him he was putting the word out that Mr. Big in Japan, Kent Richman, was back in town, that he might have a gig for him, a show in development. Renzo had left an urgent message with the Capsule Inn—Kent could no longer afford a cell phone—to meet him at a Koenji hostess bar for lunch, which Kent suspected would involve no food.

I am the earth, the sea, the sky—I am the universe. On the train to see Renzo, Kent recited the mantra that had helped him survive being big in Japan, being the hot, number one *RI-CHU-MAN-SAN!* on the top-rated primetime game show *The Strange Bonanza.* Shaggy brown hair with blond highlights. Gucci shoes and Omega watch. Cristall vodka and Filipino hash. Bali tan and Hong Kong massage. The candid nightspot photo in *Tokyo Journal,* a mention in the *Daily Yomiuri,* and a stock headshot on TV Tokyo. The paying but quietly welcomed VIP at The Plum Room, one of the many but finer hostess clubs in Ginza where he was not quite among politicians and yakuza chieftains, but more likely a local construction boss and a writer popular with young people. The face of Lark cigarettes, *PECKUP!* Energy Drink, and Sankyou Instant Ramen. Some-time husband to part-time magazine model and full-time tweeker Kumiko Sato. The glimmering *gaijin* who spoke fluent Japanese and had the face of a young John Lennon. Before Monique, before Ozman.

CHAPTER TWO

—

RENZO HAS A PLAN

"*Ii desu yo*," Renzo said. "I'm optimistic." A hostess in black miniskirt poured whiskey into his glass and then lit his cigarette. "Lie low, let me handle it. Some of these producers are skittish of a *gaijin*, especially one with your reputation."

"I was a moneymaker. I take a little break—and who wouldn't, after what happened—and they act like Kent Richman never existed, that Kent and Kumi were never voted favorite celebrity couple, that Kent Richman couldn't sell cigarettes and whiskey and any damn thing they wanted like nobody's business. Just get me something. I don't care what."

"Patience. I have a plan," Renzo said.

Renzo wore dark glasses indoors, and Kent could never tell if his agent was lying to him or not. "What's all this urgency then? You said it couldn't wait?"

"Oh, I suppose you have time to waste now? Blink and this country will forget you forever. Still, we have to let the stink wear off a bit more before we go charging in and asking for lead roles. It hasn't been that long since you dropped everything and split."

Kent was reminded that he'd done the same thing when he came to Japan the first time, dropped everything

11

at home and run, leaving what was left of his family in America—"left us," his mother reminded him when two years earlier he'd called to tell her he was getting married, that he was a celebrity in Japan. Divorced now, his parents were more alien than ever. His mother described his father's adventures traveling from park to park in a colossal RV with his new wife, evenings spent staring up at the sky through a telescope.

"Your father think's he's a writer now, published some silly book called *Quantum Suicide*, all about life beyond earth and his own brand of quantum mechanics. Seems he talks with the dead, claims to have even spoken with your brother." The book encouraged people to find their alternate solar system, commit suicide, and prepare for a new life there.

His mother was remarried, too, after giving up a lifetime of religious pursuit—finally jumping ship after Catholicism—and setting up residence in a South Florida nudist colony with her new husband, a student of massage therapy. Kent hadn't spoken with either of his parents since he called from Tokyo in a panic not long after Kumi left. His mother answered, woken early morning, Florida time; it took her a moment to realize her only surviving son was on the other end.

"Kent? How did you find me? Where are you?" she said.

"The internet—what's 'Liberty Lake?'" Kent asked.

"It's where I live. Don't you find it odd that you don't know where your own moth—"

"Yes, I do—but not for the same reasons you do." Kent heard her light a cigarette, inhale, exhale.

She spoke in whispers to her new husband—"It's all right." Then to him, "Where are you?"

"Japan." His voice was barely stilled by alcohol, cigarettes kept his hands from shaking. "But I think I need to come home."

His mother answered with surprising calm. "Come home where, Kent? Nothing's like you left it. Never really has been, not since your brother died." Kent had expected anger, recriminations, and another speech about how he abandoned her after the divorce, when she needed him most. About Allan, about the urn Kent took from her mantle. But she was all business. "I don't know what you expected." But Kent heard the tremor behind the calm, the uncontrollable voice that flew from her like the pots and pans she'd thrown at him once for reminding her that Allan was dead.

"I don't know, either. Just things aren't so good right now," he said.

"What have you done?"

Where would he start? "It's complicated."

"I have no doubt." She exhaled noisily, as much a sigh. "Life's funny that way. Have you talked to your father?"

"No."

"There's a complicated one for you."

"Is he all right?"

"As far as I know—as far as any one of you tells me anything." This triggered something, seemed to remind her that she was still angry at her one-time family. "So what is it, Kent? It's three in the morning and you call, Roger's still asleep, he's got an early tee time. What do you want?"

Come home, it's all right? You're forgiven. You were seven and it was an accident, no one would ever blame you, especially your own mother who's always loved you.

"I'm sorry. I just wanted to say hello. If you hear from Dad, tell him hi for me," he said and hung up.

"And, remember—" Renzo snapped his fingers in Kent's face. "—hey, hey, *hora!* Listen to me, you left on your own. I had things going on when you split. What happened with Ozman was bad, yes—*choberiba*, but he put you in the papers, man. You were notorious. You can't buy that shit. Can't act your way in to that shit. Can't get a degree in that sh—"

Kent slammed a hand over Renzo's yawning hole. "*Wakatta yo.*" He knew notorious. He'd grown up notorious.

Renzo wrenched Kent's hand from his face. "I had good stuff in the works for you, *ne.* Before you left, that business with Ozman actually helped you—" Renzo chain smoked, tap-tapping the end of his cigarette against the side of his ashtray between drags. "Of course you needed a break, but this business has a short memory. Just do me a favor, stay out of trouble. Get a haircut and shave off that ridiculous beard—you look like a freakin' wookie."

His hair had grown to his shoulders and his patchy beard was the most he'd ever been able to grow. "I'm broke. I'm a month behind on my rent." Kent had pawned the last of his prized CD collection for food money and ten grams of *shabu,* methamphetamines that would carry him through until the weekend then three days of bottomless sleep. Years of an astronomical income and a weakness for buying stuff were reflected in his collection, nearly two thousand CDs stacked in boxes before he began to sell them in stacks of twenty and thirty. But he'd resisted smoking before meeting Renzo. One: Renzo would know. Two: he hoped for good news and wanted to save some for celebration, a little surge to keep his good mood bright for at least three days. Kent wished now that he had smoked. In place of a *shabu* buzz, and thus a means of quelling hunger, all he could think of was his empty stomach. The hostess had brought only small bowls of mixed nuts, wasabi peas, and mini servings of *tsukemono*, slender slices of pickled radish. Kent had emptied each of the bowls and shook one at the hostess in the hopes of getting more. The whiskey left his hollow stomach burning.

"*Shinpai nai,*" Renzo said and blew smoke at Kent. "I got a plan. But we need to move fast."

"A job?" Kent had to shout over the tuneless karaoke from a salaryman.

Renzo patted their hostess on the bottom as she walked by. "Some more nuts, sweetie." He turned to Kent. "Something like that."

"What is it?" Perhaps he'd have reason to celebrate today.

"Some things came up. So, we need to capitalize on these *things*."

"What things?"

"First, no more Mr. Bad Example, right? Let's give them a Kent Richman they recognize, not this Chewbacca look-a-like."

"Just get me back on TV. And, can you give me a little advance?" Kent's rent was cheap for Tokyo but still ¥4000 a night.

"Advance?"

"How about royalties? Don't I have anything coming in?" Kent said.

"You won't need money where you're going," Renzo said.

"Sounds like I'm going to rehab," Kent said, concerned it might be true. "Come on, you know I'm good for it. Before they kick me out of the Capsule Inn."

"Let them." Renzo pulled Kent close. "You're leaving that salaryman shithole anyway." He waved the hostess over for a top up on their whiskeys, though Kent never got the nuts he hoped for.

"Because I am not doing another stint in—"

"You're going to like this."

A place where Kent would no longer have to climb down a short ladder to take a piss in a public bathroom at three a.m. Where he wouldn't wake to the sound of salarymen hustling in the hallway each morning. Where he'd no longer knock his head on the ceiling when he forgot, which was daily, that he lived in a one-by-one-by-two-meter pod.

"You don't mind high ceilings, aged cedar, and *tatami* mat floors do you?" Renzo's smile grew, as if he were about to drop a punchline.

"As long as I can stand up." Kent felt his day, his week, his entire month turning for the better.

"With the smoke of burning joss sticks wafting through your room. Bells tolling in the afternoon. Crickets chirping at night."

"Sounds like the country."

Renzo touched his index finger to his nose. "*Pin pon.*"

"I don't follow."

"Buddhist meditation resort." Renzo held his hands apart. "In the mountains of beautiful central Japan."

"Resort?" Kent scooted out from under Renzo's arm and slid to the end of the leather bench. "I'm not going to rehab, no matter what you call it. That last place, that seaside prison, sucked. Besides, I'm clean." Kent held his palms up as if to show Renzo he wasn't hiding a gram of *shabu* there. "Couldn't afford it even if I wanted."

"Relax, Richman. It's not rehab." Renzo put his face before Kent's. "Promise."

"I don't know. A Buddhist thing in the mountains? What about that Lennon biopic? I'm perfect for that. You ever hear more from those folks?"

Renzo's mouth set and he pulled his arm back. "It's a hold right now."

"A loan then? Just to get me through the month. I'll make it back, you know that. I'll do commercials for retail, fast food chains, whatever. Just let me stay in Tokyo. Out there is death."

"Who's my favorite *gaijin*?" His voice rose again, a voice through a megaphone. "Don't worry, Richman. You'll be licking wasabi off of young girls' titties again in no time. If not on *The Strange Bonanza*—in my humble opinion a dying show anyway—then on another program. Trust me, *ne*."

CHAPTER THREE

—

THE OZMAN INCIDENT

Kent did trust Renzo—if *RI-CHU-MAN-SAN!* did well, then Renzo did well, but he wasn't sure the Japanese wanted him back on television. His career had stalled with his extended absence and he needed to get his face back on television before the Japanese forgot him altogether. After what the press had since called *The Ozman Incident*, Kent and Kumi's new celebrity had done wonders for their careers as they became national icons of courage.

RI-CHU-MAN-SAN! & KUMI-CHAN SURVIVE
NIGHT OF TERROR
Offbeat Aussie Comic Takes Hostages, Shoots Wife

Kent and Kumi told the story of their abduction and deliverance two dozen times to television and print news across Asia, and four times to a Tokyo detective who, while skeptical, closed the case within a week as a "domestic incident." The stricken faces of the brave pair leaving their building ahead of police, Kent holding a blanket over Kumi's shoulders, were shown next to old stills of Ozman with his mouth open in a trademark howl and an unflattering passport photo of Monique, about whom little was written or spoken. She was, after all, the villain in the tragedy, according to the media, the temptress who had come between husband and wife.

She'd returned to Montreal where she faced a year of reconstructive surgery, agonizing rehabilitation, and a modeling career in as many pieces as her jaw. Despite Kent's early efforts, she never talked to him again or let him see her before returning to Canada. He'd hovered over her hospital bed as she slept one evening, whispering apologies and regret. But the two never spoke directly, and, after her return to Montreal, Kent gave up.

Kumi joined Estée Lauder as their Asian rep and cohosted her own cultural oddity program with a former sumo wrestling champion. Kent returned to *The Strange Bonanza* where the audience received him with frenzied applause. He was no longer the *gaijin* talent; he was one of them, permanently pasted into their scrapbook of tragedy. Then Kumi left. Two days before she kicked him out, Kumi stood in panties with one of his dress shirts thrown over her shoulders and stared out of their floor-to-ceiling window at traffic below.

"Do you think Ozman would've killed you, I mean if Monique hadn't shown up?" Kumi said and lit a cigarette.

"*Shiranai*. She did, so it's impossible to say, isn't it?" Kent wanted only to hold her.

"Do you think he'd have killed me, too?" She blew smoke up to the ceiling, her back to him.

"He was there to hurt me, not you," Kent said.

He was Denis Ozman, who went by "Bigu Sukai" (Big Sky) on *Airship Japan,* the new frontier for Japanese variety programming. Ozman, an Australian student of the Japanese school of shock comedy, little he wouldn't do for a laugh. Kent hated him and his act, the lit cigarettes up his nose, the samurai sword across his forearm, the stupid live snakes—Ozman was a child. Then there was the farting episode. Ozman on his back in ridiculous green leotard, legs in the air with baby powder sprinkled over his ass as he piped out the first remarkably recognizable notes of "Yesterday" into a microphone. The Japanese roared their betrayal when they laughed at Ozman's sendup of Kent's trademark song. Didn't they love Kent's "Yesterday," demand his "Yesterday"? And hadn't he given them "Yesterday," even though it was a Paul McCartney number, when they asked? The new breed of *gaijin* talent was bringing things down to a more pedestrian level.

But Ozman hadn't been in Kent and Kumi's apartment to discuss stage notes.

Comment ça va, Monique…? It was all about the stunning Quebecois. Flawless Japanese, a bachelor's in Asian studies, a master's in linguistics, a sense of when to speak and a talent for the rhythm and nuance of languages, her currency in Japan where a sense of sympathy and thus understanding could go a long way towards endearing her to the Japanese. Monique Martine, of Montreal. A real talent even if her husband was a spastic comic willing to sacrifice anything for a laugh. The Japanese loved him and probably would have loved her, too. But what had

Kent and Monique done but meet in love hotels? When Kent did remember particulars, he wasn't always sure they even belonged to Monique.

Ozman would have killed him and Kumi both, or at least hurt them badly—Kent believed that. Kumi, he suspected, needed to believe that, too, to help her understand the things Ozman had done to her, to see herself as a survivor instead of a victim.

"Because of what you did to him, he hurt me to hurt you." She let the dress shirt fall and pulled on a sweatshirt with "Wild Honey" in oversized letters printed on the back. One of the many products Kumi shilled for, this one a feminine hygiene spray. "You should watch more yakuza movies. He obviously did."

Kent stepped behind her and placed a hand on her shoulder. *"Yari naoshimashou ka?* I thought we were starting over." He wasn't sure if he ever believed a new beginning was possible, but he never stopped hoping.

"Hai, we are." She put her hand over his without turning around.

"Then make love to me. Help me help you put this behind us. Tell me that you forgive me or, at least, that it's possible. Or tell me what to do. I'm lost here. I know I screwed up, but how—?" Kent heard his mother: *what have you done now?*

She laughed and dropped her hand, stretching her arms to the sky. "You had the chance to make things right, but you didn't. After what Ozman did to me—most men would have killed him, but you're not made of such stuff."

Kumi was right, but she spoke of his inability to kill as if it were a failing rather than a virtue.

She went on, fueled, it seemed, by her own recollection of what happened. "If Monique hadn't shown up, Ozman would have killed us both. Torture was just the warmup act, *ne*. You wouldn't have been able to stop him. And he probably would have used that stupid gun of yours to do it." Kumi let go of his hand and turned to Kent. "I never understood that. A gun in Tokyo? *Nani yo*? And then you couldn't even use the thing. But, hey, Monique took the bullet for us. She's the real loser in all this. Poor Monique. No face, no career, no nothing. All she got was laid by *RI-CHU-MAN-SAN!*"

"You're right, I didn't pull the trigger." What could he say? "Ozman did."

"Don't you ever wonder how things might have turned out with a different set of circumstances? Different people, different place." Kumi stepped away from him. "Different people fucking different people."

Kent wanted to bring Kumi close to him again. He wanted to fix what he'd broken, to repent, be forgiven. Here was another rock in the pond for the Kent Richman story, another disaster on his watch. He'd come to Japan, as far a place as he could think to go, to start over. A romantic fable, nothing more. But he'd begun to doubt fresh starts were possible; here he'd come full circle. Starting over, yes, but with just what he'd tried to leave behind.

"Yeah. So? Don't you wonder if you weren't meant to do something else in our apartment that day? Maybe you were meant to kill Ozman or maybe he was meant to kill us. Do you wonder how things might have turned out different?"

"Every day," Kent said.

"I'm not Allan, you know," she said, her eyes glassy, cheeks flushed. "I'm not your brother. What happened to him was an accident, a childish game gone wrong. That's your baggage, not mine." She could no longer keep from crying, something Kent had only seen her do once, when her grandmother died. "What you did to me, that was no accident, no child's play. What happened with Ozman was no accident. You did that. And you can't unravel yourself from that mess, Kent Richman. You should've killed Ozman when you had the chance."

Kent leaned in to hold her. What she said made sense but didn't matter. The end was the same—people got hurt because of him, people he loved, accident or no. With Allan there was nothing he could do to fix what he'd done, no way to bring him back. But Kumi was there in front of him, alive. He held his arms open; she leaned in, letting him hold her and leaving him hopeful.

She whispered in his ear, "I found the video, Kent, the one of you and Monique in our bed."

Kent knew the video, the one that had set his fall in motion; it had gone viral for months after someone— he'd always thought it was Ozman—sent it to the online celebrity rag *Star-Gazer*. Before he met Kumi, Kent might have seen the sex tape as a career milestone. It was a milestone, of course, and briefly lifted his career, but not one he welcomed.

Then she was gone.

And, as if a wave of nausea swept over Tokyo soundstages, leaving him deaf and dumb behind his studio console, unable to understand what he was expected to do there, Kent could no longer perform. Where Tokyo had once been an open playground the city felt claustrophobic. He couldn't escape his own celebrity, fame built on scandal. Wherever he went he walked in Ozman's shadow. No script could revive his smiles, no icy methamphetamine concoction could prop up his spirits or make him believe again in what he did for a living.

Now he wanted it all back.

THE NEW
KENT RICHMAN

CHAPTER FOUR

—

THE NEW KENT RICHMAN

"A monastery? *Honto*?" Kent imagined himself in a cloth diaper curled up in a solitary cell, no booze, no drugs, no women, nothing.

Renzo smiled and finished his whiskey. "It's not a monastery. It's a resort or a retreat or a temple, whatever the hell they call it. Buddhist temples all over Japan are set up to accommodate guests. Helps them stay solvent. You're going to love it. This is what celebrities do now."

Kent recalled a trip to the Noto Peninsula on Japan's western coast with Kumi a few months after they had married. They stayed in a temple by the sea, sleeping on futons, eating traditional Japanese breakfasts of cold eggs, *sunomono*, and miso soup. It was winter, but they rose early each day and walked the empty beach, ate quiet lunches in the small fishing village, and took long soaks in the mineral baths. Their stars had just begun to rise and the time away from Tokyo was a welcome respite, a moment when their relationship had been about nothing but being together, before *shabu*. Kumi had chosen the place because she was there as a child with her father and brother, a time she rarely spoke of, much as Kent spoke little of his childhood, that time marked by the singular event of his brother's death.

"It's supposed to help chill you out. Up in the mountains, nice and quiet. Very chic. I'm telling you: all the biggest stars go to places like this to meditate, get centered, all that horseshit."

The hostess held the whiskey bottle before Kent, his last one inexplicably vanishing. He swore he hadn't touched the drink but there his empty glass sat. Renzo touched the hostess's arm, and she smiled. Kent returned her smile and held up the empty bowl of wasabi peas. "More nuts, anything, *kudasai*?" She took the bowl and bowed.

"Quit worrying about the damn nuts. There's more," Renzo said. "I've got some people who want to make a documentary, about you."

Kent liked the sound of it. Serious subjects were chosen for documentaries. "Documentaries are cool." Kent couldn't remember the last one he'd seen, but he liked the idea of telling his own story, his way.

"Exactly. So we get you up in the mountains, *hayaku*—don't screw around. You leave in two days. Get you all Zen-ed out and let them record it all. The public sees Kent Richman getting his shit together, show those studio assholes you're back in business. You can even tour the film festival circuit with them when it debuts. Put you in front of critics and fans."

"Sounds like serious cinema."

"Sounds like free publicity. If you play this right. *Gaman shiro*."

The idea of solitude and simplicity was appealing. Kent thought of his short time on Ko Chang in the Gulf of Thailand and what it was supposed to have been, his first attempt at a fresh start, at getting away from it all. After *The Ozman Incident*, and the flash of his rehabilitated celebrity, Kent tossed out his pancake makeup and sailed for open waters. He purged his life of the clutter and vice that had exhausted and nearly killed him to live a simple, clean life. But paradise hadn't been. Instead, he was asked to leave his bamboo hut, a sanctuary of sun and sand and an instance of timelessness where he believed he could erase the smear of what had happened in Japan.

"I don't have to be dry all the time, do I?" Kent put his glass to his lips but returned it to the table without taking a sip. "I mean, it's not like I can't go without, but if I don't have—"

"*Ii desu yo, ne.* They're Buddhists. Take a little something to keep you steady but remember what you're there for. Do *not* screw this up."

"Give me some credit."

"Just follow my lead, keep it simple, and stay away from the press for now. We do this on our terms."

"Simple, right. No press."

"Take the train to Azuma-mura, a little town in Gunma-ken, about two hours northwest. You'll meet a representative from Cedars who'll drive you to the mountains. I'll put you up, cover your expenses. Everything's arranged." Renzo handed Kent a manila folder. "I had Maki type it all up for you. Talk to these, what do you call them, documentarians, and when you get back to Tokyo, you'll be ready for prime time." Renzo raised his whiskey glass. Kent did the same and tried to be optimistic, but couldn't forget the chilly reception he'd received upon his return to Tokyo. He found only remnants of his former life, of his alter ego. *RI-CHU-MAN-SAN!* was forgotten. Other *gaijin* talent had taken his place. The city that once embraced Kent Richman with such affection would hardly grant him an audition now.

Renzo waved the hostess over for a refill. "Fill them to the top, sweetheart." He turned to Kent. "There's one more thing." He raised his glass and seemed to have forgotten what he wanted to say. He cleared his throat, then spoke. "Ozman's escaped from Fuchu. And it looks like he's coming for you." He touched his glass to Kent's before Kent could respond and cheered, "*Kanpai!* To the New Kent Richman!"

From *Star-Gazer.com*

BRRRR!
SHOCK COMIC & INMATE
DENIS OZMAN VANISHES
FROM PRISON CELL, TURNS UP
IN KITCHEN REFRIGERATOR,
THEN ESCAPES!

Is our favorite bad boy up to his usual shenanigans? Reports from inside Fuchu Prison, Tokyo, offer a glimpse of Japan's most notorious penitentiary and how Australian madman Denis Ozman has adapted to life on the inside, by *escaping*!

Sentenced to fifteen years forced labor for his revenge assault on wife Monique Martine and her lover Kent Richman, aka *RI-CHU-MAN-SAN!*, Ozman had reportedly adapted well to life in Japan's top-security prison, what he reportedly calls "Fuck-You Prison."

Insider reports describe the shock comic as spending his days smoothing out aluminum cupcake doilies, standard labor for inmates. One iCU reporter, who prefers to remain anonymous for fear his fellow inmates will turn on him for revealing secrets of inside life—secrets guarded by inmates and guards alike—reported that "Ozman is one tough guy. Even with his initial solitary confinement, he acted as if he was on holiday. He has impressed the guards with his tricks, illusions, whatever you call them, and quickly established himself as a prison leader. He's a pretty cool fellow and a good friend to have on the inside."

Cool is right! According to unconfirmed reports, Ozman once disappeared from his cell and was thought to have escaped. However, when the shock comic turned up inside a locked refrigerator in the kitchen where he is stationed, he was given a month of solitary. Reports suggest that guards, so impressed with his stunt, smuggled chocolate, magazines, and an iPod into his solitary cell.

One inmate suggested that a foreigner like Ozman would have quickly been labeled a troublemaker, but the resourceful comic was instead praised for his superior marching skills, humor, and endurance during forced labor drives.

But Mr. Brain Salad Surgery himself didn't turn up in the fridge this time. Oh no. He has apparently disappeared for good. Japanese authorities are mum on exactly what happened and will not confirm his escape, citing special investigative procedures. But we have it on even better authority—YOU!, our trusty iCU reporters inside Fuchu Prison—that Denis Ozman has not been seen inside his cell for three days. Is it just more solitary confinement, or has our mad Aussie actually pulled a Houdini from Fuchu?

All we can say is: Watch Your Back *RI-CHU-MAN-SAN!*

Are you a future iCU Reporter?

If you have photographs you would like to share with *Star-Gazer.com,* visit:

www.Star-Gazer.com/iCU.html and click on the iCU! link.

CHAPTER FIVE

—

MIDORI

Will the *Real* Kent Richman Please Stand Up!
A woman he didn't know positioned herself beside him at the bar and spoke a name he had grown to loathe, much as he also longed to hear it. "*RI-CHU-MAN-SAN! desu ka?*"

The scent of her perfume coated his tongue like a varnish. Kent would taste it for the rest of the night as it mixed with his drink, his smoke. Even the roasted wasabi peas on the bar lost their sting to the woman's fragrance. He refused to acknowledge her, but was pleased that even in small-town Japan people knew *RI-CHU-MAN-SAN!* He'd made it to Azuma by train, per Renzo's instructions, glad to have something to do, glad to be out of Tokyo, Ozman's most likely destination. He grew weary of looking over his shoulder every five minutes, wondering if Ozman were tracking him, ready to plant another firecracker between his lips. The thought of a couple of weeks in the mountains gave him hope, but his body told another story, so much so that his bones actually ached and his head hurt, lights popping before his eyes when he stood too fast. A local express, not even the speedier and more expensive *shinkansen,* brought him two hours west, his hockey bag at his feet. Renzo booked him in the Terminal Hotel next to the station, its name alone leaving Kent suspicious. Would a gray, unremarkable hotel on an rail line to nowhere be his last stop? Too restless to stay in his room, Kent found the small Club Tamarindo only a block away.

"*So desu ne.* Your hair's longer and you have the beardy thing, but I thought so," she said, this she of a thousand shes, the sea of shes that had once advanced on Kent in restaurants, bars, elevators, department stores, hotels, trains, planes, and even club restrooms. She sat on the bar stool next to him. "Though, you don't really look like John Lennon at all, not like on TV."

But Kent *was* a dead ringer for a young John Lennon. He knew that. He'd been told so most of his adult life. His resemblance made him a star. Before Ozman, Kent represented a Japanese coffee house chain the real John Lennon had visited. He broadcast for a Tokyo network from the opening of the John Lennon Museum in the Saitama Super Arena. He manufactured a Liverpool accent that was more Scottish than English. He met Yoko Ono, an experience Kent found unsettling when she whispered to him, "Fortunately, you look like John. Unfortunately, you are not."

She was unremarkable save for layers of makeup over an acne scarred face and an amateurish attempt to dress Tokyo. The Japanese were fond of the expression: the nail that sticks up gets hammered down. Kent guessed this woman had been hammered back into place a few times. Her eyes were shadowed in amber, eyelids brushed with glitter. Her lips painted chocolate. Her hair straight and long, frosted with streaks of vanilla and brown, the tips rust colored. Platform shoes lifted her to five feet seven inches. She smoked menthols, lipstick staining the filter, a light chocolate frosting passed from mouth to cigarette and glass. The cigarette never left her fingers, a sixth digit on her hand, practiced at remaining in flight as she smoothed her hair down or dabbed at her mouth. She held her drink with the same hand, inhaling between sips of her Calpis and vodka, tapping her ashes to the floor. When she talked, she looked over Kent's shoulder but never at him, as if ready for someone more promising to turn up.

"Did. I don't do TV anymore." He studied his drink, this moment of déjà vu, wishing he could drain the bottle. He colored his answer to imply more than the truth: that, yes, he no longer did TV, that inferior medium, but was engaged with more artistic endeavors, but didn't think the young woman understood him, though his Japanese was fluent. Even here in the countryside, one hundred and fifty kilometers from Tokyo, he couldn't escape the errant signal of his past. Still, a flutter beat in his chest with the sound of the woman's voice.

"Isn't that you?" She pointed to a muted television above the bar that aired an old clip from *The Strange Bonanza*. Kent Richman had been one of the most popular *gaijin* talents since the "two Kents": Kent Gilbert and Kent Derricott. This could have been any episode in the two years he'd been a regular on the program. The Real Kent Richman looked to see if others in the bar were watching, but only the unremarkable woman in chocolate tones beside him had noticed. The scene froze just as TV Kent looked into the camera, mouth gaping, eyes half open, narrowed as if giving the camera, the audience, all of Japan the stink eye. *Kanji* were stamped dramatically above his frozen head to the sounds of gunshots: *Where—is—he—now?* Good question, Kent conceded.

"Have you left 'the business'?" The unremarkable woman said "the business" as if she too were in *the business*, and spoke in some celebrity code.

Kent couldn't keep his eyes from the television, despite the ridicule. Better days there. When he'd been a star. "What do you mean 'left'?"

"Their question, on the TV: 'Where is he now?'" she said.

"What do they care?" Kent knew he sounded bitter but couldn't help it. He was tired of being a punching bag for the celebrity gossip biz.

"Are you hiding out? I heard about Ozman." She winked. "I promise I won't tell."

As if timed to answer for him, an image from Kent's last Tokyo gig popped up next to his disembodied head: a subway poster for a second-rate English language school franchise. *You still stink of Ozman*, Renzo had told him when rationalizing why he couldn't get better gigs. Kent rubbed at two neat, round scars on either side of his right forearm—each pink blemish the size of a shirt button. They seemed to throb and swell with the thought of Ozman. The television image was replaced with a pixelated photograph of Kent leaving a convenience store in a baseball cap, a full-length raincoat over gray sweats, and cheap plastic slippers, as if he'd accidentally walked out in his bathroom shoes. His hair was already longer and his beard growing out. The angle suggested he was leaving the store cautiously, as if trying to hide what he was doing. Another photograph emphasized his hollow cheeks, while another showed him putting a bottle to his mouth.

As the show's host prepared to segue into a commercial, they reran another clip of *The Strange Bonanza*. A rail-thin goof in enormous black glasses screamed, *RI-CHU-MAN-SAN!* as Kent's trademark loop played: a hip-hop mash-up highlighted with beatboxing and a chorus of soulful women singing: *Baby, you're a rich man!* Kent didn't remember just when he'd abandoned any sense of control over his career, but he guessed it might've been when that loop was created. TV Kent dropped his head, his Lennon glasses perched at the end of his narrow Roman nose, and smiled. The audience clapped and cheered on cue. *Hello, Ty-foo. You're looking sexy tonight,* TV Kent said.

"Oh, Ty-foo. *Suki yo*." The woman sitting next to him clapped her hands quickly, lightly, like hummingbird wings. "What's he like?"

Hey, hey, RI-CHU-MAN-SAN, you want me, you want me, you want, you want, you want me! Ty-foo sang on the television, one hand holding a microphone, the other running over his chest and crotch. Ty-foo screamed or sang just about everything. The audience laughed on cue. TV Kent yanked his glasses off, smirked, and said *A-re?*, a trademark gesture and tagline that had made him popular with audiences. Kent had said the line once, a comical rendering of *What the—?*, and when the audience laughed without a cue, he was encouraged to throw the line out whnever he could. Within six episodes, the line and the accompanying gesture had become his for an easy laugh. TV Kent had stylishly messy hair, a pale complexion and a bony face, dark folds under his eyes. The Real Kent guessed the episode was near the end of his career. He also guessed that behind TV Kent's smile were a clenched jaw and receding gums, a vinegary odor and teeth rocking in their roots like trees shaken in loose soil. Symptoms of the inevitable physical decline that came with smoking *shabu*. He'd stopped watching his own television appearances long before. Kent wished now he'd seen himself on television like that, wasting away for his art in public. Maybe the shock of his appearance would've sobered him into fixing his troubled life. If he guessed right about the time, Kent recalled he was probably paid about ¥200,000 for his appearance that evening, which he likely blew in a night on smoke and drink and dining out.

"Pretty much what you see is what you get with him." Kent turned from the television and stood, prepared to leave the bar. As much as he wanted to he couldn't encourage the woman. This was supposed to be his getting away, again. But even what should've been an uneventful train ride had been fraught with unpleasant reminders of his past. Halfway to Azuma, a big-haired Japcore wannabe in tight black pants and red cowboy boots unintentionally kicked Kent's bag as he passed in the aisle. Kent bent to check Allan's urn when he saw the stain growing along the bottom of his bag. Then he smelled it. The *Kent!* scent was too much in the crowded train car. Other passengers opened windows, held handkerchiefs over their mouths and noses. The woman sleeping next to him woke with a gasp, knocking her head against the window. She sniffed, looked at the tall American, his bag, then stood, covering her mouth with hand. An old woman scolded him for his disrespect. Another waddled on at Omiya Station, wrinkled her nose, and stopped in front of him. Already short, her bent posture put her face squarely in front of Kent's. She smiled a leathery smile, eyes twinkling, and leaned in close. She held a plastic bag before him. "*Umeboshi ikaga desu ka?*" Kent took a pickled plum, thanked her, and ate the sour fruit with a smile.

Kent still smelled the cologne—everything he owned soaked in it, like oranges drenched in rubbing alcohol. His recollection of the scent had been different. But then he remembered the review in *Perfumer and Flavorist Magazine*. "With hints of vanilla and mandarin, this celebrity inspired scent might as well be a cheap flavored vodka. God forbid you take it straight."

Kent sat again on the barstool, looked at the bartender, and pointed to the television. "Do you mind if we watch something else?" Kent wasn't ashamed—he'd worked hard to carve out a role, to find a personality that appealed to the Japanese. But the reminder was too much. The Japanese-Brazilian bartender switched the channel.

"*Watashi wa Midori desu.*" The woman held out her hand, which Kent took. "*RI-CHU-MAN-SAN!* here in Azuma. Wow. Don't worry—I won't tell anyone you're here. It's just that I've never met anyone famous before. Nobody comes here for anything, unless it's to work in the adult video plant." She seemed determined to stick it out with him. There'd be nothing unique about this exchange. She'd ask the same questions about Kumi, about what had happened with Ozman, about where Kent had been for the past year. The questions themselves were indicative of his new life, each concerned only with his past. Kent wished she'd tell someone he *was* here, let the rest of Japan know he still existed. He could make his little trip to the mountains look like the planned refuge from celebrity life Renzo had envisioned. But he had to keep his trip a secret. They would announce his visit to the temple after the documentary had been filmed, after he left, after Ozman was captured and returned to Fuchu. If this woman wanted to talk, Kent could listen, as long as she didn't ask him to sing "Yesterday," or sign her napkin, or tell her what the real Plum Petite looked like underneath his mask. He no longer owned a guitar, had sold his own signature rights to a Japanese online autograph site for ¥250,000, and he didn't know what Plum Petite, a former costar and popular drag queen, looked like underneath his trademark mask. "Were you famous in America too?"

The newspaper headlines had read, *Life Imitates Art: Boy, seven, kills brother while copying pro wrestling moves.*

The doctor explained to Kent's dazed parents that a direct blow to the chest directly over the heart at a particular time in the heart's cycle can produce catastrophic consequences, something called *commotio cordis*, a form of ventricular fibrillation. The heart's electrical activity becomes disordered and its lower chambers contract in a rapid, unsynchronized way, allowing little or no blood to pump. Collapse and sudden death can follow. Such cases are rare and always tragic, the doctor told them, sorry he couldn't do more. *If only*—

For weeks, seven-year-old Kent Richman, of Chapel Hill, North Carolina, had been famous, the story rippling across the country, sparking debates about the effects of television violence on children. Kent was the example *de jeur* for Parents Against Violence on TV, who used his case in congressional hearings and in television ads, and even tried to coax his parents into joining them on a nationwide tour to promote responsible television viewing. Kent had been big in America long before he was big in Japan.

"No—not really." Kent knew where this went. "A Tokyo casting director picked me out of an audition for extra work. The role of ROWDY AMERICAN SAILOR #3. They recognized I looked like John Lennon. Next thing you know I'm on TV as *RI-CHU-MAN-SAN!* "

"All because somebody thought you looked like John Lennon?"

"Don't I? Maybe they saw something more. A diamond in the rough."

"Of course."

"To be honest, I think I was only on TV because I speak Japanese."

"So modest." She smiled weakly.

Kent couldn't tell if she was mocking him or was just uncomplicated.

"We Japanese appreciate when foreigners bother to learn our language."

Kent had heard the complaint many times. But he knew how to study; homework had been just a matter of getting to the desk every day. Memory work, words and patterns and rules filling the rutted tracks of his mind, tracks that had always led to Allan, until he found study. Learning Japanese had given Kent something to do once he reached the farthest place from home he could imagine, kept his mind from revisiting a summer night on Nags Head. Kent studied by day, hours at a time, and taught conversational English in a community center by night, every hour occupied so that he did not return to his thoughts, every hour of study both distraction from and penance for his crime. In his study of Japanese, he'd found the logic his life lacked. And when he finally allowed himself to return to the house at Nags Head, to the family he'd abandoned, there was Allan's urn, speaking of all the things his brother might've been had he lived.

"Doesn't do much for me these days," Kent said.

"What do you mean? What *do* you do?" Midori said.

"I'm considering my options at the moment."

"Like for a movie or something?" She beamed again.

Would a movie star be a notch up from TV? Was she dreaming of real celebrity now? "Some film people want to do a documentary on me—you know, life after *Bonanza*." Kent recycled what Renzo had fed him. "I'm not sure what the public wants to see these days. I've got to make the right choices for Kent Richman, but I want to keep the fans happy, too." Kent looked to Midori for verification. She stared, expressionless—no answer there. The initial transparency in her face was gone. Sarcastic or sincere? There had been a time when he would never have been suspicious of a woman like this in a bar. But he could no longer tell.

"But you sing, you play the guitar. What about that?" Midori said.

Kent's singing should've been saved for the karaoke box, but the Japanese liked his repertoire of a few Beatles songs. They liked his earnest versions of "Imagine" and "Yesterday." His guitar playing was limited to a few chords from *The Beatles Fake Book,* a collection of easy arrangements.

"And weren't you on that show *Changes in Love* with Reiko Miyahara?"

"There were script changes."

CHAPTER SIX

—

SHOCKALICIOUS

Someone switched the television back to the celebrity gossip program, which now flashed images of Ozman: popular grinning mug shot, publicity stills from *Airship Japan*, manga and other comic likenesses of the shock comic in full howl. Ozman had been sentenced to fifteen years in a Japanese prison. Fans, however, had decided that what happened with Kent and Kumi was another of Ozman's *shockwaves*, as they had taken to calling his outrageous stunts. Instead of a needle through his cheeks, he'd put a bullet through his wife's face.

"Shockalicious!" hailed *Tokyo Journal*.

"Mohawk with a Bullet," wrote the *Japan Times*.

"Cock of the Shock," proclaimed *Robot Monkey*.

Reports of Ozman sightings popped up on internet fan sites following his arrest, and blogs scrolled with theories of the Australian's imminent return. T-shirts with Ozman's face in an open-mouth assault were sold in the Koenji Flea Market. One read "Brain Salad Surgery," another "Use the Illusion," yet another "Like a Hole in My Head." New legions of shock comics turned up on variety shows. One ambitious young Japanese tried to run a coat hanger in and back out both sides of his nose on live television but put himself in a wheelchair. When the wire hit his brain, the amateur comic fell to the stage, flopping like a fish. The audience went wild with laughter.

"I swear I remember seeing you on that show." Out of pity or kindness, Midori seemed to ignore the chance to ask about Ozman or the "changes" he'd referred to. She certainly knew what had happened; the incident had made national headlines. He and Kumi made the news in Taipei and Shanghai. No matter what he did or who he was with, what happened with Ozman always surfaced like some bloated dead whale.

It's payback time. Kent recalled Ozman's fist slamming into his windpipe. Now, whenever he thought of him, his throat tightened, and he had trouble swallowing.

"I met a celebrity, like you, in Australia a few months ago," Midori said, and had no idea how much Kent appreciated her changing the subject. "He was a musician. His band was about to make it big. They won a contest on TV."

"Is it stars you want then?" Kent asked.

"I'm not a groupie." Midori frowned. "If that's what you mean. Just making a comparison."

"I see. Groupies are in it for the long haul, aren't they? Professionals. You don't seem like the professional type."

"I have a job." She switched to English. "I teach English, sometimes."

Kent switched to English. "And very well." He returned to Japanese, where, he realized as if he'd never considered it before, he felt more comfortable. "Seems we have something in common then. I did a subway ad for NeoGeo earlier this year, you know the language school chain that went bust?" The photographer had wanted to exploit Kent's alter ego, encouraging him to pull his glasses down his nose and stare at the camera earnestly. Kent did what he was told, took his paycheck—considerably smaller than those he'd earned from Lark cigarettes and Sankyu Ramen—and bowed to the advertising director. Three weeks ago, the CEO of NeoGeo had disappeared, leaving a shell of a company and empty bank accounts. Like Kent, he surfaced in Thailand, only to be deported back to Japan.

Midori looked up again at the television. "It's not a career. It's just something that I do in the community, to help my uncle."

On the television one of TV Kent's costars had maneuvered around him, then over the console and wrapped his arms around Ty-foo's legs in mock supplication, suggesting the act of fellatio as much as network television would allow. Ty-foo leaned his head back and closed his eyes, his arms out at his sides. The audience roared. Midori laughed.

"What's he like?" She asked. "Ty-foo? He's so funny."

"He's short."

Midori was drawn to the silliness that made *The Strange Bonanza* a hit.

Kent had always thought of himself as the straight man on the childish show, yet not above a gag or two. Turned out the show was all gags. "So you're not a groupie. What then?"

"I like people who are on TV."

"Is that why you sat next to me?"

"I wanted to see if you were the same person on TV. I've never met anyone famous."

"What about your musician?"

"He tried to rape me." Midori said this as if attempted rape were one of several reasonable outcomes.

Kent yanked his glasses from his face. "*A-re?*" He knew before he finished his sentence how wrong his reply was, how desperate he must sound.

But Midori laughed, a genuine chuckle. "*Suki yo!* I love it when you do that." She picked her story up without interruption. "I thought he was nice. He was good looking. Aren't you a nice guy?"

"Don't I seem so?" He was grateful for her generous assessment. Midori knew what everyone knew—that he'd cheated on Kumi and nearly got them both killed because of it. Kent suspected a part of what she knew about him was what drew her to him. This is what celebrities did, this is what made them celebrities, voodoo dolls made for pin sticking and altar worship.

"You seem nice on TV. Funny. Good-looking. Everyone loves Kent and Kumi."

Kent appreciated the "good-looking." "There's no Kent and Kumi, not now. No Kumi, no Kent. It's a fickle business."

"I know. You were such a good couple. Everybody thought so."

This is what she'd sat down for. Kent believed she might even be an iCU reporter for *Star-Gazer*, her cell phone at the ready to capture him in some state of ridiculousness, or when Ozman found him.

Kent stood. "I better go." The tiny bar felt tinier, the noise overwhelming. Any minute Ozman would kick in the front door.

"It's romantic, your story, like Shakespeare or something." She lit another cigarette, washing the first drag down with the last of her Calpis and vodka, one hand handling the whole maneuver. "Of course I read about what happened, but I don't know what's true."

The bartender refilled Kent's glass and handed him the bottle. "Keep it," he said and winked. Kent sat again.

"Romantic, huh? And where did you read that?"

"In a celebrity magazine."

"I didn't realize I still rated such attention." This was true, but only because Kent feared it more than he wanted to believe it. "Does it say where my wife has gotten to?"

"It said she left you. Said she's with a Taiwanese movie producer in Shanghai. That she's going to star in his next movie about a Japanese heiress in China before the war. There was a picture of her stepping out of a fancy car."

"They know more than I do then." Whiskey rose in Kent's throat. Shanghai seemed as likely a place as any for Kumi. Why not? But he doubted the bit about the movie—Kumi had no interest in acting. Take her picture, sure, but she wasn't going to pretend much else for anyone. And the photo, Kent knew from a succession of his own ill-timed candid shots, could've been taken anywhere at any time. Kumi had stepped out of hundreds of fancy cars.

CHAPTER SEVEN

—

HEY, COWBOY

Through the mirror behind the bar, Kent watched as a table of ladies looked his way. They appeared drunk, each mixing *shochu* with grapefruit juice and soda. Kent recognized the bottle because the light alcohol had become popular after a television drama featured a family of *shochu* distillers fighting against the mob and corporate Japan. Renzo had negotiated a role for Kent on the show, one of many opportunities that popped up in the wake of *The Ozman Incident*, one of many that Kent had turned down in the belief that he could walk away from his career without regret, perhaps one day come back refreshed, embraced by a forgiving public. He'd have held a recurring cameo as an American businessman eager to exploit the US market for imported liquor.

One of the women held a cell phone up for a photo. They'd likely send their photos to *Star-Gazer* or some other celebrity chaser, about the only media outlets that gave Kent any attention these days. A few days before he'd been ready to believe that any publicity was good, even if it reinforced his playboy status—a joke only he and Kumi had ever been in on. Kent was no playboy, never had been, Monique his only transgression. Yet that's all anyone remembered, Midori included. He'd be better off heading back to his hotel, leaving this country girl to worship celebrities from afar, and avoiding photos of any kind.

But Kent was unable to resist the attention. If the women were determined to photograph him, he'd offer a generous celebrity smile, the one that said, *All's well. I'm happy to oblige you lovely ladies with a photo.* He'd invite them all over for a photo, have Midori capture them in a group hug. He turned. The woman with the cell phone caught him just as he pushed the edges of his mouth up for a smile. Beep, flash. Kent smiled and waved the four over. They looked to one another for approval then shuffled to the bar, hands cupped over their mouths.

Now that they were closer, Kent realized they were older than he first thought, probably wives and mothers all of them. No problem: Kent Richman embraced all of his admirers, though he recalled a much younger fan base in his *Bonanza* days. Midori stepped aside while the women crowded him. Kent stood nearly ten inches over the tallest woman.

"*Sumimasen.*" The woman held up her cell phone, nodding. "So sorry to bother you."

"*Daijoubu, daijoubu desu yo.*" Kent stood between two women, his arms over their shoulders. Their heads barely reached his chest and he saw gray hairs at the roots. They smelled of rice wine, powdery perfume, and cigarettes. The woman with the cell phone looked at Midori, offering a faint smile and a nod. Midori shuffled on her feet and backed away; she looked unsure of where to stand.

"Midori, do you mind taking our picture?"

She brightened. "Sure, cowboy."

Cowboy? Where had she pulled that from? Her use of this intimate handle unsettled him. Kumi had called him *cowboy,* a joke after he'd donned western attire for a Lark cigarette billboard. Midori sounded as if she'd known him for years as she yelled, "*Cheezu!*" The women all flashed the familiar V sign; the cell phone snapped. Kent was caught frowning and looking to the side. *Cowboy?*

Midori held the cell phone before her. "Oh, Kent, that's no good. What a frowny face. You have to smile. Another." Again, with the familiar tone from this woman he had just met.

After two more tries, Midori captured everyone with eyes open and a smile. Kent even mouthed *A-re?* as he pushed his glasses down his nose. Midori returned the cell phone. The woman nodded. "*Arigato gozaimasu.*" She leaned in. "Are you his girlfriend?" The other women turned to each other, surprised by their friend's pluck.

Midori stared at her feet. "We're just friends." She looked to him as if to seek approval.

"Now, do me a favor and keep these photos to yourselves. Don't go sending them to some celebrity magazine." He pointed to the television where the celebrity gossip program had moved on to other stories.

The women nodded and grew serious. The one who had originally approached Kent, spoke. "Thank you, thank you so much. May I ask—how is Kumi-chan?"

There it was: the familiar *–chan* the Japanese applied to their favorite stars, an honorific used informally for children and females. They didn't care about him or an escaped Ozman so much as they wanted to know about Kumi. Kent wanted to tell the woman the truth: he didn't know. But the music went loud as a group of Japanese Brazilians swarmed the dance floor behind them, the soft bossa nova giving way to a spirited samba. Kent pretended he didn't hear the woman's question, waved at no one, and laughed before he turned back to the bar.

The women returned to their table, nodding approvingly at the photograph on the cell phone. Kent and Midori sat again. He didn't ask about *cowboy*. They sat in silence as he refilled his whiskey and ordered another Calpis and vodka for Midori, hoping the bartender would comp her drinks, too.

A Brazilian soccer match was projected onto a concrete wall. A large black and white photograph of the bartender, shirtless and sweating, hands above his head and mouth open as he danced, hung by the door. He looked like a congregant of the Pentecostal revivals Kent's mother had taken him to as a child, desperate men and women taken by the spirit. Kent recalled his mother's transient religious tendencies that followed Allan's death, from Vipassana to Wiccan to Catholic in a matter of years, anything to fill the crack her son's death had made. Kumi too experimented with various faiths, searching for something to believe in beyond the flash of cameras and the hum of strangers at a photo shoot. She held no faith in celebrity nor did she have any affection for her fans. Kent recognized that part of her allure was the aloof image she presented, but wondered how and why she did what she did for the cameras at all. Kumi could walk a room as if she were a regular, enjoying everyone's curiosity. She was good at touching men just enough to arouse in them contempt for Kent, and lust for her. She knew men, women too, were attracted to her: her looks, her celebrity, the fantasy of sleeping with her or being like her. Kumi could love someone, anyone, for a few seconds and feel no guilt or shame for creating false hopes in them, and alienation in Kent. He learned to ignore it and walk the room.

Kent first met Kumi at a charity photo shoot. She wasn't even out of her teens. She bore an innocence in her face that people couldn't get enough of. They believed her. He'd seen her print ads. He knew she was something rare, someone you didn't forget. She was taller than the other girls and sure of herself, already a professional despite her age—as if she'd known her whole life what she'd become. The press called her *neko-chan*—little cat—because of the way she walked.

She had peeled a tangerine. Even now, Kent was surprised by how much he remembered. The whole room filled with the sweet smell of the fruit. Kumi focused on eating it, as if nothing else mattered—this girl, still a teenager, surrounded by veteran actors and models, celebrities everywhere, but Kumi was oblivious. She was young, but also grown-up. One minute her tongue was lodged in the corner of her mouth and she bit at her lip as if her job that day was to peel that tangerine. The next minute she was texting someone on her cell phone.

Kent knew Kumi noticed him watching, but she sat there and moved tangerine slices around on a napkin in her lap as if she didn't notice. She picked up a juice box and slurped at it. Then she gave him the slightest smile; and however subtle, there was kindness in it. Kumi was known for her pout, which Kent at first believed was phony, a part of the role she played for photographers. He soon realized it was unconscious. Her bottom lip was always swollen and red from her biting it. Makeup artists complained that they couldn't hide it. Directors and photographers couldn't get enough of it.

Kent imagined Kumi by the bar door, *Hey, cowboy*, her forehead to its glass as she stared into the street and smoked a cigarette.

Ku... mi... ko...

To acknowledge the sound of each syllable, so unlike its brothers and sisters, such a solitary sound, equal in emphasis but peerless in combination. Not *ka* or *ki*, but *Ku*. Not *ma* or *mu*, but *mi*. And finally, the character for child, that also told you she was a *she—ko*.

There were fifty-five characters in the hiragana syllabary, but there was only one combination that formed *Kumiko: forever beautiful child.*

CHAPTER EIGHT

—

KUMIKO ONLINE

When Kent returned to Japan after being deported from Thailand, he hit the internet in search of her: images, news, whatever he could find. He reasoned that if anyone knew where Kumi was and what she was doing the gawking wide world of the web would. Kent sat for hours in internet cafes spending money he didn't have reading through Kumiko Sato fan sites, blogs, celebrity gossip, and the dozens of other sites. He also found that his sex tape with Monique was still available from a variety of voyeur and celebrity sites, the same excerpt for free on all of them. ¥2000 for the full-length version— forty-five minutes of Kent and Monique in his bedroom. The prevalence of the video left him discouraged and he nearly quit the computer and his online search for Kumi altogether. The video was everywhere, but Kumi seemed to be nowhere.

He searched for her like a parent searches for a lost child in a crowded supermarket, panic, desperation, and *shabu* when he could afford it, fueling his extended stays in the cafés. All he found were echoes of the woman he'd known, Kumi in print ads, on television and red carpets, clutching coffees in sweatpants. Kent googled every qualifying proper noun variation on Kumiko Sato he could dream up. Sitting in the air-conditioned internet cafes of Shibuya, Kent witnessed Kumi getting a haircut on YouTube, a digital short caught by a stylist's assistant with a cell phone. Again and again, he watched a music video she did for the band Gorillaz, each time wondering if the woman dancing in an animated version of a Japanese house was the same woman who had collapsed on their bed and wrapped her arms over his chest one morning after a long photo shoot and said, "I'm so tired. I don't think I can be me anymore."

Kent returned each evening to his capsule with bloodshot eyes and a headache from staring at a computer screen all day. Outside, he wore out his eyes scanning the faces of every woman he passed on the street, in a store, a park, or at a train station. Occasionally, on a crowded train or in a queue for a movie—evenings in which he sat alone with his popcorn and soda, wondering if Kumi were in the audience with her own popcorn and soda, falling asleep like she did through every movie they ever watched together—he spotted a "Kumi." Kent looked at the world around him so carefully he wouldn't have been surprised to see her anywhere nor would he have cared how she appeared to him, via the swirl in his coffee or a puffy white cloud, as an angel or in the guise of a child. Perhaps she'd speak to him from the big screen, step right out of the celluloid and into the theater, a holographic Kumi, her voice full of reverb, an image of dancing light. Some of the "Kumis" Kent spotted had straight, dark hair, subtle figures and benign smiles; others in zero-sized blouses above capri pants and enormous platform shoes that left them bowlegged and clumsy, eye shadow and expensive perfumes; a few wigged devotees of cosplay.

baby, you're a rich man

One day as the train left Gotanda Station, Kent scavenged a discarded manga from an empty seat. *Yuri manga*. Girls Love. *Yuri manga* was designed for women, the love between them as much emotional as physical. As he read the story of a young girl experiencing life abroad for the first time, in Australia as a runaway, Kent saw Kumi in the protagonist named Apple, despite the characteristic manga features—large, glistening eyes, small mouth, the overlapping and nested hair. Apple had to be an allusion to her famous subway ad. In this series, the Apple roamed New South Wales in a Land Cruiser, finding adventure and kindred female spirits wherever she went, finally teaming up with an Aboriginal dreamcatcher. With his guidance, young Apple experienced vivid and disturbing dreams of great violence that she couldn't understand. She sought the help of spiritual leaders around the world, but none could help her. In Australia, she hoped she'd found the one person who could.

Kent was certain this Apple had been modeled after Kumi, but when a drunken salaryman entered his car from another and demanded the manga, he reluctantly gave up the comic. Kumi's wide-eyed image half and quarter-framed in simple cinematographic black and white lines haunted him for days afterwards, the panels like a motion picture that revealed action in slow motion, and rapid zoom-ins to close-up shots. Kent spent the next two weeks in manga stores looking for the series but he never found it again. He even asked *otaku*, anime and manga geeks, in Akihabara and Kanda if they knew the series, but no one had heard of it. They suggested it might have been *doujinshi,* amateur, DIY manga. Had some *otaku* fan created a manga character just for Kumi? And, if so, why couldn't he find it?

Kumi was everywhere but nowhere, on the street, in store windows, restaurants and movie houses, no shortage of images, video and blog blather on the internet to satisfy a fan's hunger for all things Kumi. But there was nothing for Kent. Just one photo—a tour group assembled in front of a raft prepared to float the Kali Gandaki, a tributary of the Ganges River in Nepal. In the photo, Kumi kneels in the front row, a life vest over her bathing suit. She wears a baseball cap and sunglasses so her eyes are veiled. A hint of black hair pokes out from under the cap, just behind her shoulders. On the inside of her left wrist is her tattoo. Kent and Kumi inked matching tattoos of the *kanji* for heaven, 天 *ten*, on the eve of their first wedding anniversary. Flush with new money and racing along on champagne and speed, they impulsively stopped at *Ten Ten Tattoo* in Shibuya. "It's a sign," Kumi said. "A message meant for us." She took Kent's hand and turned his palm to the sky.

"Heaven," she said and drew short, determinate strokes across his palm—left to right and left to right again beneath the first line, and from a common point, two longer lines from top to bottom, one curving left the other curving right. The elementary, invisible strokes lay moonlit in his hand.

"Do this three times," she brushed the strokes with her middle finger again and blew, brushed and blew again, "and you will realize your dreams." She took the cigarette from Kent, put it to her mouth, and inhaled, then placed the cigarette back between his fingers, as he followed her into the tattoo parlor.

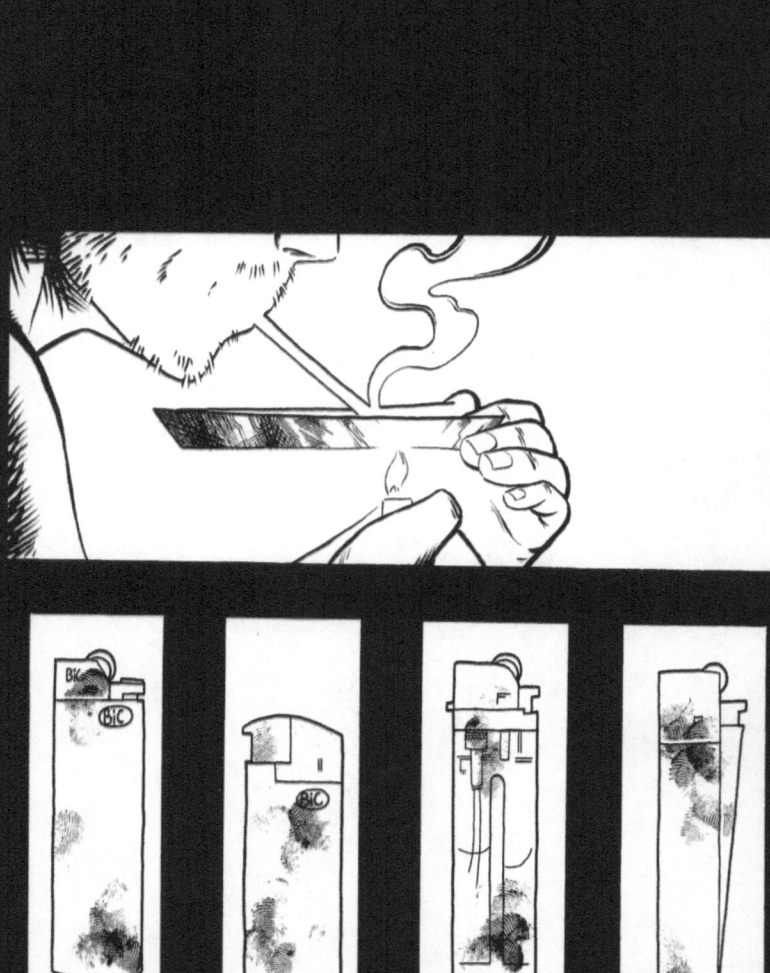

CHAPTER NINE

—

THE SURGE

Since the photo episode, the club patrons all seemed to recognize Kent with their whispered glances. It was him, wasn't it? *RI-CHU-MAN-SAN!* back from the dead? And didn't they all want to know the same thing too: where was Kumi? Kent asked the same question every day. And with each day, he held on to the hope that she'd walk up behind him, poke a finger into his ribs, and laugh over his shoulder. *Hey, cowboy.*

Kent looked to Midori. "What's the verdict? Nice guy or not?" His smile had carried him far within Tokyo circles. He hoped some of the glow remained.

"Nice guy. But we just met." Midori lowered her eyes and sipped her drink. She stubbed out her cigarette, applied a fresh coat of lipstick, and turned to Kent. "*Ikimasho.*"

Kent appreciated Midori's guileless invitation. "You sure? I'm a hunted man." He smiled but realized again that he was indeed—hunted. If he were to do anything but go back to his hotel and lock the door, he'd need help to get through the evening. "Give me a minute."

Tamarindo's dark bathroom was designed in Nepalese fashion: wooden masks and tapestries with the eyes of Buddha on the walls; works of silver and jade; a floor covered in black stones. Incense burned and indigenous music played—chanting monks and deep horns, wood on wood—as a small monitor over the urinal showed gay porn. Japan was like that, surprises hidden throughout the country, remarkable places tucked away in the oddest corners.

Kent tugged a small plastic baggie from his jeans pocket. Inside, four small rocks of *shabu*. He placed a quarter-inch rock on a tinfoil square and burned a lighter underneath. When the rock bubbled, Kent sucked up blue smoke through a drink straw. He hadn't smoked in a week, mostly because he couldn't afford it and because he planned to save the last bits for the mountains. Tomorrow he'd have to find more, even if he also wanted to be free of the stuff that had stripped him and Kumi of their health and good sense.

Midori, unremarkable despite too much makeup, seemed kind, and a night in bed with her might boost his spirits further. He liked what he thought of as her *obviousness*. Besides, he hadn't slept with a woman since Monique, his one stumble, and that affair had turned on him tragically. He hadn't even slept with Kumi for months before he met Monique. They hardly saw each other. And when they did, they were exhausted and high: one surging upwards while the other melted down.

The *shabu* surged, pulled his head straight and tightened his neck, speed rushing through his bloodstream. His heart rate and blood pressure shot up, and with the second hit he felt increased focus, a familiar alertness and energy that had been absent. His nose itched and his fingertips tingled. He felt grand. And with thoughts of Midori waiting outside, he forgot about Ozman as another surge lifted his spirits and gave him an erection. Any appetite for food was erased. He'd be up all night and well into the next day.

Kent glared at the mirror, searching for someone he knew. He lowered his head, pulled his glasses off and smirked. He auditioned his once popular line for the mirror. "*A-re?*" A familiar face scratched with fear and fatigue returned the smirk. Midori had been kind to laugh when he so wrongly tried the line on her. Perhaps there was more kindness where that came from. He squeezed Kumi's Saint Christopher medal around his neck. She'd always worn the medal—a gift from a childhood pen pal in Peru—despite protests from photographers, handlers, and her agent. It eventually became an iconographic piece of the Kumi brand. Young girls all over Japan, with no understanding of Catholicism or saints, wore the medal, which became known as the *Seinto Shi*—Saint C.

With his jaw clenched and his heart racing, Kent returned to the bar and Midori, who smiled and took his hand as if she had done so a thousand times before.

CHAPTER TEN

—

HOTERU

From October to May, Azuma took a beating from a northern coil that stormed across Russia and journeyed down through Japan from the Kuril Islands, sweeping in cold air. *Karakaze,* empty wind, cruised over the mountains around Azuma, licked through the channel of the small-town main street and shot over the southern mountains. The To-ne River, a shallow, rocky stream, wide and cold, ran through town and journeyed southeast, one of the longest rivers in Japan. In summer fishermen in wide straw hats stood up to their knees in the cold water, nylon lines gleaming. Now, the river ran full and fast with what the Japanese called *plum rains*, a seasonal downpour that lasted for weeks.

Kent and Midori hunched under her umbrella and made for a taxi stand in front of the train station. A woman in an office worker's stock blue suit glanced at Kent as she left the train station then again as he and Midori passed. Kent guessed her peek at him was more a reflexive gesture than recognition: he was over six feet tall, a foreigner, and with a young Japanese woman. This was not Tokyo. For the few others who passed there might have been the spark of recognition—a blatant double take—but only an uncertain flicker and not enough to light the stage Kent had once enjoyed. He must teach at one of the local schools, they guessed, and moved on out of the rain. They'd seen dozens like him before. After Tamarindo, and with Ozman loose, Kent was grateful for the only kind of anonymity a foreigner in Japan could attain: he blended in with others like him, tall with fair skin and brown hair. He kept his eyes ahead and dug his hands into his coat pockets as Midori tucked her arm inside his.

Under the station awning, a wall of glowing vending machines hummed the promises of beer, cigarettes, and a dozen different sodas. An aging sweet potato vendor, a small, fragile man draped in wool sweater and nylon jacket, stood behind his converted ice cream cart, his hands wrapped around a hot canned coffee. He chanted *Yaki imo!* as train passengers disembarked. Salarymen, office ladies, students, and construction workers poured on to the platform opening umbrellas as they headed for the smoky confines of *pachinko* parlor, *yakitori* bar, and home. A determined barker shouted solicitations from under a nearby club awning, encouraging salarymen with glossy pictures of women in lingerie, pushing them to join his tiny hostess club for the night. *Dozo! Dozo!*

From the train station, Kent and Midori took a taxi to one of the dozens of love hotels that dotted the hillsides above Azuma. Kent considered inviting her back to the Terminal Hotel, but thought it best to keep the arrangement simple, like Renzo had ordered. Midori pointed the driver to Tropicaria, its neon heart watching over an elaborate façade of mixed architectural messages—tiki torches and Corinthian columns. They rode in silence, the driver in neat blue uniform, cap, and white gloves, glancing at the foreigner in his mirror. Kent couldn't keep still. He could have ridden to the ends of the Kanto Plain tucked inside the taxicab as rain fell outside and Midori pressed her body to his. Within the gated parking lot, the driver stopped, quoted the fare, and popped the door for them as an old man in a gray jumpsuit rolled a mobile metal barricade behind a parked car to conceal its license plate. Inside, muzak echoed in the empty lobby.

Any other time the song would have sent Kent into the doldrums, "Yesterday" another reminder of the life he no longer enjoyed, of moments under hot lights and before attentive audiences, and of the stagnant life before him. But with *shabu* surging through his veins, he almost liked the song again. He didn't hear Paul McCartney singing, but his own voice and what he thought of as his own smart arrangement, his own flavorings. Midori hummed along; Kent nearly joined her. His arms ached for the feel of his guitar, his mouth tightened at the memory of the lyrics, and his legs trembled to be on stage again. He considered sprinting from the love hotel, but light popped before his eyes like a night sky teeming with fireflies and his legs went wobbly. He had lately suffered such starbursts until his head hurt. He assumed it was nerves, poor health, the drugs.

"*Daijoubu?*" Midori put her hand on his back.

"I'm tired." But he wasn't tired; he was nearly jumping from his skin, ready to talk, ready for a good twelve-hour *shabu* spree until he had to leave for the mountains.

"You can leave if you want," Midori said. "You won't hurt my feelings."

Kent pointed to the hotel menu panel with its lighted photographs of available rooms. "What do you think? The Bali Room?"

Midori studied his face. After a pause, she nodded and pressed a red button to signal their choice and unlock the room electronically. Kent squeezed his eyes closed, waiting for a sign, a warning to bail on his new friend. He didn't run. Where would he go but the Terminal? Even if Renzo was paying for it, Kent didn't want to be there.

In the room, the telephone rang, Midori was given a price, and she sent cash off in a plastic tube. Kent had money but couldn't afford the luxury, though Midori never asked and paid for the variation on a nature theme, large tropical plants and a cabana-style décor. She treated him as if he were a guest again in Japan. For one hundred dollars, Kent and Midori could enjoy a large round tub, a body shower, video, karaoke. And anonymity. Besides the parking lot attendant, they hadn't seen another person. The last time he'd been in a love hotel he shared a bed with Monique. The day ended with a surgeon trying to piece together the puzzle that had become her face. *Comment ça va, Monique?*

Kent first met the Quebecois expat at a club opening in Shibuya. He smiled at his good fortune. He'd never cheated on Kumi, but flirting with beautiful women was part of his job. And at 5'11", with blond hair to the middle of her back, the woman from Montreal glowed a ghostly white in the club's darkness. She seemed to believe that Kent might serve as a springboard for a career in television and the movies. He let her believe it, though he couldn't do much for her. He worried enough about his own career. His role on *The Strange Bonanza* kept his bank account healthy, but he was being offered fewer and fewer roles beyond his regular gig. His renditions of "Yesterday" and "Imagine" were included in the script less and less. Negotiations for the nighttime drama he hoped for had stalled, and Lark had not renewed his endorsement contract.

That went to Ozman, smoke streaming from his ears in the train station advertizements. Kent sold the cigarettes with class, at least in the beginning, before they asked him to wear chaps and a cowboy hat on a horse in a fake desert. In the beginning, he wore a gleaming blue suit as he swaggered down Tokyo streets. Kent looked a giant, his walk of success photographed at street level, an angle that reminded Kent of John Travolta's opening scene in *Saturday Night Fever*. His gait was like an alien's who had conquered the city as pedestrians, frozen in the still shot, stepped aside and pointed in recognition and awe. *That's RI-CHU-MAN-SAN! and he smokes Lark!* He knew the whole scenario meant little, but believed the approach did the trick. The next time smokers, particularly men, went for a pack at a vending machine, they would hear that groovy song and recall Kent Richman striding down the sidewalk. They'd press the button under Lark and, for a moment, believe they were that cool.

Ozman, on the other hand, looked ridiculous, a cartoon, a clown with smoke shooting from his ears. Who wanted to see that? Who wanted to be that guy? By sleeping with Monique, Kent had returned Ozman's many insults and cautioned him that the *RI-CHU-MAN-SAN!* brand still held some sway in Tokyo. Two months later, Kent and Monique were still seeing each other, still cheating on their spouses.

Kent and Midori sat in overstuffed leather chairs before an oval table, the king-sized bed made up with a condom on the pillow in a neat plastic wrapper. Alert and attentive as most tweekers were for a good twelve plus hours, he poured whiskey and water and listened dutifully as Midori talked about herself, of teaching English to senior citizens and school kids studying for college entrance exams, of living with her parents, of her desire to one day live abroad again.

"You'll still have the same problems there." Everything he said sounded breezy and erudite, optimism tempered by experience. "Love where you are."

"Didn't I read that you moved to Thailand? How's that loving where you are?" Midori said.

"I needed a change of pace, of scenery. That so bad? Considering."

"Maybe I want a change of scenery, too. Considering."

"You have to get in line to abuse Kent Richman, sweetheart." The "sweetheart" felt wrong as soon as he said it. He'd never talked this way. Modesty seemed the best approach with Midori. Kent was happy to oblige. In his heightened state he'd listen all night, really listen, and care. Midori didn't seem to be the fan girl he first took her for. He wondered why she even left the bar with him. The smoke from her cigarette wound up and spread across the ceiling, which was painted in a motif of green leaves. They sat quiet, sipping their drinks. *Shabu* helped with silence too; anything and everything was all right.

"Are you scared?" Midori looked Kent in the eye for the first time he could remember.

"Of?" But he knew.

"Ozman? Him coming after you? The news said he—"

"The man's insane. He tried to kill me and my wife. Of course, I'm scared." This again. Maybe she *was* a reporter.

The same day Ozman had stormed through Kent's apartment with a desire for vengeance, Monique reached him with a text message: *YARU KA? (You want a piece of me?)*. He answered: *N 30*. They met in front of the Parco department store in the Shibuya District where they both liked to shop. She wore a taffeta blouse, a sequined miniskirt, and a pair of simple leather mules as if she had just stepped from the pages of a fashion magazine.

They spent the afternoon in a love hotel near Shibuya Station called Hotel Cinematic, choosing the 8 ½ Room from the menu. The photos reminded Kent of a restaurant in Florence where he and Kumi had eaten nearly every night during a one-week stay while Kumi shot a Vespa commercial. In the room, black and white photographs of Roman landmarks and stills from Fellini's movie hung on the walls. A hip-high replica of a rocket ship that looked more like an ancient Roman phallus stood by the bathroom. Faux columns were placed around the enormous bed, beneath the mirrored ceiling. Kent loved every gaudy detail. Hours later, they'd see each other again in Kent's apartment, and a few hours after that in a Tokyo hospital.

"I'm sorry. It's not exactly a strange question." Midori's mouth pinched as if she held back other questions. "You know, I don't just go to love hotels. I'm not the person you think I am."

"I guess that makes two of us," Kent said. He didn't know if he believed her—she was here with him after all. "If we're not who the other person thinks we are, then who are we?"

"You tell me."

"What do you want to know? I can talk about myself all day." Kent hoped he sounded sarcastic.

"Did she really leave you?"

"What's the difference where my ex-wife is?"

"When people meet they talk about themselves, their lives. That's how this usually works. Or do stars do it differently? Listen, I'm not that person you're thinking. I can see it; I can hear it in your voice. Just like my Australian friend."

"You think I'm a rapist?"

"You looked lonely sitting at the bar. Big deal. And you seem, sorry *seemed*, charming on TV, like a real nice guy. Plus, I don't see a lot of new people in Azuma. And, yes, because you're famous. So what? Why are you here?"

Kent realized he didn't want her to go—she calmed the *shabu* that kept his foot bouncing and jaw clenched, but he wasn't sure anymore why he was here with her. "I'm sorry. Let's start over."

Midori put her drink down. "Tell me one thing. You know, what I read in the papers, what I see on TV, I guess, I believe it, like everyone else. I never stopped to think if it was true or not. Why wouldn't it be? Isn't that what makes people like you and Kumi stars? You have these wild lives. You're so far away from my life and me. Most of the time you seem so glamorous, so eager to be what we want you to be—beautiful, talented, rich."

"It's a curse." Even Kent couldn't stomach the sarcasm. "Do I look like any of those things?"

Midori acted as if she hadn't heard him. "When we think you've gotten too big for your britches, we need to dislike you. We need to believe that we're the real people, not you, that we, with our boring little lives and bills to pay and ramen to eat, are the salt of the earth. And when we're done with you, we find someone else to admire, someone else's life to covet. Just never our own. Nobody wants that." She knelt in front of Kent, her face inches from his. "Everything you did looked so effortless, so much better than our own lives. When you fell, it was that much easier to shake our heads, cluck our tongues, and make ourselves feel better about the kind of excitement we thought we wanted in our boring lives."

"It's an act, you know that." His appearances on stage, TV, and in magazines were self-conscious performances that promised sincerity. The expression of ease that charmed audiences, the heroic facades of grace and confidence were contrived and practiced. But Kumi had been different. She didn't care what she revealed, didn't care what audiences saw. There was no self-consciousness, no act. And audiences loved her for not pretending.

"Who watches TV like that? Thinking it's all fake. Takes the fun out of it. Would you be so special without TV, without fancy clothes and fan clubs?" As Midori leaned forward, perhaps to kiss Kent or sniff him for authenticity, she lurched at him like a drunk. Then the floor moved, and his chair bounced on its legs. Their whiskey glasses rattled on the table and a ceramic statue of a Balinese rice goddess wobbled from its bedside perch, shattering on the bamboo-patterned tile.

"*Jishin*." Midori felt her way back to the chair, sat and gripped its arms. Did he look as odd as she did, as if she were being zapped in an electric chair?

Kent had experienced slight tremors before but nothing like this shaking. The walls swayed. Everything vibrated. What surprised and troubled him most was how long the quake went on. He waited for the shaking to stop, clinging to his chair. When it didn't, but grew stronger, he feared it would go on until everything around them collapsed burying them beneath plastic tropical plants and cheap ceramic statues. Finally it stopped, and the stillness unsettled him too, as if the lull were a ruse to put them at ease before the quake shook again and brought everything to the ground.

Outside the neighborhood pulsed with car and building alarms. Fire and police sirens wailed. Kent and Midori stood under an umbrella as other guests buried their heads beneath jackets or hurried away in cars. Midori clutched a hotel blanket around her shoulders. Kent had given up on staying dry; he held the umbrella over Midori.

The earthquake added to the sensation that he was no longer in control of his life and hadn't been for a long time. It's simple, Kumi said to him once: move on, be done with this version of our lives and start over, just as she'd said when he moaned about his brother. She was the only person he'd told about what still seemed to him a recent tragedy. So why was his ruin so hard to accept?

"What if someone recognizes me?" Kent looked around. Renzo had told him to stay out of the press.

"You're kidding?" Midori looked up at him as if he were.

"I've got to be careful."

A woman in a hotel uniform scurried through the main entrance, surveyed the parking lot, and announced through cupped hands that it was safe to return to the hotel.

"*Ikimasho.*" Midori looked tired.

"You don't think the building will fall down, do you?"

"What if it should?" Midori walked from under the umbrella so that Kent had to catch up.

At the elevator she shook her head like a dog. A young couple beside them stood silent, studying the floor. When the elevator doors opened and Midori stepped in, Kent paused to let the young woman on but she kept her head bowed and didn't move. Midori shook her head. She pressed the Close Door button and ran her fingers through her hair. "I need a bath."

CHAPTER ELEVEN

—

YOU DON'T LOOK LIKE
JOHN LENNON AT ALL

Midori redressed in panties and bra, and crawled into the king-sized bed. "No hard feelings, Kent. *Tsukareta.*" With *shabu* still doing its work, Kent wouldn't sleep for hours.

Sounds of Fresh Nature, a selection from the bedside console, came from speakers built into the ceiling—water trickling, surf grumbling, and trees swishing. Still in his clothes and on top of the covers, Kent chain-smoked, his reflection in the mirrored ceiling a ragged version of himself. His long body stretched out over the bed like an X, Midori's narrow frame rolling hills of red satin. He needed a haircut though he'd given himself one with a pair of chicken shears lifted from a grocery store. His head seemed to lean to the left, accentuated by jagged, uneven bangs, and riotous waves at his ears and neck. To repair the damage, he'd have to buzz his head like he did when he went to Thailand. Would this symbolic start turn out better than the last one? Was Midori a hint of things to come? As if in response, she hummed in her sleep, then breathed in great, frenzied heaves. He should've reached out and touched her the way he'd have reached out to any human in need; but he didn't. He'd probably never see her again. Midori had been kind to him, laughing when he needed her to laugh. Even if Kent recognized his gesture as desperate afterwards, he was grateful she didn't make fun of him. She could have.

You don't look like John Lennon at all—

In the morning, Kent prepared to leave the Tropicaria just before sunrise, waking Midori to say goodbye.

She rolled to him when he whispered her name. "*Nan ji desu ka?*" She squinted up at him.

He glanced at the glowing alarm clock on the bedside table. "Five-thirty."

"So early." She rubbed at her eyes.

"I've got to meet somebody," he said.

"Somebody? Sounds glamorous." She winked. "Or romantic."

"I suppose." Kent returned her wink but he didn't feel glamorous or romantic.

"Kidding." Midori sat up and smiled. "Are you going to be around later?"

Kent studied her bare shoulders, her cream-colored bra. The desire he'd felt at the idea of her naked body returned for the first time since Tamarindo. He enjoyed the longing. Instinct led him to lie. "Sure."

"You're not very convincing." She lay back again and rolled away. "Take care of yourself." Then she turned and looked him in the eye. "Be careful. And I hope you find your wife."

"Who said I'm looking?"

"Aren't you?"

"What's the point, right? She left me, you said so."

"Yeah, don't you?"

"Sometimes, yes. Other times, no."

"I'm sorry, don't listen to me. I don't know anything about you or your wife, except that the idea of a Lolita in boy's underwear is more perverse than usual."

Boy's tighty-whities had made Kumi famous. Or had it been the other way around? Kumi in tighty-whities was an iconic image throughout Japan and Taiwan, in subway cars, department stores, and oversized billboards. Kumi forever bounced before him in boy's underwear to The Ramones' "I Wanna Be Sedated." It was a nighttime photo shoot for cell phone covers embossed in plastic with images of Winnie-the-Pooh and Disney princesses or Smiley Smile liquid dish soap. Kumi bounced, her clean-cut bob flapping like wild but useless bird wings on the side of her head. Each bounce appeared an attempt at flight, at bouncing herself right through the roof and out of their Tokyo apartment. She bounced in the kind of undress that crowned countless boys's and men's school- and work-desk daydreams across Japan. Two green apples covered her breasts. Advertisers believed Kumiko Sato's oversized underwear would sell laundry detergent, which it did. But it wasn't just her oversized underwear that sold apple-scented alkaline compounds and made her an idol. With Kumi's brand pout, the nation's favorite pair of lips, she could wind up a wholesome, toothy smile for anyone's clothes, gadget, or soft drink. Her swollen lips, clumsy skinniness and wide, sinless eyes sold anything. Kent joked that you could put shit on a plate in front of Kumi, and consumers would crawl the department stores asking where they could get some of that shit for themselves. It was perverse; the world knew nothing of Kumi, nothing of the woman he'd fallen in love with. He wondered how many different ways he might be reminded of the woman he'd lost.

"See, you know a few things." Kent leaned in for a kiss, but Midori rolled away.

"Goodbye, Kent Richman."

Azuma was small but Kent had trouble finding the Terminal Hotel and train station on foot. The rain still fell so he took the only umbrella he could find from the stand in front of the love hotel, a practice common enough in Japan so that he didn't feel too bad: a pink Hello Kitty model, barely broad enough to cover his shoulders and in some disrepair. Most Japanese streets didn't have names but worked from a system of hierarchical divisions, from the prefecture down to the block. Nearly everyone relied on visual landmarks when giving directions. Worse, neighborhoods were dense, irregular, and all alike. So Kent hoped intuition might lead him to his hotel. He decided against a taxi to save money and in the hope that the walk would help him wind down and stop the shakiness that came in the waning hours of a *shabu* surge. And he wasn't scheduled to meet his liaison until early afternoon.

After an hour down a narrow, winding road, Kent was back in the center of town. The morning was damp and cold, and the umbrella did little to protect him from the rain. His clothes were soaked, his shoes sopped, and water ran from his wet hair inside his shirt. His glasses fogged over and he feared the sad umbrella would lose its battle with the wind. Rivers rushed by him in the gutters, so many streams of water and debris that he gave up avoiding them.

The sky grew brighter as Kent followed a river tributary through a small park. Old men and women in polyester athletic suits shuffled along a tarmac path; dogs trailed on leashes. He was eager to get back to the hotel and clean up, look presentable for whoever he was supposed to meet, especially if the documentary crew was with them. Then there he was: Ozman, weathered and torn on the side of an abandoned building in an old poster advertising *Airship Japan*. Kent stopped and bent, his hands on his knees as he struggled to breathe. That face through a fish-eye lens, trademark mohawk rising in the sky like a shark fin, his eyes bugged, his mouth in a scream, his pierced tongue lapped over his bottom lip. A short samurai sword—a *chisa katana* used in ritual suicide—ran in one ear and out the other.

After wandering lost for another hour, suspicious of every footfall, every shadow, every corner he couldn't see around, Kent spent thirty minutes in a 7-Eleven bathroom trying to throw up with nothing but dry heaves. He couldn't even be sick. A young clerk finally knocked on the door, his voice low and nervous, asking if Kent was all right. Kent pulled himself from the sink and dried his face with a stiff rag from a rusting metal bar. This left the taste of chlorine in his nose and a burning in the back of his throat. As the clerk watched him withdraw from the bathroom, Kent thanked the teenager with a weak smile and a weaker apology. When he asked if he knew where the train station was, the clerk responded right away, curiosity and awe in his voice.

"Aren't you—?"

"I'm in a hurry—can you tell me where the train station is?" Kent said.

"*RI-CHU-MAN-SAN!*" A teenaged girl on her way to school in navy uniform and black Mary Janes stood , grinning. She held a cell phone open and spoke in English. "Excuse me. Yes, may I have a photograph?"

Kent caught himself in the cigarette display glass above the counter. "Sure," he replied in English. "Why not."

"Thank you very much. It is very kind." Then in Japanese to the young clerk. "Will you please take our picture?"

Kent placed his arm around the young girl's shoulder, tried to recall better days and pushed his lips up in a strained smile. He was flattered, even this early and degraded morning, that he could command a photo op.

The young girl spoke through her smile, forgetting her English for Japanese, "Are you scared?"

"Scared?" Kent remembered to lift his chin, brighten his eyes.

"Of *Bigu Sukai?*" She looked up at him.

"Don't believe everything you read." Kent squeezed the young girl closer, wishing such a platitude were true. "Nothing to fear. Now smile."

Click.

The girl reclaimed her cell phone and showed Kent the picture. His hair, made worse by his improvised haircut and rain, was greasy and tousled—and not in a stylish way. His face pale and pasty, his eyes bloodshot. He gave the young girl a thumbs-up. "Looking good."

CHAPTER TWELVE

—

DORAMA

DORAMA PART I

Kent finally found the Terminal Hotel after taking a taxi. Reception had a message from Cedars Temple. A Ms. Watanabe said that his departure had been delayed. He was to meet her the following day. This was a reprieve. Kent had nothing to lose by venturing into the mountains for some quiet time, but he was uneasy over what awaited. At least in his pod he'd been in control of his days, even if his days were empty. Still, he dreamed of himself through a camera lens, in black Zen robes, like Keanu Reeves in the *Matrix*, eyes closed, his long hair pulled up in a bun, his beard trimmed to a goatee. *Shakuhachi*, bamboo flute, played over images of Kent Richman in private meditation, side by side with the Buddhist master, and speaking to the cameras over green tea and miso soup.

Unable to sleep but headed for an eventual collapse, he decided to ride *shabu's* breakneck pace up into the mountains—he could crash later. Wasn't that what the retreat was supposed to be? A holiday. He also needed to stay alert while he was still so close to Tokyo, never sure what waited for him around the corner. Ozman was out there somewhere, and Kent had been sloppy last night. He imagined cell phone photos were already circulating the web.

He would need more of what he was sure to run out of. And, if he were going to follow Renzo's plan, he'd have what he needed. Kent had no idea how secluded the retreat might be and no interest in taking chances. A 7-Eleven near the hotel offered cheap whiskey, cartons of cigarettes, rolls of tinfoil, and lighters. He also bought a copy of *Shukan Gendai*, a weekly celebrity news magazine, to see if he or Kumi had made the pages. Finally, he found breakfast in the form of *onigiri*, rice balls with tuna and mayonnaise, an apple pie, and three bottles of a vitamin drink made up mostly of nicotine, caffeine, and glucose. He had only one more stop. And even in a small town like Azuma, he knew where to find it.

Kent's friend Shin, a popular underground manga illustrator, had introduced Kent and Kumi to *shabu*, which kept him going through days illustrating, hunched over his drafting desk, cigarettes piling up in the ashtray, never changing his clothes, never eating or sleeping. His girlfriend Umeko understood and tolerated his needs, and stayed out of his way. Shin routinely worked for two or three days without sleep or food, crashed for another two, then woke up famished and eager to be with Umeko, an artist herself who spent hours in the darkroom, though she never hit the pipe.

Shin managed *shabu* well, never seemed to crave it. The impressive volume of his hit Boy Wasabi serials and spin-off installments grew directly out of his creative sprints. For Shin, *shabu* more than paid off.

The fold of cash from Renzo helped Kent revive the confidence he'd felt after talking with his agent about career opportunities, so he treated himself to an over-the-top selection of beef and vegetables and two cold beers from a steak house chain. As he ate, or tried to, the beef tight and bulky in his stomach, he flipped through the celebrity gossip magazine. He found only a quarter page mention in the "Briefs" section describing Ozman's escape, and Kent's departure from The Capsule Inn.

The confidence Renzo had generated was quickly replaced with disquieting predictions of missed opportunity, of failure before he'd even made the starting blocks, of having his fingernails pulled out with pliers. How many offers had Renzo phoned in since Kent's return to Tokyo? He remembered two in particular for they appeared so unattractive and unlikely. One, a proposal to host a program on makeovers, in which Kent approached candidates on the street with offers of new hairstyles, clothes, and even plastic surgery in extreme cases. Audience members voted via text message for the candidates they believed most needed them. *Congratulations! You're so ugly the voting audience thought you deserved a complete and utter makeover.* Kent had no interest in carrying that kind of karma around.

"It's a starting place, Richman. Get your face familiar again. Probably go a season before you get a better offer," Renzo had assured him.

The other offer had Kent hosting a travel show in which he toured male-oriented tourist sites around the world. Bangkok had been first on the agenda. When the producers found out he couldn't get a visa to Thailand, they went with someone else. Kent discovered later that the show had become popular with salarymen and made the host, Jean Claude Chishu, a young half-Japanese, half-French man, an emerging star. He later discovered Renzo also represented the skinny French-speaking host with his ragged razor cut, perfect sideburns, and angular face.

A third offer of voice work for an animated Miyazaki film fell through when producers decided Kent's voice was not deep or abrasive enough for the villainous character he was to play, even when Kent insisted he could do villains. He'd played Rodrigo from *Othello,* he told them. In Tokyo. He hadn't even had to audition. The director, who'd come to him and believed Kent Richman was born to play Rodrigo, was doing a contemporary version of Shakespeare's play set in Iraq with a heavy metal soundtrack. Othello as a US general and a Muslim. Iago as a college boy riding a rising star in the CIA with Rodrigo his trusting attaché.

What he didn't tell them was that the director fired him after a week of production. People were gasping in the audience, but the director said Kent Richman was ruining his play, portraying Rodrigo as what he called "a pop idol on a USO tour." He told Kent after his last performance, just before he sent him packing: "I have no idea what you're thinking or doing up there. Rodrigo's a fool, an idiot. Not a movie star." Said when he watched Kent on stage it was as if he were performing in another play. "Do you even know what this play, this character is about?" the director asked. That's how Kent felt lately: as if he were playing a character he didn't really understand.

Beside Azuma's train terminal and under a pedestrian bridge, Kent spotted a group of Iranians huddled near a telephone booth. At train stations all over Japan, the immigrants had fashioned a surrogate world. They assembled around minivans and kiosks, peddling cheap silver and gold, phony telephone cards, hashish, prescription pills hard to come by with Japan's conservative national health program, and *shabu*. Kent fingered the bills in his jeans pocket, thinking about how far he could go if he spent a little more than he should. Walking past the group of Iranians, he looked for recognition from any one of them. He pretended to use a pay phone nearby and when finished with the charade nodded to a man who nodded back but didn't speak. He was tall and wiry, his black hair shaggy over his weathered face. He fidgeted beneath an oversized black silk shirt in gold damask. A gold medallion in the shape of a dollar sign on a thick, braided chain hung from his neck. Following a practiced assessment of the white *gaijin*, the Iranian smiled and held out his hand. With the handshake, he and Kent were old friends, the imminent exchange understood.

The Iranian patted Kent on the back and spoke in English. "Hello, my friend. How are you? I am Oscar." A light wind seemed to circle him in the shade of the station, his shirt rippling like a sail.

Kent stood sweating in the humid air, reduced to squinting in the dark corner. "*Nani ga arimasu ka?*" He didn't care what Oscar had, only what he wanted.

Oscar switched to Japanese. "*Nihongo wakaru?*" Thus began a dance of efficient nods and gestures that signaled Kent's purpose and the beginning of a buy. It was a choreographed routine, other Iranian men nearby appearing then vanishing inside a minivan. The terminus speakers broadcast a waltz as if in time to their movement. Within seconds, Kent had lost sight of all but Oscar as the others vanished.

Oscar pulled Kent by his arm into the shade of the stairwell. "Do I know you? You have been here before?"

"No." Even in the shadow of Azuma's train station under the cloud of a drug deal, Kent felt a tingle of satisfaction at being recognized. He nearly swept his glasses from his face.

Oscar took his hand again, squeezing it for another five seconds, as if searching for credibility. "I think I do know you, but it's okay. Maybe I don't. So, you want something from Oscar?"

"Yes, I want something from Oscar. Whatever you got."

Like a magician pulling a quarter from mid-air, Oscar opened his hand, a matchbook-sized plastic baggie in his palm. "Is this what you want?"

"That's a start," Kent said.

"What are we talking about?"

"About five times that. And some hash. Whatever you got."

"Come back at six. I'll meet you at Uncle Bob's Burger House. You know, up the street?"

"I can find it. Can you give me what you got now?"

"Take it all, friend. I can take off work early and go see my girlfriend. She's always complaining I don't spend enough time with her."

In a telephone booth, Oscar left two grams of *shabu*, a gram of hash, and an assortment of painkillers, their identities for Kent to sort out. Kent replaced it with ¥15,000 inside the pages of the telephone book after pretending to make another call. Oscar's compatriots reappeared from the shadows, huddling and nodding to Kent. The sweet smell of cheap cologne found in most public *onsens* lingered around the telephone booths and over the sidewalk, clouds of it under the stairs. As Kent turned to leave, Oscar smiled, his mouth growing wider until Kent thought it would stretch to his ears, and waved him off as if they were old friends.

DORAMA PART II

Kent returned to the hotel and smoked a pinch of what Oscar had sold him. One by one, lights went on. Contentment, so familiar but so perfectly new every time, rose within him, from his thighs through his belly and chest, to the tips of his tingling fingers, and up and up and up until the liveliness set his shoulders straight and jumped into his jaw. Fatigue, anxiety, dejection lifted as he shed his wet clothes. He could spring from his feet into the air he was so unburdened, as if gravity ceased altogether. He felt as if he were staring into the sun, transfixed and drawn upward by its heat, its glow, his body and mind in need of nothing, craving satisfied. He was happy studying the texture of the curtains or chitchatting with the hotel housekeepers, time sifted through *shabu*'s fingers. Nothing could stop him from buying more of what had raised him so high. What he wanted and what he felt were good things.

After a long soak and an hour of watching without following CNN International, Kent bounced his way to Uncle Bob's Burger House where he waited outside for Oscar. Eager to put the business behind him and secure a promising stash. Midori's Hello Kitty umbrella had barely kept the rain off and its stem was bent despite Kent's efforts to straighten it. He didn't care. He wore an overcoat from a Tokyo thrift store, his arms poking clownishly out of the too-short sleeves, and a Yomiuri Giants baseball cap. The rain felt right. *Right as rain*, he repeated the phrase all the way to town like a mantra.

In school uniforms, shouldering backpacks and texting on cell phones, the teenagers gathered at Uncle Bob's for American burgers and fries, milkshakes and nuclear green melon sodas. Kent was wary of being recognized in the restaurant where marathon screenings of *The Strange Bonanza* were a likely choice on Bob's wide screen television. He looked for recognition anyway. What harm could come from throwing a few winks at gawking high school girls? Despite his caution, Kent wanted to talk. Or not. He could do anything and be content. He had the urge to sit at one of the big booths modeled after those in American diners, order a root beer float, and practice his *kanji* reading a Japanese study version of Murakami or Tanizaki or one of Shin's Boy Wasabi serials as he went through half a pack of Larks. He'd spent his early days in Japan like this, isolated and alone but happy, a disciplined life of study and bicycle days in which he explored the countryside then haunted a coffee shop for hours with his books and dictionaries.

Kent watched the boys and girls inside through the large front window. He wanted to embrace them all, to share their energy, their glee. He peered through the glass. A television showed a celebrity gossip program. It took Kent a second to realize it was his face again on the screen—one of his better publicity stills from the early days—leaving him both grateful for, and afraid of, the media's endless speculation. And again his face paired with Ozman's, also an old publicity still, from *Airship Japan*. Ozman in profile to Kent's portrait, as if the lunatic Australian were screaming at him still, open-mouthed, mohawked, tribal-tattooed goon in full shriek. Then someone did scream at him. Kent jumped and turned, certain to find the Australian shock comic racing for him in steel-toe boots, a knife between his teeth, his mohawk in full sail, payback time.

"Hey! *RI-CHU-MAN-SAN!*" Three young men approached from the other side of street. Not Ozman, thank God. But yakuza. Still better than Ozman. Kent knew it. They had to be. Some punkass *bosozoku*, some motorcycle shitkickers pissed because he'd gone to the Iranians for drugs and not them. The man who screamed at him wore cheap aluminum glasses, blue polyester sweats, and white sneakers that would've been new were they not soaked and covered in mud. A Bluetooth earpiece stuck out from the side of his head. He was thin, more teenager than adult, with a buzz cut, the stubby bristles forming a square on top of his head. And clearly upset with Kent. *Bosozoku*, surely, but this guy didn't *look* like a *bosozoku*. No punch perm, no ornate women's house slippers, no baggy workman's pants, and no pompadour. *Bosozoku* made themselves known. But Buzz Cut didn't look like any *bosozoku* Kent had ever seen. Maybe they were goons sent by Ozman.

Kent was ready to pull down his glasses and go for an *A-re?* to diffuse whatever had upset these men when Buzz Cut swung his umbrella at Kent, missing.

"You stupid," he said in English. Swung again and caught Kent on the knee.

"What the hell?" Kent responded in Japanese and searched for something to brandish in defense. He thrust his umbrella at the man like a short sword. Buzz Cut swung again, both hands wrapped around his own umbrella. And again. Missing both times. Until he connected with Kent's umbrella, bending the poor pink thing further at the middle.

"I don't have any money. I got nothing." Kent held his hands up, and turned his palms out. "*Nani mo.*" And it was true—he had nothing.

"I don't your money," the peculiar fuzzy man continued in English.

"Then what do you want?" Kent shot back in English and searched the sidewalk for Ozman. If these were his goons, then he might be watching, just out of sight.

"Motherfuck." Buzz Cut thrust his neck forward as if spitting the mangled English at Kent.

"Motherfuck?" Kent laughed.

"Motherfuck!" The other two men moved in closer and swung their umbrellas. He wondered if they belonged to some club where the uniform involved tracksuits, sneakers, and glasses.

"I speak Japanese." Kent said in Japanese and pointed to his mouth. "*Nihon-go.*"

Buzz Cut dropped the umbrella from its swinging position. He looked defeated despite the fact that he was the one attacking Kent. He sighed and switched to Japanese. "Of course. You're on television." His shoulders sagged and he kicked a soda can across the sidewalk. "Stay away from Midori." His voice rose and cracked. "I mean it."

"Midori?" Kent kept his arms up in case Buzz Cut started swinging again. "Who the hell is—?" It took asking the question before Kent realized the man was talking about the woman he'd met last night. "Midori? Dyed hair, about—" Kent held his hand horizontally at his chest "—this tall?"

"I knew it!" Buzz Cut swung his umbrella at Kent, missing again, but enough to push Kent against Uncle Bob's plate glass window. Teenagers gathered to watch, a few girls screaming as he smacked against the glass.

"Hey, nothing hap—"

"I know you were with her, *RI-CHU-MAN-SAN!*"
Kent looked around to see if anyone else had heard
them. He didn't want trouble or attention here with Oscar
so near by. He knew the police knew of and probably
tolerated Oscar, but only if Oscar and his dealings were
done quietly. Kent felt too good to be afraid, but he didn't
want to jeopardize his own score. And in Japan if the
police caught you buying drugs, you got a long, harsh
prison sentence. He could end up with Ozman in Fuchu.
He'd hardly last a day.

"What did you do with her?" Buzz Cut and the other
men closed in on Kent, a move that seemed rehearsed, their
umbrellas bumping his. Buzz Cut appeared emboldened
by the presence of his comrades and the teenagers who
were pressed against the other side of the window.

Kent swept his glasses from his face and in his most
comical voice said, "*A-re?*" Who knew? He hoped the
tagline, a self-deprecating stab at his own clownish
personality, would allay the tension. When his routine
failed to evoke a reply, he acted as if his glasses needed
wiping and did so with the tail of his T-shirt. When he
replaced them, he'd only dirtied them with his unwashed
and oily shirt. Buzz Cut and his friends appeared as greasy
blurs. "I don't even know you. I have no idea what you're
talking about."

"Bullshit." The tough guy talk didn't match the man
with the earpiece and bent aluminum frames whose lenses
were fogged over by the humidity.

Kent couldn't see the other men, who flounced
behind and nipped at him like hyenas at a wounded zebra.
He waited for umbrellas to rain down on his head. He
gripped the handle of his own, ready to duel if necessary,
to get rid of these clowns.

"Don't play stupid." Buzz Cut rocked on his feet and licked his lips.

"You've got nothing to worry about. Midori doesn't—"

"Stop saying her name!" Buzz Cut stepped closer. "She's not your groupie slut, your celebrity toy."

"My wh—?" Kent stepped back only to be shoved forward again by the other two.

Teenagers gasped behind him, drawn to the glass by the commotion, their cell phones capturing every second.

"She doesn't want anything to do with me. Really. *Nothing* happened. No hard feelings." Kent turned to see the other two men who now shuffled nervously on either side. "Ask her yourself. She'll tell you."

"Shut up! Stop talking!" Buzz Cut's eyes bulged, bouncing from side to side. Kent wondered if he were jacked up on *shabu* himself. He looked ready to burst. "She told me."

"Told you what? There's nothing to tell."

"In Tamarindo, the love hotel." This reminder seemed to push Buzz Cut even edgier. "She told me everything."

"Oh, man—this is all wrong." Why would she tell this man that? "This is between you two. I had no idea. But it doesn't matter, nothing happened."

"You're a liar." He inched closer. "I'm going to kill you like Ozman should have."

"I gotta go." Kent searched the sidewalk for Oscar. "You guys are messing something up." Kent made to step away, but stumbled when a sharp edge from his umbrella caught the webbing of Buzz Cut's, entangling the two.

Buzz Cut jerked his umbrella away. "Get off."

Kent pulled at Hello Kitty, tearing a hole in Buzz Cut's umbrella webbing.

"Look what you did, asshole." Buzz Cut waved the torn umbrella at Kent. The aluminum stems raked over Kent's face, sweeping his glasses to the ground and scratching his eye.

Kent screamed, dropped his umbrella, covered his right eye with one hand, and fell to his knees.

He heard one of the two men behind him. "Oh shit, Kenji." Then scuffling, footsteps retreating, Buzz Cut nearby still. "Ass—hole." The umbrella hitting the sidewalk and footfalls.

Kent opened his good eye but even that hurt. He thought he might pass out from the pain. He imagined his eye as a ragged mess of tissue and blood, the eyeball dangling from its socket, attached by a loose red thread as if he were a cartoon character. But he wouldn't be able to pop his eye back into its socket and move on. He might be blinded forever. He managed his good eye open enough to search for his glasses and catch a smear of people gathered around him on the sidewalk. Every movement, every glance from side to side to see who might rain umbrellas on his head. When he tried to keep the wounded eye still, he understood it was impossible.

Someone handed him his glasses. "Are you all right?"

Teenagers rushed from the restaurant to his side, encircling him, cell phones flashing.

"That guy poked my eye out." Kent held one lens of his glasses up to his good eye, and, despite the smudge across it, he saw Oscar, his drug dealer with a pocketful of what Kent had come for, of what he wanted more than anything else, walking briskly away.

CHAPTER THIRTEEN

—

TYPHOON JUDE

O N *SHABU* Kent believed he could find a way back to what he'd once been, the only thing in his life besides Kumi that ever made him feel that way. Kumi had saved him from what he'd left in the States. From Allan's death and his mother who fell deeper into an already dangerous alcohol dependence and seemed unable to forgive him. From his stargazing father who offered no solace beyond the possibility of reincarnation via suicide. Kumi's love and his popular success as *RI-CHU-MAN-SAN!* had convinced him that he was better than the person he'd left in America, that he was capable of being someone beyond the seven-year-old infamous for fratricide.

On *shabu*, Kent believed his life would turn around. Kumi would take him back, and they could start over for real this time. Ozman would be captured, his sentence lengthened, security in his cell heightened. Kent would return to Tokyo, rebuild his career, and forget Monique and Ozman. He'd forget Kumi had ever left him. Forget Renzo's ridiculous publicity stunt. Together he and Kumi would once more become "Tokyo's Favorite Celebrity Couple."

On *shabu*, Kent sorted out the disorder of his life. His thoughts marched along single file.

On *shabu*, Kent trusted his life was fixable, that the chain of events which had led him to Japan and on to Tokyo sound stages and his life with Kumi, and, finally, to a small town in the mountains of central Japan would also point him right back to Tokyo and the good life he once enjoyed.

After his clash with the three sweat-suited men, Kent stumbled back to the hotel in the rain, refusing offers of help from the strangers who gathered around him. He didn't want the police or the media turning up and asking questions. He still had a handful of *shabu*. He saw no sign of Oscar or his pals, their vans and vending carts gone. His eye was a puffy mess, enflamed with rivulets of red. A washcloth and ice helped with the pain and swelling, but he couldn't see out of the eye and when he tried to move his good eye, the wounded one moved as well. All he could do was close them both but even then they moved involuntarily behind his eyelids, *shabu* still surging through his veins.

To keep out the painful light and offer some protection, Kent fashioned a makeshift eyepatch by cutting out one side of a green, airline sleeping mask, an artifact of his tenure in first class cabins. He smelled of *shabu*, as if he'd gargled with hairspray, and of cigarettes, and the curry-flavored potato chips he bought on his way to meet Oscar, a halfhearted attempt at nourishment. His jaw ached from the relentless grinding. He knew his teeth were the worse for it, too. His canines were sharpened to spear points. Where once there had been two rows of straightened and whitened front teeth, now hung chipped, tobacco-stained relics. The exchange had somehow always seemed fair. Poor health for pain relief.

This rainy day, however, Kent hurt. The *shabu* helped to distract him from the eye pain, but not as much as he'd hoped. He took a couple of the mystery painkillers from the baggie Oscar sold him, which calmed but did not douse the pain that lit up his eye. He'd have to ration the *shabu* he bought earlier, make it last much longer than he'd anticipated, unless Oscar returned before he left. There was enough to last a week, if he were patient and allowed what he'd smoked to carry him as far as it might. Even then, Kent knew if he looked hard enough, he'd find someone else who'd sell to him. Despite Japan's reputation as a drug-free nation, there was no shortage of the stuff if you knew where to look and didn't mind the risks. Still, with his eye raging and his nerves threadbare, Kent hit the pipe again, pushing blue smoke to the ceiling with a long, slow release.

From his hotel window he observed an old man in pajamas watching television in the apartment complex next door. The old man smoked a cigarette, sipped tea and routinely waved a fan decorated with an image of the popular and furry Totoro holding an umbrella over his head. The old man rested against a pink pillow on the floor, his legs underneath a coffee table. Blue and white images reflected onto his sliding glass door. The old man caught Kent watching, so Kent waved. The old man smiled and dipped his head. Otherwise, the old man didn't move but to smoke his cigarette and sip his tea. Kent stopped watching when what appeared to be the old man's grandchildren swept into the room. They didn't acknowledge him and he didn't move as the children changed the channel and settled inches from the television to watch. A woman, his daughter or daughter-in-law, entered and left with the old man's ashtray and teapot. She returned with an empty ashtray and a fresh pot of tea without once speaking to the old man. Kent could have watched the domestic theater all night. The old man's home was not perfect but it was a home, something Kent hadn't enjoyed in some time. He even considered crossing the alley between them and inviting himself in. When the kids started jumping on a spongy love seat, all he could think about was his own ascent and jump from a couch years before, a fall that never seemed to end.

Unable to sleep, Kent took advantage of the dry spell outside, despite the waves of pain from his eye: crest to trough, trough to crest, pain and more pain. *Shabu* kept him up and eager to be somewhere, to do something, and he believed distraction might help. He sat in a city park a few minutes from the hotel, swatting at mosquitoes and drinking one vending machine beer after another to calm his jitters and dull the pain in his eye. The To-ne River flowed with a great whoosh in front of him. Kent found it revealing how little he needed to survive. Since leaving Tokyo, he'd eaten little, *shabu* suppressing his appetite. He could go on his little suck-pipe of energy without food or sleep. At just over six feet, he'd dropped to one hundred seventy pounds from his usual one hundred eighty-five.

The television news announced a rare early and powerful typhoon was heading their way, on top of the already heavy plum rains. A swirling mass of feathery white clouds the size of Mexico sweeping northeast towards Japan. The storm had been named *Jude*, the first of the season. The weatherman had walked across a satellite image of Southeast Asia, predicting Jude's path with a pointer, thick yellow arrows driving towards Japan like a military offensive. But for now, the rain was held at bay by a canopy of unseasonable heat. While he was content to sit on a bench by the river and wait for the rain to wash away his blues, Kent didn't know how long he could continue outside, the air so saturated there was little left to breathe. He pushed himself up, dizzy, beer sloshing in his stomach. Lights popped before him and he leaned against a maple next to the cool of the narrow river. At the railing along the river's edge, an assembly of green metal pipes that ran the length of the river through the city, Kent leaned over and threw up into the dark, rushing water.

Back in the hotel again, restless but weak, he removed his wet clothes and filled the tub, his body and brain exhausted from the day's range of dismissals. After his bath, he boiled water for tea, rolled a cigarette with hashish, and watched television in his hotel-supplied *yukata*. The tea and hashish left him warm in front of the evening programs, at rest for a change; maybe he'd sleep after all. He flicked past NHK educational shows—a cooking show where they cut scallions for a thin soup and an Australian program on dog training—until he found an evening drama about a family in which the father in the midst of an affair is discovered with his mistress by his teenaged daughter. The players overplayed, falling to the floor amid denials and moans, closeups that revealed inner turmoil and a wellspring of tears. The show left him aching.

Changes in Love was the show he was being groomed for before Ozman. He was to be the next plot twist. A *gaijin* love interest on Japanese television. He planned to break new ground, cross boundaries, show the Japanese that he could do more than sing orchestrated Beatles songs and perform as a talking energy drink. With every death, ritual or otherwise, he was inevitably drawn to the image of Allan across a beach house floor. Thanks to Allan, Kent had a story now, too.

KENT RICHMAN IS *RI-CHU-MAN-SAN!*
In the morning, Kent was eager to leave, to get out of the Terminal Hotel before the room swallowed him whole. He'd been unable to sleep, but twitched and squirmed on the bed before an endless supply of satellite television channels. Renzo called at eleven to grill him about new cell phone videos turning up on the web, and to detail another opportunity in the works.

RI-CHU-MAN-SAN! would return to *The Strange Bonanza* at the end of the summer. But in voice only. Kent Richman, the actor on stage, would be replaced by an animated version of *RI-CHU-MAN-SAN!*, wide-eyed and big-haired with a triangle mouth. Kent Richman would supply a scripted voice for *RI-CHU-MAN-SAN!* from a production booth. Kent Richman would never again appear as *RI-CHU-MAN-SAN!* Kent Richman would sign away his rights to the character. The actor Kent Richman could not appear at *Bonanza*-related events. Only *RI-CHU-MAN-SAN!* could appear, via computer animation, at *Bonanza*-related events. After one year, Kent Richman's voice of *RI-CHU-MAN-SAN!* would be withdrawn and replaced by an actor as yet undetermined.

"You get this, Richman, and you're making cutting-edge television. You'll be a pioneer. Talk about a comeback. And you can finally shed the *RI-CHU-MAN-SAN!* persona. You'll be able to branch out into more serious roles that don't rely on your Lennon likeness or that idiotic tagline." Kent heard music in the background; Renzo sounded as if he were eating a sandwich.

"What about the documentary? Can't we use that to shed all that and start over, tell my story the way I want to?" Kent said.

"It's happening, Richman. But you need to keep your head down—can you do that for one more day, *please?*—and get your ass to the mountains before another asshole catches you doing something stupid, before Ozman follows your snail trail to Azuma. What the hell was that all about anyway?"

Kent hadn't seen the videos, but guessed they were captured outside Bob's. "Just some zealous fans, no big deal."

"Yeah? Looked like somebody was beating the hell out of you." Somebody was speaking to Renzo over the music—*another for me and*—. "Are you all right?"

"I'm fine. A misunderstanding. Don't worry."

"And why would I worry about you, Richman? I'll be in touch."

Kent kept seeing himself in animated form, occupying the console seat on Stage B he'd once held. A comic book version of Kent Richman: skinny and long-legged with spiky hair, protracted and angular face, cheekbone lines extending into his pointed chin with the hint of goatee he once wore, and thin lips. And, of course, round glasses with rose-colored lenses at the tip of his Roman nose. From neutral to slight up angle. Slight down angle with eyes on camera. A hyperbolic grin, one eyebrow raised, and *A-re?*

MIDORI REDUX

At four-thirty in the morning, Kent put on

his gold smoking jacket and his Yomiuri Giants cap and went in search of a convenience store. He felt better in the jacket, which reminded him of better days. They'd gone to the roof of their building to watch the sunset, a rare clear day in the city. Kent lifted the gold jacket from the box. Collar and cuffs of black velvet, hand-finished braiding, a sash. He tugged its arms like a puppeteer. "It's a beauty. Where did you get it?" He put the jacket on over his sweatshirt.

"A vintage store in Tokyo. You like?" Kumi placed her hands on his shoulders, straightened the collar, and picked a piece of lint from the lapel.

Kent found Kumi so beautiful in the afternoon sunlight that he got his camera. They took pictures of each other. Kumi against the skyline. Kumi with the sun behind her and her head bowed low. Kumi holding a Japanese fan in front of her face, her eyes coy and cool over the top. Kumi smoking a cigarette, eyes nearly shut, a breeze before her. Kent comically stiff in his new smoking jacket. Kent as lounge lizard with cigarette and bottle of wine. Kent and Kumi laughing as the self-timer beeped to a close. Kent and Kumi, wine-stained and careless.

He was supposed to meet his liaison at 7:00 a.m. but needed again to get out of the hotel. He liked Japan in the morning: narrow, serene streets through a maze of neighborhoods, no street signs to guide your way. The neighborhood nearby offered a uniform habitat of one and two-story residencies side-by-side-by-side, a few multi-storied apartment buildings, blocks of them pinched between prewar rice fields and small businesses, drainage canals and small parks, a highway overpass, once the path of samurai. Houses sat quiet, the occasional light blinking on as its residents woke before the sun rose over the traffic of diesels, the smokestacks of the Haraguchi Copper Mine and the pimply green logo of the Akiba Pickle Factory, the larger-than-life pickle like a colossal green penis. Even heavy rains could not wash away the pervasive scent of vinegar that rose from the factory flues and clung like a glaze to the town.

Kent waved to indifferent monks as they swept soot into the gutter and collected trash from in front of a nearby temple gate tucked between a vegetable market and a bicycle repair shop. Early risers shuffled along in slippers holding umbrellas over their dogs. Students wearing book bags pumped at the pedals of their bicycles as they held umbrellas in one hand, handlebar in the other. Storefronts sat dark, while vending machines for rice, sodas, and cigarettes cast glowing light to the street and hummed along, never dark. Mountains peaked over the top of the low, dark clouds Jude had swept in. The To-ne River swirled between its soaked banks, throngs of vine and wild rice bobbing with the swift current. He sat under an old train trestle as the roads came alive with cars and trucks, bicycles gliding by unhurried.

At five, a man in a blue smock opened the doors and swept the front walk, the parking lot. Kent bought bananas, oranges, and rice balls in the hope that he might be hungry later. As he left the convenience store, a group of four teenaged girls in plain blue school uniforms rushed past him, giving him a glance. Kent smiled and winked at the girls in response, certain they had recognized him, until he heard a tall girl in knee socks say something about a pirate and he remembered the eyepatch.

He spent the next hour and a half walking the town perimeter, a steady pace and a feeling that he was moving forward, that his life would improve.

When he returned to the hotel, the desk clerk stopped him.

"Mr. Richman! Excuse me, Mr. Richman."

"Yes?" Kent's paranoia, a guaranteed consequence of too much *shabu,* no sleep, and no real sustenance, left him expecting the police and questions about an Iranian named Oscar. Or worse—Ozman.

The young clerk pointed behind him. "Someone is here for you."

Before Kent could turn to look, a woman's voice echoed in the lobby. "Nice jacket." Midori held out her hand in greeting. "Ready to go?"

ONE OF THE BEAUTIFUL PEOPLE

PART TWO
ALMOST, AT TIMES, THE FOOL

CHAPTER FOURTEEN

—

REST STOP BLUES

Had he told her where he was staying? "What are you doing here?" The mock eyepatch didn't fit under his regular wire-rimmed glasses, and he was forced to wear a pair of large, black frames left over from a brief stretch in which he looked more like Elvis Costello than John Lennon. He seemed to be suffering his own aftershocks since the earthquake. Without warning, the earth tipped one way then another, leaving him unnerved and off-balance.

"Midori Watanabe, at your service." Her hand remained outstretched. "I'm here to take you to Cedars Temple." She took off her sunglasses and leaned in. "Oh my, what happened to your face, your eye? Did Ozman—?"

"You?" He felt as if he had been played, but he wasn't sure how or for what reason. Nothing—Midori, the attack, his trip to the mountains—and everything seemed to add up. But to what? Was this Buddhist resort so exclusive that they vetted their clients? Had he then passed the audition?

"I'm sorry." She dropped her head. "I should have told you the other night." She looked up again and reached for Kent's face. "But what happened?"

He jerked his head away. "Don't you know? Your goon boyfriend, if that's who he is." Kent stepped forward, one hand on the makeshift eyepatch. "This how you treat all your guests?"

Midori stepped back as if she thought Kent might swing at her. "You saw Kenji?"

"Is that his name? And a couple of his goon buddies." Kent stepped closer as Midori bumped up against a lobby chair. "You hire a hit squad, because these guys seemed pretty unhappy with me."

Midori looked deflated, her mischievousness gone. "But how did—"

"Why didn't you tell me who you were the other night and why is your boyfriend out to get me? Your name *is* Midori?"

"Yes." Midori dabbed at her eyes with a handkerchief. "My uncle runs the Watanabe Cedars Temple. It's been in our family for over four hundred years. I help out part time, teaching English, this and that, but my family lives here in Azuma. I live with them. It's a long story, but we have half a day's drive, and I promise I'll explain everything in the car. I feel so stupid."

Kent softened with Midori's tears. "*Ikimasho.* I can't wait to hear this story."

In the confines of Midori's compact Subaru, she smelled good, no longer the overwhelming vanilla from Tamarindo, but a scent of white flowers and musk mixing in nicely with her menthol smokes. Kent recalled a phrase from the Bible his mother used to throw out when it suited, though it never made any sense to him. *Our lives are a fragrance presented by Christ to God.* Windshield wipers and rain made everything blurry; the car was cozy and warm. Midori wore fresh make-up, though not nearly as much as before, her lips clear and glossy, her eyes missing the pale glitter. She wore loose blue jeans, a black belt squeezing the over-sized pants around her small waist, a man's undershirt and a black sweater over her shoulders, black leather shoes with high, thick heels. Her hair was held up in arbitrary folds by a plastic clip.

After fifteen minutes of silence, of looking out the window at the early morning drivers, people getting away like them, Midori spoke, asking Kent to pick some music for the CD player. She kept a steadfast path along the expressway. He chose Japan's Mr. Children from a CD case on the floor. He tapped away at the infectious pop music and hoped like hell that they could drive for hours more. His earlier pinch of *shabu* kept him alert and contented but his increased heart rate left him sweaty, his blood flowing a little too fast. A handful of painkillers ensured his eye was only a dull throb under the eyepatch. They climbed a steep grade and were quickly engulfed in a dense fog, gray with rain and steam, everything a lush spring green. With each kilometer under them Kent felt better, despite the odd circumstances. He was getting away from Azuma, a town that had lobbed bombshells at him.

The prospect of real work ahead helped him to put his blunders behind him. For the first time in weeks, Kent saw a future. He'd go with this unremarkable girl to the mountains for a few days, rest, relax, and try some meditation, talk about his life, make a film. His career would turn for the better. He'd take the voice-over gig, get his face out again the way he wanted, do some interviews, and make some club appearances to establish his return. Once casting agents knew of his comeback, he'd land a coveted role on a Japanese soap opera and break real ground, just as Renzo had promised. With his soap opera success, he'd receive sponsorship and movie offers, again be given VIP memberships and welcomed into the best clubs in Tokyo. After a year, he'd leave *The Strange Bonanza*. The schedule had always been a challenging one and the real reason he'd relied so heavily on *shabu*. Every day from noon until six he was in makeup as *RI-CHU-MAN-SAN!*, whether on stage or elsewhere. And following taping, he was still *RI-CHU-MAN-SAN!* on the street, in a restaurant or club, shopping for dinner. Kent always viewed the role as apprentice work before he took on more specialized roles. And with his career revitalized, Kumi would take him back. Kent and Kumi—it was certainly possible—would once again walk red carpets, their story an inspiration to all—rise, fall, and rise again.

Kent tapped out his optimism on the floorboard. The rain, the *shabu*, the J-pop, the mountains, the smell of Midori's flowers and menthols took him higher, as if lifted to the sky by a nest of hot air balloons. Kent saw his future. The Japanese might build a shrine to the pair as a memorial to the industry and triumph over tragedy the public so admired. In a city park. Name a school or a theater after them. Love, endurance, and rebirth prevail. The glow of sunshine rose behind the mountains and the clouds, and Kent was ready to forgive.

"So—talk already." He made sure Midori heard the lightness in his voice. She was the only person in his world right then, and it didn't matter what she told him.

"I don't know where to start." She pulled a menthol from the pack on the dash, punched the car lighter, and turned to Kent. "I feel so stupid. And do you mind if we don't listen to that CD. Kenji gave that to me. I never liked it, but it was one of his favorite bands." Midori switched on a morning news program as they drove northwest and deeper into the Japanese Alps.

"Why? Because you got caught or because you got me beaten up?" He still felt the burn of her duplicity.

"I'm sorry about your eye. Is it—can you see?" She rolled the cigarette between her fingers unconsciously, like he had seen school kids do with their pencils.

"It hurts like hell. But I'm not blind, if that's your concern."

"I'm sure he didn't mean to hurt you. He's not—he's got his faults but I've never thought of him as a violent person. I mean the idea of Kenji hurting anyone is laugh—"

"I get it. But he's sure got a thing with umbrellas. Scratched the hell out of my eye. I suppose he accidentally beat me over the head with the thing too? And he accidentally brought his buddies with him? I thought yakuza had come for me. Or maybe Ozman had hired some goons to take me out."

"Kenji and his buddies, yakuza? Goons?" She laughed. "*So na.*"

"Easy for you to say—you weren't being beaten over the head on a public sidewalk."

"With—an umbrella." She laughed again.

"Funny. You've no idea." Kent removed the homemade eyepatch, struggling to open his puffy eye. Midori put her hand to her mouth to hide a gasp. Kent's eye had been draining uncontrollably since the accident. Tears streamed down his cheek, leaving him sniffling.

She reached a hand out to him but stopped short of touching him. "You should see a doctor."

"*You* should drive." He gently replaced the eyepatch. "It's like someone's pouring acid into my eye every time I move it. But I don't want to see a doctor." Kent was afraid of what a doctor might find in addition to his rheumy eye.

"I'm sure Kenji just meant to scare you. He's harmless—but upset."

"So, what's the story with this guy?" A tear rolled to the tip of his nose. Midori seemed poised to wipe it away with her finger but again stopped short of touching him. There was no indication that the two had slept half-naked beside each other in a love hotel.

"There's not much to tell. Kenji and I dated for two years, but we broke up two days ago. He's very unhappy about it. Made a big fuss, crying, begging. I couldn't stand it."

"Unhappiness I got." Kent dabbed again at the tears on his cheek with a paper napkin.

"He's a sweet guy, but I didn't see the point in staying with him. I met him after I came back from Australia. I felt unglued from my life. But Kenji was—safe, secure, easy. I knew what to expect from him and I needed that, and he treated me nice. He's a high school physics teacher. Everyone expected we'd get married, including Kenji."

"Not for you?"

"Not now, not to him."

Kent held his hands open and smiled. "Need someone a bit more exciting?" He caught his reflection in the window, the eyepatch, the large black frames, the puffy cheeks and reddened skin. *Exciting*.

"Maybe. I broke it off one night and ended up at Tamarindo the next night. I don't know why. I needed to get out of my apartment, needed someone to see me, tell me I'm pretty, and buy me a drink. You handled most of that, all except the pretty part."

Kent felt guilty for thinking Midori so plain. In the light of day without makeup, she wasn't the plain girl he remembered.

"Is that so bad? Kenji's so insecure he just doesn't know how to deal. He hasn't had a lot of girlfriends. He still lives with his parents. I was following the path of least resistance and, suddenly, I didn't like where it was leading. It was a shock for him. He had our whole life together planned out. Then we broke up, he found out I was with you and lost it."

"You mean you told him?"

Midori ignored him.

"He told me you told him."

She turned, her mouth pinched. "So, I told him. Big deal. I was tired of his whining. I just wanted to hurt him a little, take control of things. Give him a reason."

"And that's why you were with me?"

"Not exactly. It was more of a convenient coincidence."

"I see. Nothing happened. I told him that."

Midori turned to him. "You told him that?"

Kent nodded. The gentleman. The good knight.

"It doesn't matter. I'm just tired of other people messing with my life. First this guy tries to rape me, my parents want me to get married, then Kenji and all of his insecure shit. I saw you at Tamarindo—it was a coincidence. I was supposed to take you to Cedars, but I wasn't supposed to meet you until the next day. Then, seeing you there by yourself, I was curious. I was having fun and thought if you knew who I was then—"

"Who knows?"

"It really wasn't about you—I don't even know you."

"Thanks." Kent wished she'd stop talking.

"Except for TV." She turned to look Kent in his good eye. "And I don't pick up guys in bars. I know how that sounds but I don't know what I was thinking leaving with you. It just felt good to have a stranger, and you a celebrity, interested in me. I couldn't believe it. I needed that—that kind of attention."

"What's so hard to believe?"

"I'm sure it happens all the time." Midori crushed her cigarette out, blew a stream of smoke to her side, and reached for another.

"No, not all the time."

"I'm not stupid. I know how this works. And like you said: nothing happened."

She pushed her black hair away from her face—the smell of it lifted Kent's spirits again. She looked to him for confirmation. "I just thought—"

Kent couldn't return her gaze. "Thought what—?" He followed the traces of her cigarette in the air. He wondered if this, whatever it was, between them was finished.

"I thought it'd be fun to hang out with you, that's all. A change of pace from my boring life. Big deal. Call it a rebound. Have sex with a stranger, nothing more." A flush rose to her already ruddy cheeks.

"And you didn't even get to have sex." Kent thought she would appreciate his sense of humor, but she ignored him.

"I thought it would be nice to do something besides sit in my parents' stupid house on another stupid Friday night. I thought you'd be different."

"Different from what?"

"From *me*—from Kenji, from my boring life. Don't act like you don't understand, that there's a difference between you and me."

"Disappointed?" Kent said.

"In what?"

"In me?"

"I don't know what I expected. It's not like I thought you'd sweep me off my feet and jet me to Tokyo where we'd sip champagne in your Shibuya penthouse. Or maybe I did, I don't know. I just thought we might have fun, get out of here for a while. Can we just forget it ever happened? I'll take you to Cedars as planned. It's a beautiful place. It always makes me feel better."

"We had fun." Kent put his hand on her knee.

She tensed. He removed his hand.

The smell of her shampoo again. He asked, "So what now?"

"I take you to Cedars, do what I do, then go back to Azuma, and, if I'm lucky, find a job so I can get out of my parents' house. Figure my life out. You do your thing at Cedars. Go back to Tokyo. Be on TV. Whatever celebrities do."

Kent leaned forward. "Any room for me in there?" He knew he sounded desperate but he couldn't stop himself.

"Don't." She looked like she might cry. "Don't mock me. You know nothing about me."

"I know some." Kent turned again to his reflection. Just looking at the eyepatch made his eye hurt. He was unshaven and his cheeks were hollow. His eyes, nose and face were chapped from constantly wiping away tears.

"I can't tell if you're joking or just lacking self-awareness." Midori narrowed her eyes. "I told you I was sorry about Kenji. I think you have your own problems. I can't help you. I can hardly help myself right now."

"Maybe I can help. If you let me."

"Let you what? I'm taking you to Cedars, and then I'm leaving. This is too weird. What's your story, anyway?"

Where would he start? *My first real public catastrophe came when I was a wee lad of seven.* Ozman had asked him the same thing. *What's your story, RI-CHU-MAN-SAN!?* Ozman had asked him again and again, as if Kent might have an explanation for banging his wife. He didn't, but he understood he owed Ozman that. Maybe if he'd just said he was sorry from the beginning, confessed to the insult, Ozman might have left before Kumi came home. But then Kumi came home, her photo shoot postponed, her face moving from confused amusement to shocked awareness at the sight of Kent covered in blood from a broken nose and a split lip, of Ozman standing before him, his face splashed with soot from the firecracker he'd exploded between his teeth. With the memory of Ozman, Kent heard Ozman's name on the car radio, as if he'd conjured it up with some voodoo. He no longer trusted his senses. Then he heard it again.

"You hear that? Listen." Kent turned the radio up. "They're talking about Ozman."

"I'm sure it's just—" Midori reached for the volume control but Kent slapped at her hand.

"Let me listen."

"… Corrections Officer Junichiro Kawabata explained that Mr. Ozman had apparently managed to slip out of the prison, though his methods are currently unknown. 'There has never been an escape from Fuchu Prison. But we suspect Mr. Ozman may have concealed himself somehow with one of the contract services we employ, who come and go as necessary. I cannot, at this time, speculate further on how he may have escaped.'

"Japanese law enforcement, as well as Interpol and other international law enforcement agencies, have been put on full alert. 'He will not be able to leave Japan, unless he swims.' Officer Kawabata also speculated that Mr. Ozman might be looking to settle his score with fellow entertainer Kent Richman, who famously had an affair with Mr. Ozman's wife, Monique Martine of Canada.

"Mr. Ozman had been in Fuchu Prison since his arrest following the shooting of Ms. Martine in the Crystal Palace Apartments, where Mr. Ozman abducted and tortured both Mr. Richman and Mr. Richman's wife Kumiko Sato in an apparent revenge scenario. Ms. Sato separated from Mr. Richman soon after—"

Kent still believed Ozman's escape had to be a hoax, another of the prison pranks he'd read about, some publicity stunt designed to keep him in the papers.

"Jesus, he's still out there." Kent tried to light a cigarette, his hands shaking so much that Midori had to help with her free hand. "You have no idea what that man is capable of."

"I'm sure there's nothing to worry about. Cedars is very remote."

The scars on Kent's arm bothered him, swelling and thumping, as if blood might pour from the hideous puckered marks. *I've been practicing really hard for this one,* Kent heard Ozman say, gloating as he had pulled the aluminum knitting needle from a sports bag on the floor. *One very sharp knitting needle.* He rolled up the shirtsleeve of his left arm. *One very soft arm.* Ozman plunged the needle through the thickest section of his own meaty forearm, blood spurting from each side. Ozman didn't take his eyes off Kent. Kent, on the other hand, stared in horror at the blood splashed across his Armani slacks. *Now you.* Ozman cut tape from around Kent's wrist with an X-ACTO blade, released his right arm, and turned up the underside. Kent squirmed and kicked, trying to form words with his muffled grunts. The chair rocked and slid against the marble floor. But Ozman held Kent still, his grip remarkably strong around Kent's free arm, and jammed the needle in from the side, pushing with his palm until it had cleared two inches of skin and muscle.

"That monster would have killed us, if I hadn't—" Kent turned to Midori, slapped his hand over his forearm, and pointed to a fast approaching rest stop. "Stop here."

Kent stumbled from the car as if he'd forgotten how to walk. Everywhere he looked, he saw Ozman's mohawk, the bizarre tribal tattoos, and steel-toe boots. His right forearm ached, and Ozman's mad grin flashed before him. Good God, the man was still loose in Japan, and coming after him. Kent felt certain it was all a joke, and, if not, that Ozman would have been captured by now. Japan was a small country. How long could a man like that roam free?

Kent started again with the understanding that he'd lately been captured by every cell phone in the Kanto Plain. He'd broadcast his whereabouts since leaving Tokyo. All Ozman had to do was search the web. Stargazer. com alone probably had a map of Japan with a red line tracing his path, a series of cell phone photos marking his passage northwest. And the corrections officer had verified that Ozman was coming after Kent. For revenge.

This time Ozman wouldn't waste his time with torture; he'd kill him.

Kent's gun had sent Ozman to prison, the 9mm an impulse buy in a Roppongi bar from an American sailor stationed at Yokosuka with the US 7th Fleet for $2000. A high price, but the easiest way to find one in Japan. When he first held it he knew he wanted the pistol. Though he'd fired the gun only once—an accident in which he shattered the floor-to-ceiling mirror in his bedroom, he liked having it. That day with Ozman, Kent had held the gun for all of ten seconds, slamming the clip into place before it fell from his trembling hands. As he had reached to retrieve it, Ozman appeared at the closet doorway and kicked Kent in the gut, sending him to the floor. Kent remained hopeful—he could do this, he could outsmart, outtalk, and outthink this Neanderthal. He rummaged for another weapon, coming up with a shoe—a Gucci loafer with a heavy heel. But Ozman was already there, pointing the Beretta at Kent's head. He disengaged the safety and pulled the slide, loading a bullet into the chamber. *Looking for this?*

Ozman now had nothing to lose. How long would it be before he tracked Kent down? And his idiot agent had sent him on this errand to the mountains for some meditation and a documentary, as if Ozman couldn't find him here. Kent should've been on a plane to Hong Kong or Taipei, a safe haven from loonies with no passport. Kent lit a cigarette and tried to think. But his eye throbbed and his hands shook so bad he had to stuff them in his pockets. He folded his fingers around his copper pipe. He waved a hand at Midori. "I'll be back." And walked toward the restroom.

Inside the expressway bathroom, he stood over a squat toilet, the hot air balloons of his future dropping so fast so he had trouble breathing. He squatted in the stall so as not to be seen over the door, one leg bent across the hole in the floor. He pulled the copper pipe from his pants, packed it with hashish—something to calm his nerves, stop his hands from shaking, and inhaled, as his cigarette burned on the toilet paper dispenser to hide the pungent smell. Kent inhaled again, coughed, coughed again, an all-consuming series of noisy hacking, his lungs and throat on fire. With the wracking cough and unsteady squat, he lost his balance. The pipe dropped to the floor with a metallic clang, spilling the rest of the hashish. He tried to scoop the sticky black ball up but it had already rolled into a puddle of piss on the bathroom tiles in the neighboring stall. He reached for the hashish, but a man entered the stall, mumbled at the sight of Kent's hand and kicked at it. With the hashish out of reach, Kent switched to the *shabu*. He needed a bump, a surge of confidence, buoyancy. As he unfolded the wad of tinfoil, a man nearby grunted as he struggled to urinate, another dragged his feet across the slippery tile floor.

Ozman still ran free.

Kent placed the small rock in a square of tinfoil and lit the lighter underneath. The squawk of a walkie-talkie. Kent panicked, fearing his luck had run out, the police come to get him, finally. He tossed the *shabu*, the tinfoil, and the glass tube into the toilet and flushed. The shiny lot twisted its way down but didn't flush. He pulled the handle again, the squawking radio closer, the uniformed blue ready to appear over the stall door and scream at him to place his hands above his head, a nightstick ready to crack his skull, a white-gloved policeman digging that incriminating mix of illegal drugs and paraphernalia out of the toilet. A list of criminal narcotics charges and a notorious Japanese prison sentence would follow. He'd end up in Fuchu after all—once Ozman realized Kent was in Fuchu, he'd turn himself in. He'd enjoy the irony and focus his energies on destroying Kent Richman for good. A man like Kent wouldn't survive such a sentence. He'd die there, on all fours with his pants around his ankles and one of Ozman's famed *chisa katana*, the kind he sliced his arm with, cleaving his ass.

The radio squawked again. Kent knew he'd gone too far. Killer bees swarmed his head. Stopping had been a mistake. He wanted only to get back to the safety of Midori's car and drive on; he'd do anything to get out of this muddy rest stop toilet. Perhaps the mountains were a good place to hide. Had he told anyone else he was going? His left leg straight out to the side nearly into the next stall, he reached to fish the stubborn mess from the toilet trench. His hands shook and sweat ran into his eyes. He struggled to see through the yellow flashes of his new swarm and his head spun black. His stomach lurched, bile rose in his throat. Someone kicked his foot from the other stall, grumbling a complaint. Kent jerked his leg up, but the stall wall was too low, and he hit his shin against it causing more pain and flash after flash of his killer bees. He toppled, his head catching the corner of an aluminum toilet paper dispenser. Bees buzzed as the dispenser popped open releasing two rolls of toilet paper. The radio cried. And Kent Richman slid to the cold tile into what he hoped would be darkness free of fear and pain.

FROM *Star-Gazer.com*

THE GREAT OZ

LOOSE ON THE KANTO PLAIN

A Fuchu Prison official has confirmed that Denis Ozman, Australian shock comic and Fuchu Prison inmate, has escaped. Speaking off the record because he was not authorized to represent the facility, the corrections officer confirmed that Denis Ozman had not been seen in the prison for over a week and was presumed to have escaped.

Determined iCU reporters have been flooding our inbox with possible sightings from Hokkaido to Okinawa, though no one has yet to capture the daring escape artist on camera.

One report described a muscular, bald Caucasian on a train heading west from Tokyo on the Joetsu Shinkansen. He was seen getting off at Shim-Maebashi station with nothing but a gym bag.

Was that you, Ozman? Do us a huge favor and send us a photo. Don't worry: we won't tell. We're going to find out soon enough anyway—we always do.

And, hey, if you want to know where you-know-who is—*Shhh!*, we might just know that, too.

Click here again to find out where Ozman has been spotted next.

To send your iCU reports visit:
www.Star-Gazer.com/iCU.html and click on the iCU! link.

CHAPTER FIFTEEN

—

SANCTUARY

Kent woke feeling as if he'd fallen asleep only minutes before and was disturbed by a nasty dream or a thump in the dark, reviving an ache in his head so awful he could open neither his bad nor his good eye. Speed sleep or no sleep, he couldn't tell. He shivered underneath a sheet soaked with sweat. The buffered sound of a bell rang. Kent smelled cedar smoke and the dust of decades so that he could hardly breathe at all, his tongue dry and swollen, his throat sore. His jaw and neck ached and his teeth were so sensitive he could hardly touch the tops and bottoms together without pain. A crust of mucus had dried around his cracked lips.

Kent sat up and surveyed himself and the room. He wore no pants. A Band-Aid had been fitted over a painful knot above his right eye. He fingered the Saint Christopher medallion around his neck, its presence comforting, reminding him that he was in some way safe. He found a crumpled pack of cigarettes in the front pocket of his t-shirt: one broken cigarette and a pack of matches inside the cellophane. With the initial drag he coughed until he thought his lungs would tear open. But the nicotine got his blood flowing, and though his head and eye throbbed, he felt better.

The room was large with tall, shuttered windows, a high ceiling lost in shadows. Behind cloaked windows, the light of daybreak crept through at its edges. His futon was rolled out over the *tatami* floor. There was the dust he sensed, old age trapped in *tatami* straw. School desks were lined up three-by-four in front of a white board. Kent leaned against a low, wooden table, his hand resting against a portable compact disc player. Someone had rendered a manga character Kent didn't recognize on a white board. On a smaller table, a coffee maker, a gray, hot water vessel, and a few teapots. Kent took an aluminum ashtray from a stack and sat on a pillow by a window.

Voices seeped in from another room. In the crack between window and shade, day began, however dismal and gray, so that Kent saw the old building better, its high ceiling and worn wooden beams exposed to a large flat room. Outside, water poured from the roof above, a steady stream, and splashed into puddles that had formed in the gravel underneath the window, a narrow moat growing deeper and wider around the part of the house Kent could see. Gravestones dotted the landscape below the foothills of an ascending forest of giant red cedars. Voices again, what sounded like radio squawks, and he suffered a flashback of the rest stop bathroom, the smell of disinfectant. His stomach soured and he couldn't finish the cigarette.

From behind. "*Ohayo gozaimasu.*"

He turned to find Midori behind him in blue jeans and T-shirt, her hair down, her eyes red, a Kool burning in one hand, his pants folded over her arm.

"How do you feel?" she said.

He ran his fingers over the Band-Aid. "Like I went head to head with a truck."

"You hit your head when you fainted. You were a little out of it, so some gentlemen helped me get you in the car." Midori handed Kent his pants, stabbed out her cigarette in the aluminum ashtray, and began to roll up his futon. "You were a little crazy, talking about things I couldn't understand. Who's Allan?"You really freaked out the people there. Once here, my uncle helped me bring you in, stitch you up—you're lucky, you only needed three."

"Stitches?"

"My uncle's pretty handy with a needle. Was a medic in the Self-Defense Force years ago. It was either that or the hospital. You wouldn't let us take you."

"I can't seem to stop hurting myself." He struggled for balance as he slipped one leg into his pants.

"Makes you wonder, doesn't it?" she said.

Wonder what? Kent fell over as he tried to get the other leg in.

Midori looked down at him with hands on her hips, but looked away as he labored to get his pants over his knees. He'd seen that look before, the look away, from Kumi, in those last days before she asked him to leave. Disgust.

Midori unrolled and rolled the futon again, then once more, her back to Kent. "The cleaning lady found you. She was pretty upset, this huge foreigner with his foot in the toilet and his head against the stall, bleeding. She thought you were dead. She was ready to call an ambulance."

"Cleaning lady?" His policeman had become an everyday janitor. "Great. What else?"

Midori placed the futon on a stack of others inside a

closet and turned to Kent. "When I saw all these people at the bathroom door, I knew it was for you." She pumped her eyebrows up and down. "Big surprise, huh?"

"I suppose not." Kent recalled a sketch he'd done in the first months of his career before *RI-CHU-MAN-SAN!* took off, the night Plum Petite was introduced to Japanese audiences. In the sketch, all you saw were Kent's feet behind the bathroom stall, pants down around his ankles. In the stall next to him, a women's black heels, her white hose around her ankles, the hem of a yellow dress. Plum Petite also had a role on *The Strange Bonanza*, a shrill transvestite in a Snow White costume and a big wig that evoked the Bourbon kings of France. Plum Petite's wig had required scaffolding to keep it upright for the sketch in which the punch line was the transvestite's introduction.

"One of the men who helped carry you to the car, I think he recognized you," Midori said.

"Recognized?" Kent saw himself held up by two men, one holding him under his arms, the other supporting his legs. His arms hung to the ground, knuckles dragging over the sidewalk, his eyes rolled white into the backs of their sockets as drool dribbled from his mouth.

"They wanted to take you to the hospital. I almost let them. You looked so white, like all the blood had been drained from your body."

"That's all—the hospital?"

In a screen test for the soap opera *Changes in Love* a mobster had stabbed Kent's character. Kent lay on the ground, his face made up in an unflattering, greasy gray, holding his gut, as his love interest, Nami Panda, a J-pop star whose only real hit was the theme song for another weekly TV drama, knelt over him. Believing he was dying,

Kent's character confessed the love for her that he knew was forbidden. Uncomplicated, embracing love and life at all costs.

"A few had their cell phones out." Midori mimed taking photographs.

Kent imagined the crowd of travelers gathered around, the rubberneckers with phones held high, the whispers of recognition. "I'll be all over the net. What about Ozman?"

"I tried to stop them but—"

"Yeah, but—so, they definitely recognized me?" Kent said.

"I'm sorry—I guess that's bad," Midori said.

"Not *good*." Renzo would hear of this. And, so would others. "And Ozman?"

"You saw him at the rest stop?"

"No. At least—" Kent tried to relight his stubbed-out cigarette, but his hands shook. "I don't know what I saw. But you have no idea what that man is capable of. If Ozman's still loose, it doesn't matter where we are—we should worry."

"What did he do to you?"

"Another time." Kent saw that Midori was genuinely concerned. "Listen, I'm sure there's nothing to worry about." But there was, wasn't there? Ozman was mad, capable of great violence. And this time, he was more than motivated. "And I'm sorry about the trouble. I don't know what happened."

"Don't you?" She held out a small paper bag. "You're lucky I found this."

Kent took the paper bag, peered inside, and saw his copper pipe. The bag smelled like burnt leaves. The nearly sweet smell left Kent craving.

"I told my uncle you were drunk."

"Nothing to worry about." Kent shook the bag, looked inside, and shook it again. "You didn't find— anything else, did you?"

"No. What might I have found?"

"Just asking." Kent rolled the top of the bag closed. "I mean, you wouldn't keep anything that you found, would you?"

"Why would I do that?" Midori turned from Kent and raised the shade on the window. The room filled with a dusty silver light. Without turning, she said, "Your bag is under the desk there."

"Thanks." Kent wobbled towards the rumpled hockey bag.

She turned. "Why do you have an urn in your bag? It is an urn, isn't it?"

Kent stopped before the bag. "You saw that?"

"Why do you have it?"

"It's a long story."

"You have many long stories."

"All good ones, too. Listen, my head's pounding. I need—"

Midori wiped her hands on her jeans. "This temple has been in our family for almost four hundred years."

"This is the temple?"

"No, the temple's next door." She lit a cigarette. "This is a study room: for classes, for *go* or mahjong games, group meetings, or just sitting and talking. Anything's okay." Midori lit another cigarette and pointed outside. "That's a cemetery for the community. It's all very old." She smiled, the first time she had really looked him. "My uncle will have prepared breakfast, if you're hungry. We'll eat. Then, maybe the rain will stop today."

What Are You Made of, Rich Man?
Kent felt as if he were on another sort of retreat—more of a camping trip for misanthropes in the solitary mountains. Or worse. Had Renzo duped him? By retreat he meant rehab? Midori the group leader about to guide him through a twelve-step program or prep him for some bizarre plastic surgery, a dramatic identity-altering procedure. In the bathroom, Kent tried to piss but nothing came; still his bladder and kidneys ached. Had the *shabu* ruined him so? The bathroom was basic, a mineral-stained ceramic hole in the ground that led to a backyard septic tank. The closet-like space smelled of rotting wood and wet earth. He emptied a tin bucket of its stale water and refilled it with water that flowed brown from the faucet. This was no resort. He poured the water into the toilet, watching as it splashed to the bottom. A tiny sink, barely big enough to fit his hands into, was to the right of the toilet, above it a small mirror framed in washed-out pink plastic. He gently removed the eyepatch, his eye still an enflamed mess. And now he had a gash on his forehead, handstitched by a Buddhist monk. Kent splashed mountain-cold water on his face, careful not to wet the bandage. Dark circles had dug in under his eyes like topographical tattoos.

Midori knocked on the bathroom door. "Breakfast is ready when you are."

"Thanks." A mosquito buzzed in his ear, reminding him of the pests that had swarmed Ko Chang, leaving him a welty mess in his first week in Thailand. "Another minute."

"Are you okay?" she said through the door. Where did this stranger find such tenderness for him? Kent sniffed. Something didn't smell right. He'd never felt so *off,* so lopsided. He sank to his knees, couldn't quite catch his breath, scared of what he'd done, of the emptiness before him, not a hint in this world of what waited for him. Up in the Japanese mountains with a woman he barely knew, a madman on the loose, and Kumi, or the idea of her growing fainter each day. The prospect of a return to Tokyo for a diminished version of what he'd once been, even if the idea of making a career behind the microphone didn't seem so bad, it left him lonelier than he'd been since Kumi changed the locks on their condominium and dumped the hockey bag in the hall. He'd survive in Tokyo but there was no one save Renzo there to pick him up at the train station when he returned. No apartment to crash in for a few weeks until he got settled. He wanted out but had no home, no place he could land. Still, he guessed he'd need to leave this quiet place in the anonymous mountains. Now, if Kent looked for a starting point, which he knew was foolish, not a reliable beginning but, at least for him, a point of reference, a moment at which he could point his finger and say *Ah Ha!* this or that is to blame, he ached to hold the gun once more, just as he'd once dreamed of jumping from a couch in a rented beach house on Nags Head and—missing his brother.

What are you made of, Rich Man? Ozman sang.

"Welcome to Cedars Temple, Mr. Richman." Midori's uncle greeted them in the kitchen with a broad smile. He handed Kent a warm towel that smelled of lavender and gestured for him to wipe his face. He ran his hands over his shaved head, raising square, silver-framed glasses to his forehead to rub his eyes with his fingers. When he spoke, his dentures moved in his mouth, a clicking, slurping sound accompanying his words. "My name is Rinji Watanabe. My students call me *Sensei*, but you can call me Oji-san." He held out his hand.

Oji-san was five-four at the most, with a large, round head, its rotund shape emphasized by its baldness. With his little neck beneath the balloon-shaped top, he looked like Charlie Brown with glasses and a mangy beard. His face was relaxed, the nostrils under his broad nose wide and round enough to hold marbles. His right eye seemed squeezed forever half-shut behind his glasses, like a coin slot. Liver spots on his clean head and flushed face spoke of his age. A chronic smoking habit had creased the corners of his eyes. Deep lines framed his mouth. His eyebrows had all but disappeared, what remained curling upwards in fine, fair ringlets. He wore a pale blue sweat jacket, white stripes down the arms. Underneath a more traditional waistcoat with a gold lapel and loose trousers tied with a long piece of twisted cotton rope. On his feet white socks with padded soles, individual spaces for his big toes. Colored prayer beads hung from his neck. A rich aroma of flavored coffee and tobacco smoke filled the room, while the sound of a television came from the kitchen.

"*Hajimemashite.*" Kent shook Oji-san's hand. "Sorry about—"

Oji-san smiled again, his creases growing deeper, a cigarette to his lips, and held his hand up. "No apology—requests for forgiveness are not a good way to start a new relationship. Puts us on uneven ground." He exhaled smoke without moving his eyes from Kent. With his other hand he held forth a pack of Hi-Lite cigarettes, shaking them. Kent placed his hand over his stomach and frowned, but Oji-san waved the Hi-Lites at him again.

"Why not." Kent took a cigarette from the old man's pack.

"You must be hungry then." Oji-san lit Kent's cigarette with a kitchen match.

"I don't know. After last night—"

"You look rather poorly. How's your head?" Oji-san said.

"All right, considering. Midori tells me you did the doctoring. I owe you."

"It looks worse than it is. What about your eye?"

"Short story—" Kent glanced at Midori, who turned, ignoring him. "Pissed-off boyfriend. Umbrella."

"Bad situation. Why don't you try my coffee then? Then I'll get a salve for your eye."

"Coffee I can do." Kent wasn't ready to trust whatever folk remedy the little monk might have hidden away in a kitchen jar.

Oji-san handed Kent an empty cup. "I'd forgotten how good your Japanese was."

"Forgotten?" Kent's hand shook. He steadied it with his other, wondering if coffee was such a good idea.

"From television. I'm a big fan." Oji-san pushed his glasses down his nose, and lowered his head. "*A-re?*"

Kent didn't know whether to feel flattered or ridiculed. But the old man seemed genuine as he held the comic pose. "Not bad."

"I like *The Strange Bonanza*. I like your 'Imagine.' Very soulful." Oji-san poured coffee from a pot under an expensive coffee/espresso machine.

"Fancy," Kent said.

"I like coffee very much." He placed a package on the table. "Some snacks until breakfast is served." The

package read, in English: *Burned Meat Flavored Biscuits.*
"And, don't worry, Mr. Richman—"

"Kent."

"All right, Kent. Ozman won't find you here."

For the first time in days, Kent felt safe. He believed
this old man might be telling the truth.

When Oji-san had poured Midori a cup of coffee, he
pointed Kent towards the kitchen. "Once you have eaten;
you'll find an assortment of vegetables by the large sink.
Your first duty here will be to prepare the vegetables—
clean, peel, cut, but don't cook—for tonight's dinner.
Midori will handle the seafood. We're having *nabe*. All this
rain has left me with a chill. I need winter food to warm
me up. For now, I have a funeral to prepare. Midori will
show you what you need."

When Oji-san returned to the kitchen, Midori
gestured for Kent to sit down, taking her place on one
of the floor cushions. "I knew this place sounded like
rehab. Last place I went to like this everybody had a job.
I cleaned toilets. Do I have to clean toilets, too?" Kent
had to maneuver around columns of manga, DVDs, and
VHS tapes stacked high on the floor. He imagined having
to clean the mildewy toilet he'd found earlier. Instinct told
him to run, but the coffee was good, the room warm and
comforting.

"You don't have to clean toilets, unless you want to.
My uncle would like you to feel part of the place." Midori
parted a door curtain made of linen and cherry blossom
brocade, and disappeared into the kitchen.

A tall, hand-painted glass display cabinet with brass
accents and a mirrored back was crammed with action
figures. Next to the cabinet stood a large, rectangular
mirror framed in woven rattan. A golden yellow wig,

unique for the spiked tufts jutting out from all sides, hung from a hook next to the mirror. In a corner littered with tattered scrolls, a bamboo *kendo* sword, and a tennis racket, loomed an enormous sword at least three-feet high and a foot wide, like the business end of a giant butter knife with a wooden handle, painted black and wrapped in silver tape. It appeared to be real metal, if a light variety.

"What's up with all this stuff?" Kent yelled into the kitchen.

Midori poked her head through. "It's just something he does with his friends."

"I thought he was a priest or a monk or whatever." Kent sipped his coffee, the strong, flavorful brew sparking some life in him. He'd want another cigarette soon.

"He's a priest. And a wonderful teacher." Midori returned with two plates of steaming scrambled eggs, thick bacon, and pancakes. "Isn't this what you like?" She set the plate before him.

The western breakfast surprised Kent so much that he found his appetite, the food reminding him of a home he hadn't seen in over five years. He'd grown to love the Japanese diet and rarely missed western food. Even when he ate western, it was flavored by Japanese cuisine, from burgers with soy and ginger to pizza covered in octopus tentacles. This he loved about Japan, one of the many details of daily life he cherished. He sometimes wondered if it were more likely that such everyday offerings kept him there. Not money or fame, but finding a random Shinto shrine in the middle of a busy steel and glass district or a parade of school kids in uniform, with bright yellow backpacks, in short pants and skirts. And he loved his convenience stores, his 7-Eleven, his Lawson, his Circle K, and Daily Yamazaki, where he could find almost everything he needed, from a hot meal and cigarettes to—lately—medical supplies. Perhaps his retreat to the mountains wouldn't be so bad. He had good food, the prospect of some camera facetime, a pinch of the surge to keep him going, when necessary, and Midori, whatever she meant. He guessed he was as isolated as he could get in Japan, safe, at least for a while.

Midori sat beside him on her knees with her legs folded under her. "He has hobbies and a social life, of course. And, for now, there's no one else. I believe we're expecting a film crew at some point." She stretched out beside the table. Kent admired her short but slender legs, recalled her in panties and bra. The ache to see her this way again surprised him. He preferred her morning look, without makeup and styled hair.

"So I've been told. My agent, Renzo, he arranged everything. I'm just following orders. Like a good soldier."

"Mr. Royama was supposed to fax your agenda. I'll check to see if it's arrived. Until then—relax, eat something. Then we have the *nabe* to prepare. Morning meditation is over, but there will be a noon session. Your first."

RI-CHU-MAN-SAN!
IN APPARENT SUICIDE
ATTEMPT

Central Kanto iCU reporters suggest former television star American Kent Richman was found unconscious in an apparent overdose of prescription pills. Richman was reportedly seen carried from a rest stop bathroom in the small mountain valley in Niigata prefecture, just sixty kilometers north of his last sighting in the town of Azuma.

iCU reports suggest a female "friend," who appeared distraught, accompanied Richman. A Department of Transportation source confirms that a female bathroom attendant found a foreign male unconscious. Richman, whose identity was neither confirmed nor denied by the DOT source, was reportedly in a state of undress and wrapped in a flower-patterned comforter.

One traveler, also stopped at the rest area, a 65-year-old taxi driver who declined to give his name, reportedly encountered the American as he attempted to buy a pack of cigarettes from a vending machine.

"He kept fumbling with coins, trying to find the right amount, like foreigners always do when they use Japanese money. He kept putting in ten-yen coins, one after the other, until he ran out, short by fifty yen. He just leaned against the cigarette machine and he looked like he was going to cry. I offered him the fifty yen and he snatched it from my hand, got his cigarettes and hobbled off, dragging this blanket behind him. I couldn't tell if he wore anything underneath or not. He looked like he was crazy." Headed around the bend, KR? Your fans want to know.

To send your iCU reports visit:
www.Star-Gazer.com/iCU. html and click on the iCU! link.

CHAPTER SIXTEEN

—

THE SELFISH SUFFERER

*K*ent Richman's First Foundational Meditation Sessions *Checklist*

1) *Breathing*

2) *Postures*

3) *Reflections on the Repulsiveness of the Body*

4) *Reflections on Material Elements*

5) *Clear Comprehending*

BREATHING

Oji-san hit a small gong with a rubber mallet and walked behind Kent, a short bamboo rod in his hand. Kent expected at any minute to feel its sting on his shoulder.

"Breathe," Oji-san purred and tapped the rod against Kent's arm, measuring out a slow rhythm. "Think of nothing—*nothing*—but the sound and feel of your own breath. Draw strength from stillness. Act without acting."

Kent wasn't sure what the old man preached. The words of wisdom all sounded like a bad kung-fu movie. And he couldn't be still, couldn't *not* act. How would such nothingness help him get his career back or keep Ozman from killing him, especially when there were no cameras around to capture it all? Before him, an altar was overlaid in ornate black and gold. A lacquered cabinet held golden statuettes, bowls and offering plates, candles and incense. A golden Buddha sat atop the altar, a tranquil, feminine form whose hands were positioned in harmony to one another, eyes narrow, curved lids that granted instant peace. Kent imagined a curtain behind the altar with a tiny, bald monk bent over a crank, pumping the eyes of Buddha slowly open and closed in an exhibition of compassion and consent. Oz in a puff of smoke and a tranquilizing voice: *We are sinners all of us, but with each step forward we erase a moment of our past.* Kent gazed at the Buddha's eyes, half-expecting them to pop open in a terrifying glare, the serene, Mona Lisa smile twisting into a grisly growl, flames shooting up behind the disembodied head. From Oz to Ozman.

Below the Buddha, two gilded wooden flowers blossomed on each side, a blue and white candle in the center. In a cabinet underneath sat hundreds of smaller Buddha-like forms, glowing gold in the lotus position. Tall candles and incense burned for sins past and present, flames fluttering with the breeze from an open doorway. Rice cakes and oranges had been placed in offering on a red-lacquered podium. Ceramic white and gold flowers flanked the sides of the large altar, layers and layers of beautiful sculpture. A thick, twisted rope entwined in red silk hung from a gong high above the altar. The shadowy beams of the temple were painted in bright reds, blues, and yellows, carvings that told a story of which Kent was ignorant.

Midori entered along a worn, red carpet, clapped her hands, and bowed her head. She lit a great bundle of joss sticks in a bowl of sand. Clouds of smoke rose to the ceiling. Her silhouette and the smell of incense prompted images of Kumi in their apartment and the incense she had burned each morning.

"One for each day," Kumi explained. "Like a prayer."

"I like the smell," Kent said.

"Why don't you pray then?"

"For what?"

"Anything. Say thank you for all the wonderful things in your life."

Kent wouldn't pray in front of her, but there were times when he was alone that he lit one of her joss sticks and asked for answers, for a little healing air to float his way, for an understanding of why his life had played out the way it had. He usually felt worse afterwards, ashamed, red-faced false anticipation for something he didn't really believe. Kumi would have told him that believing was the answer. If he believed then and only then would he feel better. She believed and she felt better. Simple.

Kent sat before the altar and tried to breath deeply, in and out of his mouth as Oji-san did, a low hum from his throat. His lungs and the muscles around his chest ached. And each time he breathed, his breakfast of cigarettes, bacon, and coffee resurfaced in a succession of rank bubbles.

POSTURES
    After circling for fifteen minutes, in which all he said was "Breathe," tapping out an unhurried tempo against his leg with the bamboo rod, Oji-san sat before Kent in lotus position. Midori joined them. Kent's back already hurt, a twinge along his spine and up through his neck. His legs had cramped.

"If you feel pain, bend. Trees bend, trees sway," Oji-san whispered.

Kent imagined himself as a tree, but his tree was stiff and crooked, unable to sway for fear of snapping in two, rotted and twisted by years of abuse. Oji-san instructed him to gaze beyond his shoulder, to focus on everything but nothing, a single spot that contained all, pushing light from his eyes and through the top of his head. But Kent couldn't stop staring at Midori's ears. He'd never thought of a woman's ears before but hers were tiny seashells, pink and smooth. Small, like a squirrel's, but poking out from her head. Kent thought of hobbits and elves. Midori's ears should have been the part of her you saw first, but Kent couldn't recall noticing the beauties. Oji-san guided Kent through a simple meditation: a pursuit of light. But Midori's ears. That's what kept Kent calm, focused, so that he actually forgot himself—and Ozman—for five minutes.

REFLECTIONS ON THE REPULSIVENESS OF THE BODY Oji-san said little other than the reminder that there was no separation between body and mind. Midori nodded. This was not a problem for Kent, for he felt inextricably bound to his hurting body, his red swollen eye, thumping forehead, itchy skin, and aching back. While his mind raced, serving up one horrid scenario after another, each one worse, Ozman stuffing hot coals into Kent's mouth, Ozman breaking Kent's fingers one by one, Ozman flaying Kent, beginning with the arms and legs.

His body hurt. He was exhausted, despite his long sleep, and he yearned to crawl back into bed. He'd kill for a drink, anything to keep him still, to silence his fugitive thoughts, and to calm his thrashing heart. A cigarette rolled with hashish would be just the cure, if he hadn't lost his dope in the bathroom stall. Kent wanted everything he didn't have and couldn't stop the wanting. He was in that terrible space between exhaustion and anxiety, one that wouldn't allow for sleep even as his body begged for it. He knew from too much experience that he was close to collapse, the crash that followed days of abuse.

REFLECTIONS ON MATERIAL ELEMENTS
When Midori frowned at him for staring, Kent returned to the disappointment he suffered upon realizing where he was to stay for the next two weeks, disappointment temporarily displacing fear. Cedars was no resort, hardly a retreat either, unless you considered it a retreat from light, the place cloaked in darkness by towering cedars and rain clouds. The smell of rotting wood and straw, of damp, was overwhelming. The place was falling down, *tatami* mats worn and ripped, doorframes bent unevenly, sagging floors, even the ornate sculptures and murals were faded and chipped. Yet, Midori found it beautiful. Oji-san didn't seem particularly righteous and Kent didn't know what to make of Midori, at once tender towards him and distracted by her own problems. He doubted any film crew was to show up and wasn't sure he wanted them there anymore. Oji-san had instructed Kent to wear only what felt comfortable. He had offered no Zen robe. No *Matrix*. No Keanu Reeves. He would have to meditate in his sweats. And because it was chilly, his smoking jacket. Oji-san had given Kent a salve for his eye, a clear, unctuous substance, and an actual eyepatch. Kent's only pleasant thoughts, beyond Midori's ears, were in imagining the documentary poster. The director would

shoot Kent's profile with the temple out of focus behind him, maybe even Midori or Oji-san's blurred image nearby, partially out of frame. With the documentary, Kent Richman's story could be both tragic and touching.

CLEAR COMPREHENDING

In Kent's one moment of uninterrupted contemplation, he wished for penance, to finally and forever put his bloodied past behind him. His knees bent stiff and his head still throbbed with the shock of withdrawal and his recent accident, but the sensations seemed remote, part of another self, one bound to the earth by the roots of his past. He decided he needed the sum of all his pain to atone for his sins. He called upon the hurt to lead him beyond the empty room, beyond his body, beyond Allan, beyond Kumi. The greater the pain, the greater the chance he might find answers. He'd no longer have to forfeit happiness for guilt, he'd no longer think of Allan or Kumi, Ozman or Monique. He'd no longer ask himself, yet again, what might have been different that summer night in Nags Head. He'd no longer wonder where his wife was or if she'd ever take him back.

Kent pushed his mind to prayer, words to God—a god he knew little of—and let the pain in his knees and back and head and eye roll like the tides. The smarting in his head thumped just above his good eye and he couldn't see clearly or focus any longer on the wall before him. He whispered his brother's name, then his ex-wife's, and engaged the pain, so strong in his back by then it made his eyes water. He guessed his spine might crumble, leaving him limp and crippled on the dusty *tatami*. He felt Oji-san's eyes on him, but didn't return the look.

baby, you're a rich man

A wet breeze blew through the temple, sweat cooled beneath his shirt, and a tingle rolled over his scalp. He smelled smoke from a cooking fire, a suggestion of spices that he couldn't name in the air. He murmured his brother's name again, his wife's, the only words that formed in his throat. He tucked his thumbs under his fingers, an irrational trick Kumi had shown him to prevent terrible things. He tensed his back to ensure that the hurt would roam his body without favor to him or any part of him. An eye for an eye; he guessed he'd made his deal. Beside him, Midori stirred. Before him Oji-san tapped out a rhythm with the bamboo rod against his thigh. Outside, cedar tops swayed and rain poured from the overflowing gutters.

CHAPTER SEVENTEEN

—

BIG IN JAPAN REDUX

To get out of Oji-san's way, Kent and Midori decided on a walk through the mountain village, despite the unrelenting rain. Before leaving, Kent spent thirty minutes watching the local news for updates on Ozman. But the approaching typhoon dominated the news cycle. He grabbed an umbrella, Midori draped her arm on his, and they stepped outside where he saw the temple exterior for the first time. Weathered wood, gabled roof, wave-like shingles of Japanese *kawara*, and a gold seal at the apex presented a portrait of a much older Japan. A steep slope dotted with great boulders and the immense cedars, and short crooked pines flanked the temple. At the back, the cemetery Kent had seen before, with its granite pagodas. A narrow, gravel path ran down and around the right side to the village streets below. Houses lined the path behind gray stone walls and wooden fences, squat, pruned trees along the fence lines.

They reached the town center: more rows of compact brown houses and an odd collection of stores along a narrow main street, many selling souvenirs and local delicacies. High-walled, narrow alleys wound and climbed through the mountain village of less than ten thousand. Densely-packed, wood-framed buildings with red, clay roof tiles served as homes, shops, restaurants, and traditional guest houses. The oddly stacked buildings looked like a village Dr. Seuss might have dreamt up with steep steps and footpaths leading from one level of town to the next. The smell of sulfur told of the hot springs that bubbled underfoot, making this a popular stop for tourists who believed in the water's healing properties. A shallow river cut the village in half. In the dry season, bathers floated along the rocky shore where hot water mixed with the cool river. The past few weeks of rain had kept everyone indoors and the usual stream of tourists thin. The river now ran full and fast, water rising against its high banks, results of a heavy spring snow melt and the enduring plum rains.

The broader central street originated from a tiny train station marked by a saltbox ticket office and a tin awning on each side of the tracks. A single, local train car brought tourists from larger towns. Tour buses were too large to navigate the tight mountain roads that led to the village. In front of the station stood an eight-foot bronze figure of a sixteenth-century warrior, a scowling, armored witness to the village's ancient past. Kent had been in Japan five years, but he'd forgotten how quiet life outside the city could be, how soon the concrete and glass rolled northward into wooded slopes and green mountains, into Japan's earlier glory. On trains out of the cities, when he'd passed the massive four-lane expressways that rose above patches of highland rice fields and farm houses, it was often hard to tell where the city ended and the country began. In the mountains, he felt, for the first time in years, as if he were in a foreign country.

When the drizzle turned to heavy rain again they stopped in a coffee shop near the village center but below street level, hidden behind a slatted wooden gate. A hand-painted sign read, "God of Fire." The smell of rose water and the sounds of an agitated melody greeted Kent as he bent his head through the low doorway. The café was empty. Music from a phonograph played *Krenek Piano Sonata No.3*, a name and a detached sound Kent had never heard before, intemperate and moody. The decor was prewar European. Large ferns hung from hooks on the stucco walls and worn, oak tables were squeezed in among books and magazines stacked to the ceiling in every corner. The café reminded Kent of the manga shops in Tokyo's Kanda Jinbo district, where he'd studied the vast collections of comic books and sipped coffee. Generations of customers had scratched their names into the oak-paneled walls and small, round tables—names in *kanji*, misspelled English words, dates, crude hearts, smiley faces and yin-yang symbols.

"That guy's looking at me funny." Kent squirmed on the low, wooden seat.

An old man in an apron with wild, white hair shuffled behind the counter, sneaking glances. He smiled and nodded when they sat down.

"It's Mr. Morita, the owner. He's harmless. Besides, have you seen yourself lately?" Midori said. "Eyepatch, Band-Aid, white guy." She laughed, reached across the table and placed her hand on his arm. "It's all right. You can relax here. Isn't that what you're supposed to be doing?"

"I know, and I'm used to the staring. But he's looking at me odd. Makes me nervous. Think he knows about Ozman? What if Ozman has spies?"

"Spies?" Midori lit a Kool. "*Honto?*"

"It's not that. I mean it—it's like he's expecting something of me. And give me one of those, please."

Kent held two shaky fingers up. "Can you blame me for being a little cautious?"

"I guess not, but you're on TV." She tapped another Kool from the pack, lit it and handed the cigarette to Kent, who took a series of deep drags.

"No, like he knows me." A temporary calm spread across his chest, through his arms and into his fingertips, which now tingled. "Like he's ready to whip out his cell phone and *snap*! he's on his way to upload the latest Kent Richman sighting. No one can know I'm here."

The old man shuffled to their table with hot towels. "Miss Watanabe, it's good to see you again."

"Hello, Mr. Morita." She stood and bowed before the old man.

He grasped her hand and held it. "Who is your friend?"

"Mr. Morita, this is Kent Richman. He's visiting Cedars for a couple of weeks."

"I thought so." His smile grew. "But with the eyepatch and beard." He ran his fingers over his chin. "I wasn't sure it was you. Are you—in disguise?" This prospect seemed to make him happy.

"Umbrella accidentm," Kent said.

"I'm very pleased to meet you, Mr. Richman. My name is Makoto Morita. I'm the owner of this café. I enjoyed your show very much. And we seldom get such a celebrity here."

Kent stood, his knees shaking beneath him. "*Hajimemashite, Morita-san*?" He bowed, which made the old man smile.

Midori ordered coffees.

"I will make them special." Mr. Morita shuffled back to the kitchen.

"Maybe he's got a cell phone in his pocket. It's not cool right now, not with Ozman out there, so close." Kent searched for something to focus on, but once his eyes settled somewhere, they bounced elsewhere. He was at once exhausted and irritable, hungry and anxious. He needed a bump but had only coffee and cigarettes to get him through the day. His foot bounced to the frenetic rhythm of Krenek's piano sonata, occasionally hitting the bottom of the low table, causing coffee to splash from the bowl-cup.

Midori looked up over her magazine. "I'll bet he's back there right now activating a GPS device hidden in the espresso machine so that Ozman can pinpoint your exact location."

Kent jerked his head one way then another, as if Midori had spoken in stereo. He could hardly understand what she said.

"*Kidding*," Midori said and placed a hand on his knee. "Try to relax. We'll have a soak later. I know a wonderful *onsen*. Oji-san's planning a big dinner tonight. And there's something I need—"

"I'm fine." A hot soak might settle his crawling skin and a good meal would restore some of his waning health. "But this place is claustrophobic, don't you think?"

"You wanted to be out of the way. *This* is out of the way. Besides, it would be rude. Listen, I got a call from—" Midori looked over his shoulder. Mr. Morita had returned with a plate of *petite fours*, coffee, dark chocolates, and buttered toast. Kent sat up straighter, ran his hand through his hair and brushed the cigarette ashes from his shirt. He wanted to keep himself together, rest up, so when the cameras rolled, he'd look his best. Renzo was trying to help him, Midori had thought enough to rescue him from an expressway restroom, and her uncle had welcomed him into his temple. They were so far up in the mountains he was surely safe from Ozman. Kent was tired of disappointing people. More coffee and his own pack of cigarettes might be enough to get him through to dinner. He'd enjoy a soak, let some of the appetite for the speed his body so craved sink into the hot mineral water, and let its healing magic work on his ills. His hand trembled as he tried to sip coffee from the enormous cup.

Midori helped Mr. Morita with the plates. "You didn't need to go to such trouble."

"It's no trouble. These are from Mrs. Kobayashi's bakery. They're very popular. Please enjoy." Mr. Morita placed the tray of cakes on the table then reached a hand into his apron pocket. Despite Kent's little pep talk, he braced himself to be photographed.

"Ah!" Kent's trembling hands flew involuntarily over his head, his knees knocking the table and spilling coffee over the tray of *petite fours*. Mr. Morita jumped backwards, dropping something to the floor.

Midori reached for the unsettled coffees. "What're you doing?"

"I'm sorry. I thought—I don't know, it seemed like he was—" Kent had the unpleasant perspective of someone watching himself on video.

Mr. Morita picked up what turned out to be a comic book. "I'm sorry, I only wanted to show you this." He unrolled the comic and held it before Kent. "I'm a big fan."

Kent read the title. *Big in Japan: A Chronicle of Kent Richman.* "What's this?" Underneath the title, a plainly drawn Kent Richman inside a capsule hotel pod, his knees curled up in his arms, his face in his hands. A thought bubble floated beside his head and read: "Another day in hell."

"Your comic," Mr Morita said.

Panel after panel of monochromatic illustrations showed a comic book Kent going through what appeared to be pedestrian days: along urban sidewalks, in parks, bars, restaurants, and coffee shops. Most of the panels showed Kent alone, more thought bubbles than speech. One panel presented spectacled Kent with his hands up in frustration and surrounded by Picasso-like renderings of fantastic creatures, some of them monstrous, others players in a bizarre circus—strongman, skeleton, clown. The caption read: "I thought life after Kumi would be different!" The "Kent" character was inked in what Kent recognized as the *gekiga* style of manga royalty Yoshihiro Tatsumi, though more crudely drawn, and he marveled and even took some pleasure in the likeness. But the delight vanished with the feeling that he was being watched, as if the artist had a lens into Kent's life.

"Where did you get this? Who—?" Sweat rolled down his neck and beneath his shirt. His mouth had gone dry and he licked at his cracked lips as if searching there for an answer to the improbability before him. He felt as if he'd stumbled into an alternate world where his life played out in manga panels.

"It's *dojinshi*." Mr. Morita continued to smile, though Kent noticed an uneasiness growing.

Dojinshi? Kent knew *dojinshi*, a word from long ago it seemed, a curious Japanese idiom he'd once learned then lost to more important vocabulary. He'd seen *dojinshi*-style manga when he accompanied Shin to Comiket one winter. Fans swarmed Shin with requests for autographs and questions about their hero, Boy Wasabi. Shin, whose comic book hero was copied by hundreds of do-it-yourselfers, had been invited to attend the large comic market in Tokyo as a featured guest. He sat on a panel with other illustrators, gave a keynote address on selling your manga abroad, and conducted a workshop. While most of the manga and novels were parodies, fan fiction or imitations, some artists had created their own characters.

"It's do-it-yourself manga, self-published, but very popular. *Big in Japan* is one of my favorites. So, I was so surprised and happy to see you here today. Like fate."

"Me?" Kent couldn't shake the feeling he was being watched. "Why would someone—?"

Midori took the comic book from Kent, as much, he guessed, to draw attention away from his trembling hands as to see what had caused him so much anxiety.

"Yes, you." Mr. Morita glanced at Midori then back at Kent, and offered a broad smile, which suggested uneasiness rather than delight.

"Did my agent put you up to this?" Renzo was desperate to put him back in the spotlight, at any cost. Kent's damaged eye twitched. He was nauseated.

"Are you all right?" Midori placed her hand on his arm.

Mr. Morita offered Kent a cold towel. "You have many fans. This manga artist, a woman, in fact, Toshi Haneda, is very popular at Comiket. She has almost one thousand in circulation for each issue. I am surprised you don't know."

"Can someone just do this? Make me a character in a comic book?" Kent wiped the towel across his face. "And why me?"

"It's all right, Mr. Richman." Mr. Morita patted him on the back so hard that Kent thought he might spew the coffee sloshing in his stomach across the table. He looked again at the cover as Midori flipped through the pages, laughing as she read.

"This is amazing, Kent. It *is* you. It's your life. You're a manga hero." Midori held the comic book before him. "It really looks like you." She pointed to an illustration in which "Kent Richman" stood in line outside a Tokyo club in a raincoat. His figure was arrow-straight and thin, his long shadow stretching down an alley, legs two black shafts. A cigarette burned in his mouth, his hands deep in his pockets. He was unshaven, a simple inverted semi-circle for his mouth, and his eyes were darkened with fatigue. The thought bubble read: "I used to have my own VIP room at this place." On the next page, a single frame depicted a snarling, stubbled Ozman, his round, Sluggo face, a colossal mohawk rising out of the frame, behind prison bars. "I'll get you one day, Kent Richman."

What he saw in the comic book was too close, too real. Toshi Haneda, whoever she was, had captured the real Kent Richman, and people loved it. The air in the café had grown hot and stale. The cigarette burned his throat. Kent stood, his hand over his mouth, intending to run for the toilet. But as he turned for the narrow doorway of the bathroom, he made for the door to the street instead.

Through the lashing rain and into the village center his sneakers splashed over the paving stones. He didn't know where to go, but he needed to be anywhere else. Kent's new reality, it seemed, was more interesting to the public than his former self. The comic book, Ozman, everything rose in his throat to choke him—he could hardly breath. As he hurried through the village center, Kent bumped against bicycle racks and sidewalk benches, the eyepatch reducing his vision. The few who braved the ever-increasing rain regarded him with alarm, stopping and turning to follow him with their eyes. He'd not brought his umbrella, and his clothes were already soaked.

In sight of the train station, Kent considered hopping the single-car train and escaping the tiny town. It wasn't hard to find this place, the old town popular enough among the Japanese. But as easily as they could arrive, he could depart. He'd ride the train to wherever it took him. As he approached the station and passed the warrior statue, what appeared to be a thickset *gaijin* in a green and yellow baseball cap, yellow rain slicker, and motorcycle boots exited the northbound platform with a daypack strapped to his back, orienting himself as he read a small map. Ozman. It had to be. Who else could it be? He hadn't taken long to sniff out Kent's well-chronicled trail. Through the rain and with his face obscured, it was impossible to be certain, but Kent didn't bother to find out.

As he walked swiftly towards the river, trying not to draw attention, Kent turned once more to see the man in the yellow slicker. But he was gone. He ran towards the river. He'd hide there until he figured out what to do next. The flooded river smelled of earth and vine, the effluence of fuel and fumes, a touch of some flower he couldn't name. The air grew cooler and the rain slapped his face. He descended a series of moss-covered stone steps that led to the rushing water, nearly sliding from one rock to the next. At the grassy bank, the river ripped past, filling his ears with its great whooshing. It seemed like a good place to be. And he was grateful for the encompassing sound. But at the bank Kent kept going, stepping where there were no steps, the ground beneath him not where he expected it to be. Unable to slow his momentum down the steep hill, he slid on the wet grass and mud into the river. Water ran too fast over his ankles and up to his knees.

Though it was nearly summer, the water was icy cold, and his feet numbed. At first, Kent welcomed the cold, the water shocking him sober. The river didn't care if he were on television; the river didn't care if he cheated on and failed his wife or maintained bad habits or knew not what his next step would be. The river didn't care that he'd killed his brother. The river was an absolute: water coursing over rocks and grass, full of sand and silt, cold and cleansing.

The current pushed against him, the water high and rushing; his feet slipped on the slimy green rocks. What felt good at first had become dangerous. One blunder and he'd slip under. Kent had never been a strong swimmer. How cold would it be under there, legs and arms stretched out like a big X, face up in the water, floating on to Tokyo and into the Pacific right on out of this island country? He looked to the other side, its steep bank nearly thirty meters away and covered in green grass, bobbing nests of dense green vine, and trees that leaned into the river, their branches and leaves pulled by the high water. He had to get out before something stupid happened. He stepped backward, stumbling and sliding. The water grew deeper and closed around his balls in an icy grip. He stood with his arms up and out at his sides, a ridiculous figure once again. He could no longer tolerate the life he lived, something had to change. Midori was right: *Have you seen yourself, Kent?* As he turned in the rushing water toward the bank, which seemed to stretch farther and farther away, Kent put his foot down in an overconfident search for a rock and found a hole instead. He went under, flapping his arms above his head in an attempt to stay upright, swallowing a gulp of river water.

As he surfaced, water rushed in his ears and he took in another mouthful. He coughed till his chest burned— as if matches were lit in his lungs—but he couldn't stop coughing. I'm drowning, he thought, in four feet of water. How stupid. A final stupid act to close a stupid life. Kent drummed his feet over rocks but couldn't steady himself as the river caught him in its current and pushed him downstream with the sand and the deadwood. Panic took hold, his stomach and chest tight, still on fire, his throat achy and the water sour and cold in his mouth like a bitter tea. His foot caught between a rock—a foothold—but his ankle twisted painfully. Kent bit hard into his tongue as his knee slammed up into his chin and he tasted blood. He tried to spin his body, again flapping his arms in the air and water, but the current pushed him forward, twisting his torso upriver and his legs towards Tokyo.

High up on the riverbank, Kent caught sight of a blurry figure in yellow. Would Ozman watch him drown, the river doing his dirty work for him? A wave of water washed over his head. When he looked up to the riverbank again, the yellow figure was gone. He wanted to reach up and pull Ozman, if it was him, into the cold water with him—*just the two us now, friend*, but he ran his knee into a large shallow boulder. As he reached his arms around the big gray rock, someone called his name. He could turn, he knew, and see his nemesis—how odd to have a nemesis—grabbing his crotch and laughing at Kent drowning before him in the river. He pressed his cheek to the cold rock and hung on, afraid to turn his head and look. With his name on the air, pulsating pain around his ankle and knee, the water rolled over him and all he could think about was the hockey bag that held his life's belongings, Allan's urn. How pathetic he would look to embassy officials when they gathered his body and his few possessions to ship home and discovered that he had no home, no place at all.

*(PHOTO OF FUCHU PRISON
FROM THE OUTSIDE)*

LAND OF OZ
INSIDE FUCHU PRISON

An Osaka film company would like to shoot a prison comedy starring Denis Ozman. A representative for Bombastic Productions reports talks are in the works with prison officials for a live, televised one-hour show starring the outrageous Australian, if he ever returns or is captured. Is Fuchu going soft? Or has Ozman worked his magic again?

Keep clicking as we dig deeper into Ozman's life behind (and outside of) the bars of Fuchu Prison.

To send your iCU reports visit:
www.Star-Gazer.com/iCU.html and click on the iCU! link.

CHAPTER EIGHTEEN

—

CINÉMA VÉRITÉ

S HOW ME THE GOODS
"Show me the goods, Kent Richman."

His face pale and damp, Kent sat on Oji-san's tatami floor in the room where he'd eaten breakfast with Midori. A blanket was draped over his shoulders and his right leg propped up on a pillow. Underneath, he wore the gold smoking jacket, which he now favored over other clothing. Most of his clothes he'd found in thrift stores and were too small anyway. He held a glass of Oji-san's cognac. A cigarette burned in an ashtray on the table. Rain battered the roof and wind whipped through the giant cedars, sending branches crashing to the ground and on to the gabled rooftop. Esquivel played faintly from a stereo in Oji-san's study, where the old man did sit-ups and lifted hand weights. Kent knew the lounge songs well because his father had played little else when he was a kid. He should've been astonished at the coincidence, the incongruity of hearing those dated, kitschy songs here in the Japanese mountains, but the record made sense. It could've been the cognac and the handful of the last of his painkillers.

Hideo, a young man in a John Deere cap turned backwards and oversized, and black-framed glasses, sat on the floor in front of Kent, a Sony DV camera on his shoulder, his eye to the viewfinder. "Got to show me the goods, man. That's why we came."

A soft-lighting box stood behind the young man, casting diffused light and warmth over Kent and the room. Chieko, Hideo's assistant in tattered blue jeans and a T-shirt that read *Rock Ago Grow Up!,* stood next to the lighting unit holding a boom mike. She wore a camouflage trucker's cap, with headphones fitted over the top. Hideo pointed the camera at Kent's ankle, wrapped in gauze that held an ice pack. Kent wondered if a bruised and swollen ankle really counted as "the goods." He'd also expected a much larger crew: an RV or two filled with caterers, lighting and audio crews, a makeup artist and a wardrobe specialist, perhaps even a special handler for him. The entire film crew consisted of Hideo, the director, and Chieko, the sound and lighting tech. Still, he did what he was asked, reasoning that the new school of documentary used low-tech, unadulterated methods. This might be the best way to tell his story, an ironic counter to his previously glamorous life, like the do-it-yourself comic book Mr. Morita showed him. He raised his foot for Hideo's camera. Midori, who sat nearby drinking green tea, leaned in to help.

"Excellent." Hideo returned the camera to Kent's face. "So, how'd you end up in the river?"

"Accident." Kent put the cigarette to his mouth. A panicked jump into the river was not how he'd envisioned the start of a documentary about his rejuvenated career, pretty sure that the rejuvenated career was supposed to come before the film about the rejuvenated career.

"You just fell into a flooded river?" Hideo sighed. "Why were you by the river at all?"

Kent cut his eyes to Midori. "Fresh air." He shifted on the floor and winced. He could've told them about seeing Ozman, if he had. But he didn't want Ozman to be part of his story anymore.

"In this rain?" Hideo looked around the camera. "This wasn't—something else, something to do with Ozman?"

"You mean—was I trying to drown myself?" Kent tested his swollen tongue against his teeth. "Or—" He tried to laugh but it came out as a high-pitched choke. "I suppose Ozman chased me there, or… or better yet, he threw me in the river. Is that what you want to hear?"

"All right, all right. We're just here to talk. But come on, man. Be straight with us. We understand what you've been through." Hideo smiled, encouraged, it seemed, by the possibility that Kent had either tried to kill himself or, yes, Ozman had tossed him into the swollen river. He returned his eye to the lens. "I understand you've been depressed lately, considering. People respond to that."

"Considering?"

"Considering everything you've been through, are going through—with Ozman, Kumi, all that coming back to haunt you with Ozman's escape."

"Who isn't depressed? I slipped—I got one good eye and can't tell if things are two feet in front of me or ten. Once I was in, the water just took me. My ankle got caught between a rock and here we are." Kent knew he should calm down, better manage his story. "Sorry to disappoint."

Hideo leaned away from the viewfinder again and rested the camera on his knee. He pulled a pack of cigarettes from his T-shirt pocket, tugging on his paltry goatee with the other hand. He nodded to Chieko who switched off the tungsten light.

"You want this to work? You want this to be some down and dirty cinéma vérité, right? Let people see the real Kent Richman? That's why we're here right? I'm thinking: *Crumb* meets *Porn Star: The Legend of Ron Jeremy*. *Wakaru?* Can you get that?"

Kent had no idea what Hideo meant—he couldn't remember the last documentary he'd seen, though Ron Jeremy sounded familiar. Hideo struck a wooden match across the hard shell of the camera case, lit the cigarette in his mouth, and blew smoke into the air. He wasn't sure he wanted to show the real Kent Richman. He had a different image in mind for this documentary. A serene and healthy, at least on the mend, Kent Richman in Zen robe and Lotus pose meditating while the sounds of cicadas and temple bells resonated across a rock garden. A wooden flute played as a gentle breeze lifted his hair, by then cut in a boyish but stylish shag—a collaboration between Kent and the makeup artist—his Lennon specs perched at the end of his nose. His voiceover spoke of a new dedication to a peaceful pursuit of happiness, one in which he shed his difficult past for a revival of both spirit and career. Kent was on retreat certainly, but more accurately *in* retreat.

"Loosen it up, let it go natural." Hideo inhaled deeply on his cigarette and exhaled a rush of smoke as he yelled, "*RI-CHU-MAN-SAN!*"

Kent took another swallow of Oji-san's cognac. "Let's stick with Kent." He should just feel better—try to see the day in the black, turn himself in a positive direction—but he'd need more of the cognac. If he drank enough, the painkillers would dull some of the pain for a few hours and leave him optimistic. He might feel better about the day and loosen up for the documentary. He imagined a happiness bubble rising in his belly to his chest where it spread to his shoulders and down along his arms to his fingertips. Kent felt as if someone had thrown a heavy blanket over his shoulders and placed a hand there only to remember that Midori had done exactly that.

"Don't think so much. Forget you're talking to a camera. This is not like TV—you don't have to be *on* for the camera. Let's step back a bit. We don't have to talk about Ozman, all that right now."

Two policemen had pulled Kent out of the river with a life ring, as Midori waited on the riverbank with an umbrella. Though Kent had been relieved, he missed the numbness of the cold water. How blissful it was to float senselessly for a few minutes, even if they were a perilous few. He'd been afraid in the water, but he had a limited sense of his own mortality. No threat had seemed capable of doing him in. Now, Hideo's voice pulled him from the refuge of the soft blanket and he missed the warmth.

A year ago Kent was calling the shots for interviews, where someone brought him his favorite coffee—two sugars, twenty-five percent half-and-half stirred for thirty seconds in a tall ceramic mug, not Styrofoam, not paper, not aluminum or stainless steel—and they paid for lunch, dinner, whatever he wanted, brought him gift bags, let him keep the clothes as long as he wore them in public. The questions were softballs and the photographer's lights flattering. Now, they focused the camera on his purple, swollen ankle, told him to relax, and probed him about attempted suicide. Hideo fiddled with the lens, turning it in a way Kent believed the lens wasn't meant to be turned.

"Are you supposed to do that?" Kent nodded to the camera.

"No problem. A little difficulty with the focal length. No big deal—it's not responding or something. Relax." Hideo continued twisting the lens, which released a series of disagreeable mechanical whines.

"I just got pulled out of a flooded river, a madman is stalking me and you guys show up with what looks like video equipment for a family reunion and you want me to relax, act like you're not here?" Kent adjusted his eyepatch. His eye should have been better, but his vision remained blurry and sensitive to light. Was there permanent damage? A doctor visit was out of the question—he was no longer part of the national health plan and he had no money to spend on a hospital visit. He was tired of seeing out of his left side only—the blind side left him unsteady, always anxious that something or someone would come out of right field and thump him.

"You called us," Hideo said.

"Renzo," Kent said.

"What?"

"Renzo, my agent, he called you, not me."

"Fine, your agent then. He said it was cool with you. When we got here, you said it was cool with you. Now it's *not* cool with you? What's up, man? You think we'd be up in boonies like this for no reason? We're here to help you, man. We're here to tell Kent Richman's story, man."

"It's been a long week," Kent said and went for a sip from his cognac only to find it empty, again.

The filmmakers turned out to be graduate students from Waseda University who wanted to chronicle life after *Bonanza* for Kent Richman. With Ozman on the loose, their documentary had legs. Hideo was right: they could help him. But now that they were here, Kent was disappointed. "Where's the rest of your crew?"

Hideo nodded to Chieko. "We're it, friend. This is new wave documentary. We don't need high production value to make a good film. We want people to know what it's like to be Kent Richman without all of the filters. That bullshit's for TV—no offense. This is film."

"Isn't it digital?"

"Sure, but we're making a *film*, man. Come on, Kent. Play ball, how about it? Real film, which I predict no one will be using in five years anyway, can be as much of a mask as, well, as a mask. With handheld DV we can capture you without the mask. See?"

"I guess so." Kent wanted to believe, but he'd seen higher production values for audition videos. And he liked the mask.

"Don't worry. We're good. We've trained with the best." Hideo placed the camera on the floor. "I was a PA for Kazuhiro Soda's last film. I've seen all of Errol Morris' films, some like five or six times each. Chieko was audio tech supervisor for the Sakura Film Festival. Don't you worry about the production stuff—you just be Kent Richman."

"I can do that." Kent guessed there might be value in capturing a more realistic version of himself, normally presented in the high gloss of television. "Get to the uncooked me instead of the glamorous show business side that everyone sees."

"Uncooked. Exactly. Chieko, remember that. We might use it later."

"'Kent Richman: Raw and Uncooked.'" Kent liked it.

"Yeah, raw and uncooked," Hideo repeated. "The *real* Kent Richman."

"'Kent Richman is *not RI-CHU-MAN-SAN!*'" He felt a surge of inspiration.

"Okay." Hideo fidgeted. "Maybe."

"'Kent Richman is Big in Japan.' Or 'Another side of Kent Richman'?" Kent searched for a pen and paper. "'Kent Richman: Here and Now.' Should I write these down? The Life and Times of—"

"Listen, why don't we take a breather." Hideo leaned towards Kent, his hands on his knees. "Don't want to impose a title on this thing yet. Let's let the camera tell us what to call it. We'll get there. Let's just talk a bit."

Kent believed he might be able to turn the documentary into something special. A stripping away of all his masks. Show people that being Kent Richman is not all fun and games, glamour and gold. That life in front of the camera can take its toll. That Kent Richman was down but not out.

V ITRUVIAN MAN
     The cognac and fatigue left Kent floating in a warm buzz. Esquivel's version of Cole Porter's "Night and Day" drifted in from Oji-san's study and hung in the air.

Though he felt himself swayed by Hideo's vision of what the documentary could be, Kent thought his ambitions for cinéma vérité required too much making it up as he went along. Kent was accustomed to scripted dialogue. He needed to compose himself, at least see the questions first and prepare some of his answers, find the confidence that allowed his performances a more natural appearance. He didn't improvise well. Even though *Bonanza's* witty exchanges appeared unprompted, most were carefully scripted. Improvisation on the show was not allowed—the "golden rule," they called it. He hoped the informal nature of his interview with Hideo would deflate the tension and unify the group while they got to know each other first. And it was, but once Hideo turned the camera on again, Kent broke the golden rule and began to ad lib.

"Did you know someone's written a manga serial about me? I don't remember the exact title. 'Big in Japan,' something, something. I was shocked at first just to see this cartoon version of myself, then horrified. But I'm thinking, all right, okay. It's flattering. Kent Richman's life is interesting, even this version. And, in many ways, it was my life, like I was seeing my life as it unfolded right before me. Things that have happened, maybe things that will happen. Weird to see your life all drawn out like that before you. As if—you aren't in control of yourself. Someone's out there inventing you, making things happen to you. Has nothing to do with who you are or who you *think* you are. Completely out of your hands. Makes you want to call on the author to explain what the hell they were thinking when they wrote this, wrote that."

Kent paused, switching gears as he sensed inspiration. "It's like a Mobius strip. You know the Mobius strip? One side but it looks like it's got two. Simple but complicated. That's how I see myself and that's how I want others to see me too. It's not all fun and games in TV land." Kent had read a metaphor somewhere in which celebrity life was analogous to a Mobius strip—at least, that's what he remembered. As soon as he said the words, doubt surfaced and left him wondering if it weren't some other kind of strip or metaphor. Either way, he couldn't quite remember how the comparison worked. "Does that make sense?"

Hideo sat behind the camera, which he'd placed on a tripod adjusted to sitting level. Midori sat paralyzed it seemed by Kent's words. "Sure it does, man. You're the man, Kill Bill. This is your show. Your trip."

Chieko, tired of holding the boom mike, had set it on the ground. She tried to make a Mobius strip out of the two sets of her fingers, placing them tip to tip, turning them one way then another.

Kent had no idea what Hideo meant and unraveled the Mobius strip metaphor further. "It's a paradox, right? Right. You want attention, but when you get it, you don't want it. You know what a Mobius strip is, don't you? Am I the only one? It's got one side but then it turns over and you don't know where one side begins and the other ends. Did I say that already? It doesn't matter, you know what it is, right? It's complex, I'm complex." Kent smoked nervously from his cigarette, letting his metaphor sink in. He believed he was close to recovering what he'd started with. "Your life on television appears one-sided, but it's not. It's got two sides. Simple, but not simple. Well, actually it's got like ten sides, but that won't work, that'd be like a Mobius bowl of noodles." Kent waited for a laugh—CUE—but Hideo only stared, his brow wrinkling. "Or maybe it's the other way around."

Midori gazed at the rain streaming from the roof. Chieko fiddled with the audio mixer. She seemed to set and reset the same levels. A stream of late afternoon sunlight— the sky had been nothing but gray for the past week—cut through the cigarette haze until it wound around Chieko's body like a ribbon of yellow silence. *Yellow silence. Yellow silence. Yellow silence?* Kent was stretching the arms of his brain in opposite directions, one arm reaching for his last thought while the other reached for the next. The two thoughts pulled at him, leaving him empty. An image of Da Vinci's Vitruvian Man sketched its way in to his head and deposited this equation: the span of a man's arms is equal to his height. Kent stretched and stretched but couldn't get his fingers around the thought in front of or behind him. He twisted his mind like a freestyle swimmer, one arm forward, one arm back, then came around full circle. "That's not right. The thing is, this manga about me. You just have to see it, then you'd know."

Chieko removed her headphones and stretched out before Kent, a beautiful girl of twenty-two in tight black jeans, hands behind her head. His eyes lingered over the thin, smooth pipes of her legs, the neat denim V between, the tiny mounds of her breasts cupped in a black bra under her T-shirt. Midori's plainness was even plainer next to Chieko. Hideo spoke but Kent didn't understand a word and leaned toward Chieko. Kent wanted to lie down beside her and listen to the rainfall. That would be enough. He didn't need to touch her, only to smell her, and to see the rise and fall of her chest. But the door from the kitchen slid open. Oji-san stood in a long, black robe, his feet in white *tabi* socks, and sandals.

"Excuse me, I need you all to please step into the classroom. I've got a funeral to prepare and I will need this room." Oji-san smiled. "You will have to play elsewhere for now."

C EMETERY CONTEMPLATIONS
Midori went to help Oji-san with the funeral. Hideo made phone calls from the study, and Chieko went outside to smoke on the back deck overlooking the cemetery and play a quick game of Dragon Quest Mobile on her cell phone. The rain had stopped and a dense mist

settled over everything. Birds lit on granite headstones, the braver ones ripping at the oranges left behind.

"It's beautiful here." Kent sat beside her and lit a cigarette

Chieko didn't look up from her phone, her thumbs tapping away at the tiny keys. "Yeah."

"The dead don't bother you much." Kent lied.

Chieko remained focused on her game. "I guess not."

Kent leaned in to look at the game she played. "I'm useless when it comes to those things. I only learned to text last year." Kent thought at once about the text messages he'd exchanged with Monique, who had encouraged him to use the instant messaging feature. Kumi wouldn't even carry a cell phone, though she'd done several ads for cell phone companies. "Big thumbs." He held both thumbs up for Chieko to see.

"What?" She stopped tapping.

"My thumbs, they're too big for those little phones." He moved his thumbs up and down.

Chieko released a hand from her cell phone, letting the other slide down beside her leg. "I heard Monique texted you right before she showed up at your apartment, right before Ozman shot her." She turned her face to his as if he'd spoken his thoughts out loud. "I heard Ozman was the one to answer her."

"And how did you hear that? How could you *possibly* know that?" Kent said.

"I read it online. They even had some of the text messages," Chieko said. "Hideo was trying to come up with some way to incorporate them into the documentary."

"I don't remember much." He wished he did, for Chieko seemed more interested in that story.

"It's not like I have a camera with me." She held up her hands, palms facing him. "Look."

"Ozman knew she was coming. She texted me that she was coming over. Ozman heard the phone and read her message. Bad timing all around."

She turned to him, her face now inches from Kent's. She smelled of cigarettes and soap. "What did she write?"

"I don't know. I was wrapped up in duct tape." Kent knew it sounded ridiculous, even though it was true.

"What happened next?" Her hand fell to his leg.

"He, we waited." The weight, the idea of her hand there encouraged him to talk.

"Were you scared?" Chieko moved her hand to his arm. "Was Ozman as freaky as he looks on TV? I mean, was he scary?"

"Guy's nuts and he had a gun. Of course, he's scary." Chieko's hand grew heavier on his leg. "He'd already hurt us both by that point." Kent turned his right forearm over. "Here."

"He did that?" She reached out. "Can I—?"

"Go ahead."

Chieko dabbed at the round scars.

"Whenever I am reminded of that day, they throb."

"How did he do it?"

"Knitting needle." Kent rolled the words out as slowly as the four syllables would allow.

She closed her eyes and rubbed at the scars, as if she hoped to relive the scene by touching him. "Oh, my god." Chieko raised her hand to Kent's face, running a finger over his Band-Aid and the edge of his eyepatch, as if she were exploring a delicate artifact. "You get hurt a lot."

"Seems so, doesn't it." Chieko's sudden tenderness surprised him. He hadn't been touched so affectionately in a long time. Even Midori, in her infinite patience and kindness, hadn't touched him so softly. Kent wanted to fall into the young girl but he was too aware of himself—of his labored breathing, the sweat sliding down the back of his shirt, the tonic of her sweet, smoky breath. "It's my cosmic sentence."

"You and Kumi were heroes. Your story was so romantic." She pulled her hand away. "What a perfect tragedy. Like a soap opera."

"Wish it were."

"When Hideo heard the news about Ozman, he got in touch with your agent right away, couldn't wait to get up here before—"

"Before what?"

"Hideo got the idea after reading about Ozman. He wanted to get here before, you know, in case Ozman—" Chieko stared out at the cemetery.

Kent wanted to trace his finger along the downy hairs that lay feathered across the top of her forehead. "Before Ozman got to me first?"

"It might make good film."

"Haven't had enough of Kent Richman?" Kent didn't really want an answer and believed he should kiss Chieko, that she'd possibly come out here for just such a kiss. She seemed transfixed by his story. A bottle of *sake* had been left on a large new altar in the cemetery along with flowers and cigarettes. Kent didn't think much about it—only that he needed the *sake* to lubricate the moment. He limped over, got the big brown bottle, and twisted the cap off. As he did so, the rain started again. They took shelter under the stoop of a small red shrine with a gabled roof. He gestured for Chieko to follow and she joined him inside the small shrine. No one would miss the *sake*, the bottle of what Kent recognized was *futsu*—cheap, and it would go to waste on top of the black altar.

From the edge of the cemetery he saw inside the funeral hall where a few of the last mourners shuffled in under umbrellas, the younger ones clutching bags, busy with car doors and their elders. Others slipped away in shadowy cars, while a handful stayed behind to visit the graves of their own relatives. Kent drank the tepid *sake* straight from the bottle. He passed it to Chieko who did the same. Several of the mourners did double takes at the tall foreigner with a bottle to his lips.

"This is bound to be bad," Chieko said. "You really are trouble, aren't you?"

Kent guessed she hoped he was and wanted to put his finger to her lips, just dab at them, but put the finger to his own. "Shh."

Two women in black walked through the cemetery carrying a bamboo bucket and a wooden ladle, each with a plastic grocery bag. They didn't notice Kent and Chieko. The younger woman held an umbrella over the elder. They walked to a gravestone and the shorter and older of the women pulled dead flowers from a silver vase and replaced them with fresh ones pulled from the grocery bag, then they sprinkled water over the headstone. They lit several sticks of incense in a bowl and knelt in front of the plot. With heads bowed, they put their hands together in prayer. The younger woman stood, leaving the elder who continued to pray. The younger woman: so much the daughter, as she lingered behind, gathering the bucket and ladle, wrapping the dead flowers in her plastic bag. She waited in the drizzle with the umbrella, one hand on her mother's shoulder.

Kent and Chieko drank more of the cheap *sake*, the bottle already half-finished. Chieko brushed her fingers over the scars on his forearm once more. "Real trouble."

Kent swam: through the watery day, the air so thick, he felt pinned to the earth. His arms and legs like the granite beneath him. Another swallow and he felt better, a cheerfulness bubbling between him, the bottle and Chieko. Rain or no rain, let the day go on like this, he prayed.

Oji-san was suddenly standing beside them. Chieko jumped, dropping the bottle, which broke over the granite base of the temple.

"I'm sorry," she said and ran off towards the temple.

"You scared the hell out of us." Kent began to pick up pieces of the bottle.

"That woman will stay for a long time. She always has trouble leaving." Oji-san sat on the granite railing, lit a cigarette, and nodded towards the mother and daughter.

"I'm sorry about the bottle." Kent held a jagged piece of brown glass.

"Don't worry about the bottle. Clean it up, replace it, and forget it." Oji-san clapped his hands together. "Or I might have to spank you both." Then he giggled. "At least the young lady."

"Funeral over?" Kent reeled and his good eye went blurry. He waited for his bees to swarm.

"I'm not needed just yet." Oji-san nodded again to the two women in the cemetery. "As you can see, suffering doesn't end so suddenly. That woman visits her husband's grave often. Her daughter will wait with her for as long as the old widow wishes to remain. Even in this rain."

"Did he die recently?"

"Almost ten years ago."

The widow stood at last and gazed at the gravestone, wiping her eyes with a white handkerchief. Mother and daughter walked away together, the elder's legs bowed and her back bent so that she stared at the ground in front of her. The daughter took a last look at the gravesite then turned to hold her mother's elbow as they left the cemetery.

"It's wrong for her to grieve so long. As Buddhists, we're encouraged to honor our family, but life is unbearably short. It should not be wasted on prolonged grief. There's a time for this, but it shouldn't go on and on. I've encouraged her to enjoy her daughter and the many friends she has here, but she clings to her husband's memory. She has forgotten how to live for herself."

Incense burned and a small stream of visitors filed from outside into the funeral hall, a separate room in the temple. At the door, they offered *koden*, condolence money in white envelopes wrapped in black and white ribbon. Some of the visitors stared at Kent.

"You weren't what they were expecting to see here." Oji-san fingered prayer beads around his neck. "Most have probably followed the Ozman story."

"Is it ok to stay? Is it safe?" Kent said.

"It's safe, but why do you want to stay?" Oji-san said.

"I'm supposed to."

"You don't want to be here?"

"I'm just not sure what I'm supposed to do. This was my agent's idea. Seems I don't have much control over what I do."

"Some things are out of our hands," Oji-san said.

Kent didn't trust the Buddhist platitudes. He nodded towards a woman just inside the door to the temple. "Is that the dead man's wife?"

"She's been up all night, keeping watch over the body after the wake," Oji-san said.

"And what do those *kanji* mean, the ones in front of the photo?"

"That's *kaimyo*, ancient *kanji* detailing the deceased's new Buddhist name. Few know what it says—I doubt anybody does but the family, since they chose it. Sort of depends on the price, what name you get. The more money you give to the temple, the better name you get."

"No offense, but it sounds like a racket," Kent said.

"A bit—but they get what they need," Oji-san said.

"What's that?"

"A sense that they've done the right thing for the departed. That they've properly honored the person they loved. It helps. It relieves the guilt they feel for surviving. Helps them say goodbye, move on as the living."

"My mother had a lot of rituals when I was growing up. None of them seemed to help her get over loss."

"How do you know?"

"I guess I don't, but she tried a lot of them."

"What was it she sought in these rituals?"

"Answers, I guess. I don't know much about her anymore."

"Perhaps it was not possible to gain what she sought in such *ritual*. Ritual is meant to remind us of our spiritual and emotional needs, help to strengthen our faith. One cannot *seek* faith or answers in ritual. That is walking in the wrong direction, towards the impossible. I enjoy many rituals for the sake of the rituals themselves. I find solace in the repetition, in the convergence of mind and action."

"All right, *sensei*. I get it." Kent patted Oji-san on the back. "This is all getting a bit too *Karate Kid* for me."

"*Do* you get it?"

"Sure—my mother was looking in all the wrong places."

"And what was she looking for."

"Her son."

"You?"

"My dead brother."

"I see," Oji-san said.

"Do you?" Kent said.

"Why did my son have to die? Was that her question?"

"I guess. Or, maybe, why did my youngest son have to kill him? She seemed to take it personally, like God, or whoever had conspired against her to take away her boy. But, in fact, it was me—I'm the one who took him away. Not God."

"You were responsible for his death?"

"It's a long story, but yes. An accident. My fault, but yes."

"This is who you carry in that urn?"

"You know about the urn?"

"Midori mentioned it."

"Full of surprises, that girl. Then you already know, *sensei.*"

"Yes, I suppose I do. And stop calling me *sensei.*"

"So, why do they get a new name? Why do you give these people a new name after they die."

"Keeps the dead from coming back every time their name is spoken." Oji-san stood. "I need to go—I have sutras to read. A funeral is long and it leaves me slow and tired. I don't really like doing them. We should soak later. We'll have to skip tonight's meditation, though I encourage you to try meditation on your own. Tomorrow, I'm having some friends over for a little party. Rest today and tomorrow we'll play."

"Rest it is, then." He looked squarely at the old man's face though he remained seated. "And I'll give the meditation a try."

Oji-san dropped his cigarette to the ground, stepped on it. "My niece likes you, I can tell."

"She's been great to me," Kent said.

"And this other young lady?" He nodded towards the temple.

"Chieko? I guess Ozman has reinvigorated my reputation. Otherwise—"

"Yes—otherwise. Midori has a bad habit of finding trouble and wanting to fix it. It's her way. And, you're trouble, I suspect, maybe more than she can take on. I don't know if she can fix you."

"No?"

"I'm really only thinking of Midori. I love my niece. You are my guest. But she is family and she is stubborn, born the year of the tiger. Like her father. My brother is stubborn, too. Stupid, stubborn man sometimes. So stubborn he asked his daughter to leave his house."

"Why?"

"Because he's an idiot." Oji-san pursed his lips, his face redder. "When Midori was twenty she traveled to Australia. For fun, to learn English and to get out on her own a bit. She's always been a good student. But she met an Australian boy there and wanted to marry him. My brother was very upset. He told Midori it was impossible. She would embarrass the family and to never to come home again. So, she didn't."

"She mentioned an Australian guy, but nothing about marriage."

"She married him, of course. And my brother refused to see her."

"Why?"

"She's his only daughter—it might be difficult for you to understand. But also, he's a tiger, like Midori. Two tigers, they fight each other. It's no good. But this boy, he was no good, too, you see, just like my brother told her. Her father knew. This Australian boy lied to her. He was always angry, wouldn't let her leave the house or have friends—very jealous and controlling. He might have even hit her, though she won't discuss it. He had girlfriends and no money. Midori worked and he spent her money. Is this your way too?"

"I have no girlfriends. No money either, but I promise I won't spend Midori's. I'm sorry for causing so much trouble."

"Just work out whatever's wrong. Don't bring Midori into it. I enjoy it when she's here. She stayed with me for three months when she returned from Australia."

"She said anything about me?"

"You are our guest. Still, I suspect something's wrong."

"She had some trouble with a guy named Kenji. You can thank him for my eye."

"Maybe I should. And what provoked him to such action?" Oji-san looked at his watch, pulled a Hi-Lite from inside his robe and lit it.

"Haven't a clue."

"Or perhaps I should thank you for the trouble. Kenji was not right for her either. Or perhaps I need to ask you to leave. My niece doesn't need any more trouble of this kind. But she's stubbornly drawn to disasters like you. No offense."

"None taken."

"You're welcome to stay for your allotted two weeks, if this is not the case. All I ask is an honest assessment of yourself."

"That's a lot to ask of someone who hasn't a clue what he's doing. I—"

But Oji-san was gone, vanished in a puff of cigarette smoke. Kent felt dizzy again from drinking the *sake* on an empty stomach. The rain came down harder yet, so he hobbled off to the classroom where he had slept, wrapped a blanket around his shoulders, and watched the rain roll over the edge of the roof. He would try meditation, try emptying his mind of everything that seemed to haunt him: Ozman, in particular. Kent thought it was time to leave, let Midori and her kind uncle be, spare them any more drama. He'd catch a train to Tokyo—at this point, Ozman would not consider looking for him there, maybe drag Hideo and Chieko with him, recover some of his old stomping grounds, and stir the kinds of memories he suspected the filmmakers were after. The rain and the mountain air chilled him so he pulled the blanket tighter and drifted off to sleep in front of the doorway.

In his dream, the temple window revealed the ocean and a bright blue sky, a mammoth white whale breaching the water. Then he was in the water and swimming, the whale bumping against him, its great body swimming past his slight figure. He waved to someone on the beach but the whale bumped him and pushed him under. Kent couldn't get his head high enough to see who was on the beach and feared he was drowning. Then Kent was on the beach watching the whale again, Ozman leaning into him with his ruddy face and spiky mohawk, poking him in the chest with his index finger, spittle flying from his mouth. *What'd you say, John Lennon? Speak up.*

CHAPTER NINETEEN

—

A PHONE CALL WITH RENZO

"**R**ichman, it's Renzo—what the hell took you so long?"

"I was meditating," Kent said, understanding how stupid it sounded before he finished his sentence.

"*Honto?*"

"I can get deep," Kent said. In fact, he'd been napping for the first time in days, blessedly so.

"I figured you might put on a good show for the cameras, but real meditation?"

"It's a documentary. It's supposed to be real."

"You don't want to show them the *real* Kent Richman. At least not what you keep showing on the internet. YouTube should pay you."

"Now I'm responsible for every jerk with a cell phone?"

"I tell you to keep it low. And what's the first thing you do? I saw at least two photos from Azuma alone. You were there two days? Then this craziness at a rest stop. Not cool, Richman, *not cool.*"

"Bad days, I know." Renzo was right.

"So, do me a favor—*do—not—fuck—up—any—more*, and stay away from cameras, except for one. Just let this

Hideo guy do the good work for you. Let him shape Kent Richman the way we want to show Kent Richman."

"But he keeps talking about cinéma vérité—"

"Cinema *what?* Listen, directors are all a bunch of tyrants, you know that. The only way good movies and TV are made is to be a control-freak. Just nod and pretend you love it. Then, give them what we need."

This was not what Kent had imagined, some graduate student telling him how to be himself, Renzo pulling strings behind the scenes. "And thanks for not telling me this whole charade is about Ozman. You knew all along—"

"Coincidence," Renzo said.

"They're just waiting for Ozman to show up and beat the hell out of me on camera, aren't they?"

"What do you want me to say, Richman? I didn't want you to freak out on me. You do have a habit. When the news about Ozman hit, the guy from Waseda called and it seemed like a good idea—"

"I wouldn't have freaked out," Kent said.

"Are you freaked out now?" Kent heard Renzo take a deep drag on his cigarette.

"No—" Kent sensed Renzo was about to counter his claim. "Can you blame me?"

Renzo exhaled noisily. "He'll never find you up there. I'm not sure I could even find you right now. And when you look like he does, how far can you go in Japan?"

CHAPTER TWENTY

—

LET'S ENJOYING COSPLAY

"Who are you?" Kent stood before a young woman in an elaborate costume with the help of an improvised cane, one of Oji-san's cosplay accessories.

"I'm 'Yoko,' from *Tengen Toppa Gurren Lagann.*" The young woman held up an imposing gun, assembled from fiberboard and PVC pipes spray-painted blue. "She's a villain." The gun stood taller than the young woman, up to Kent's chin.

"Amazing costume." "Yoko" seemed flattered, honored even by Kent's curiosity and praise. In shiny black bikini top, belted hot pants, and long, fingerless gauntlet-style gloves, white go-go boots over thigh-high stockings and a bronze-colored wig, the young woman stood out, even among her cosplay friends.

Oji-san's friends had come in from neighboring towns to dress up like anime and manga characters, drink and talk costumes and characters. There were eighteen members in the group, which they called Masquerade. Of the eighteen, eleven had turned up for the party in the temple's community center.

"Most of it—the bikini top and pants—are made of PVC vinyl. The gloves and boots—I had to buy and modify them—are leather. The gun is made of various elements." She glanced at Kent's cane, the eyepatch and Band-Aid, and his gold smoking jacket. "*Anata dare?*"

Kent didn't know how to answer—who *was* he? Former celebrity, John Lennon look-a-like, homeless and out-of-work manga character, clown, hunted prey? "Yoko" didn't seem to know who *Kent Richman* was at all.

"You look like a lord or a pirate, some sort of mercenary wizard, I'm not sure. Or maybe like Sherlock Holmes, but I don't know *this* character. What's he from?" She ran a finger along his jacket lapel. "Silk, nice."

Kent considered lowering his glasses and offering *A-re?*, but moved on to the next player, not in the mood to play *RI-CHU-MAN-SAN!* or anything else. He met Sophie Hatter from *Howl's Moving Castle*, a character he recognized from the Miyazaki film. The petite middle-aged woman played a much younger girl in a full-length linen skirt, collar and bodice, and straw hat. Her hair was braided into a long ponytail that draped over her shoulder. "Sophie" lifted her skirt to reveal actual bloomers and a petticoat.

"Tomoyo Daidoji" from *Card Captor Sakura* refilled Kent's *sake* glass and offered him a cigarette. The young man wore a standard schoolgirl uniform of blue skirt and sailor-style blouse, white thigh-high stockings over his skinny legs, and opera length gloves. He stood tall on patent leather platform heels. "Tomoyo" cared about the details.

"Her heart is my heart. So, out of respect for the character and the artist, I want everything to be just right. We are one person with two names," "Tomoyo" said and adjusted his wig. "Mr. Watanabe told us about you. But I don't understand that kind of television. It makes me feel lazy. No offense. But, you really look like John Lennon." He pushed a strand of the soft-looking fake hair behind one ear and wiped at the corner of his mouth with the same finger that held his cigarette. His bright red lipstick had stained the cigarette filter. "I'm hoping, as our group grows, to one day meet a 'Sakura' to partner with my 'Tomoyo.' They have only shared a kiss, but Tomoyo keeps a very deep love for Sakura. Theirs is a special girl love. There is nothing profane about it."

Kent had no idea who or what the young man was talking about but smiled, thanked him for the *sake* and cigarette, and excused himself. "You look great, by the way," Kent said and meant it: odd but stylish, his costume neat and not the least bit cheap.

The young man smiled and raised his glass. The encounter reminded Kent of the hundreds of parties he'd attended, where he spoke to people only in short, often non-verbal acknowledgments or pretended to listen while they spoke of things Kent Richman had no interest in or knowledge of. Once they'd finished, he told them how good it was to see them or meet them or that he'd look forward to hearing from them again about whatever it was they'd spoken of, it didn't matter. All he had to do to escape was to agree to whatever it was they asked. To keep promises he'd never remember. How many opportunities had he blown off that he'd happily accept now? Oji-san's friends, however, seemed genuine—they either didn't know him or didn't want anything from him. And Kent enjoyed the lively mood the enthusiastic cosplayers encouraged, appreciated the diversion the party and costumes offered.

"Hi, cowboy." Kent turned to find a masked woman sealed in tight, red leather and a spider-like—not quite

Spiderman—pattern of black stripes. A long pumpkin-colored wig fell down her back. Pink animal ears poked through the carroty curls. Pale yellow cups with red tips on the front of her suit left the impression that holes had been cut in the leather to reveal her nipples, gracefully firm and small. The polished leather shimmered in the fluorescent light. The pattern of black stripes pointed to the V between her legs. She had a little tummy Kent wanted to rub. This surprised him. The *cowboy*, the red leather, the pale yellow cups, the magnificent V—the potbellied tummy. The woman tilted her head at him head like an animal. The mask was plainly feminine with wide, blue manga eyes, tiny nose, and pointed chin. She moved in close, the blue gauze over the eyeholes sparkling, opaque. She laughed and pulled the mask down.

"Gotcha!" She laughed.

"Midori?" Kent drained his *sake*.

She put her hand under his chin to close his open mouth. "Are you drooling?"

Kent mock-wiped his chin as if to make sure he wasn't. "Midori?" he repeated.

"Didn't recognize me?" She rested a hand on her hip and thrust sideways, a move that worked better on a longer-legged woman.

"You're into all this, too?"

"You think it's weird?" She pinched her mouth, but Kent noticed a trace of real disappointment in the comic frown.

"You surprised me, that's all." Kent flushed from his last swallow of *sake*, the room tipped, not a jolt, but a slow-motion slip, another of the "aftershocks" he'd been experiencing. "Actually, you look—great." And he meant it.

"You think? It took me two months to put this all together," Midori said. "I'm Asuka Langley Soryu. From *Neon Genesis Evangelion*. She's American but was raised in Germany. Speaks German."

"German." Kent thought about the plump of Midori's belly under red leather.

"What are you, stupid?" Midori put her face in front of his.

"Huh?"

"It's Asuka's catch phrase: '*What are you, stupid?*'"

Kent didn't understand.

"You are stupid, aren't you?" Midori shoved Kent. "Are you high, Kent Richman?"

Kent held up his empty *sake* glass.

Midori grabbed a *sake* cup from a nearby card table.

With the bottle obtained from Tomoyo, Kent poured, her glass, then his. They toasted and drank. Midori glowed in her tight red suit. He realized he'd never touched her with any intimacy and felt worse for it, this plain girl who'd been so nice to him. This reinvented Midori, this Asuka So-and-So from the pages of a comic book. He'd been so preoccupied with Renzo, Ozman, documentaries, and his own failing state, he'd hardly noticed the lovely girl in front of him. Kent leaned in to whisper in her ear—what, he didn't know, anything to bring her closer.

The music stopped, and a man in a full suit of futuristic armor made of flexible synthetic material spray-painted silver tapped his beer bottle with the real metal spikes on his silver gloves.

"Everyone—your attention please. Let's all welcome Mr. Rinji Watanabe, our gracious host."

The guests turned towards the main door where Oji-san stood in full dress, and applauded. Oji-san wore a yellow wig, its spiked tufts jutting out on all sides and standing nearly six inches high. He wore navy blue military-style commando pants and a shirt adorned with leather belts and straps, a silver claw of some kind strapped to his leg and armor over one shoulder. A red cloak wrapped around his neck and fell the length of his torso. His hands and forearms were covered in spiked leather gloves and he wore black leather high-tops. In his right hand was the enormous sword Kent had seen in Oji-san's dining room—at least three-feet high and a foot wide. His eyes were highlighted with black eyeliner and they appeared to be blue. On his back, giant, vinyl bat-like wings floated as if he might suddenly take flight.

"Thank you, everyone, for joining tonight's Masquerade cosplay event. Once again you have all outdone yourselves. As you can see, I am 'Cloud' from Kingdom Hearts and Final Fantasy. The newest additions to my costume are the blue contacts and the improved wings, now made of a more resilient but still flexible PVC vinyl. As you know, the previous wings did not travel well, particularly when we debuted our costumes and routine at the Melbourne Preliminaries. Tonight, I will show you the full routine live, as it was performed in Australia. Therefore, without further commentary, please welcome Mrs. Kaneda." Oji-san stepped into the room and nodded to another member—some sort of Victorian Shirley Temple in pink boiler suit, white stockings and curly blond wig, who started operatic rock music on a portable stereo. Oji-san stepped away from the door. "Ladies and gentlemen: 'Sephiroth.'"

The Masquerade members applauded as Mrs. Kaneda stepped into the room in full costume. A woman of at least sixty, she stood in shiny black knee-high leather boots an and elaborate waistcoat with tails trimmed in red piping and sporting her own set of enormous blue wings. She wore a long, silver wig that parted in the middle and rose high like silky bird wings. She smiled, despite her best efforts at a fearsome grimace, revealing a gold cap on a front tooth. The music changed from operatic rock—Kent thought of Queen or some kind of glam metal—to a solo cello playing high, staccato bursts. Mrs. Kaneda's smile returned to the grimace and she drew a long, narrow sword made of a light metal. Where did they find such weapons? Who made them? Oji-san raised his own enormous sword in a fighting stance. The two squared off. As if scripted, everyone in the room retreated to the corners, leaving a space in the middle of the room for Mrs. Kaneda and Oji-san, aka Cloud and Sephiroth.

"Good to see you—Cloud. Your geostigma is gone. That's too bad," Mrs. Kaneda said in a menacing voice—a deeper growl than Kent would've imagined from a petite, older woman.

Oji-san walked cautiously towards Mrs. Kaneda. "Sephiroth." He pointed his giant sword at her. Kent was surprised Oji-san could lift the large weapon. "What do you want?"

"To sail the darkness of the cosmos with this planet as my vessel, just as my mother did long ago." Mrs. Kaneda raised an arm to the sky. The music faded from cello to driving metal. "Then one day we'll find a new planet. And on its soil, we'll create a shining future."

"What about this planet?" Oji-san said, raising his sword, which took some effort, threatening to pull him over if he leaned too far forward.

"That's up to you, Cloud." Mrs. Kaneda moved towards Oji-san in feigned slow motion, her sword raised. Oji-san lifted his to meet hers. They clashed as the music crescendoed. Oji-san deflected Mrs. Kaneda's sword with a *clank* and spun, aiming at her knees when he came back around, all in slow motion. Mrs. Kaneda stepped aside, dodging Oji-san's sword, spinning herself until she swung, catching Oji-san on the back. He fell. Mrs. Kaneda prepared to drive her sword through him, but Oji-san brought his sword up and thrust it at Mrs. Kaneda's gut. She dropped her sword, grabbed her belly, and stumbled backwards, laughing. "Where did you find this strength?"

Oji-san stood, brushed himself off and replied, "I'm not about to tell you," before running the sword into Mrs. Kaneda once more, dealing the final blow. "Stay where you belong, in my memories."

Mrs. Kaneda struggled to rise as she gazed absently at the ceiling. Oji-san knelt beside her, holding her head with one hand when Mrs. Kaneda croaked, "I'll never be a memory."

Oji-san nodded at Shirley Temple—the music stopped—and he raised his sword once more. In slow motion he brought the sword to Mrs. Kaneda's side.

She took the sword inside her arm, groaned, and whispered, "Never."

After several rounds of applause and a few hoots, the cosplay crowd mingled again and refreshed their drinks before the next scheduled performance. Hideo and Chieko walked the room, shooting footage of the cosplay *otaku*, who were thrilled to have their costumes documented. Kent wondered how the cosplay event fit in with his story. When he tottered outside to the back of the temple, neither of the filmmakers followed.

The woods behind the temple were dark, the unfailing rain producing a soothing hum. Kent breathed deeply of the mountain air. His bees threatened to buzz. He couldn't get over Midori, who had slipped away to the kitchen. He opened the screen door and sat inside its frame. Shadows from the lit temple danced on the forest. Kent closed his eyes to the calming rain and as he breathed in the damp air he noticed that the muscles around his ribs and chest were held in a cold new ache.

CHAPTER TWENTY-ONE

—

CHANNELING MICKEY ROURKE

Everyone at the cosplay event was drunk and getting drunker. Kent was no exception. The *sake* left him talkative. Seeing Oji-san's friends so comfortable in their costumed skin encouraged Kent to find some part of himself he liked. He convinced Hideo and Chieko to sneak off to the study and put the camera on him while the *otaku* cranked out karaoke. Hideo held the camera unsteadily before him, but it was to Chieko that Kent spoke about Monique.

"I don't know why I did what I did," he said, as Hideo filmed. "It started out innocent enough. Meet a pretty girl at a party, flirt. It happened all the time. But then I found out who she was, and maybe I saw it as a chance to make Ozman suffer a little. It was just supposed to be a bit of flirting, nothing more, some innocent prank on this guy who'd made a fool of me on TV, in front of the whole country."

"Yeah, yeah, the farting thing. That was freaking hilari—" Chieko stopped herself.

"I know—*hilarious*, right? Everybody thought so. And I looked like a fool," Kent said.

"No, no, no... not *you*, not *RI-CHU-MAN-SAN!* Him. *Him* was funny," Chieko slurred.

"Shut up, Chieko. Let him talk," Hideo nudged her backward with his arm until she fell on her back and closed her eyes.

"You see, Ozman had it coming. I was just going to flirt with Monique enough to make him take notice, make him suffer, like he'd made me suffer in front of all of Japan, in front of my fans. It was half of my job, practically, flirting with women, men too, at parties. People, strangers come up to you and just wanted to be with you, be near you just because you're famous, because you look like somebody famous. I look like somebody famous."

"You do, you do—John Lennon, *ne*," Chieko piped in again without rising from the floor and turned her head to Hideo. "He really does."

Kent continued. "People love that. Love me for it. Or they did. Monique just seemed like everybody else. She wanted to talk to me, stand next to me, be with me."

Chieko jumped in, still slurring, "*So desu, ne.* You're *RI-CHU-MAN-SAN!* Everybody loves *RI-CHU-MAN-SAN!* I love *RI-CHU-MAN-SAN!*" She tried to rise but got halfway up before she fell back again.

"Didn't they?" Kent said.

Chieko struggled to get upright. "I remember watching you on TV, you know, when I was in high school. Oh my god, Kent Richman, so John Lennon, so sexy. My friends and I thought you were *hot*. When you sang 'Yesterday,' you had us screaming. My parents thought I was nuts."

Hideo joined the chorus. "You're the man, *RI-CHU-MAN-SAN!* That's the truth. The *man*."

Chieko managed to sit up but rocked unsteadily. She removed her hat and waved it in the air. "*RI-CHU-MAN-*

SAN! is the man. Whoo!" She tipped into Hideo, knocking the camera from his hands. They both laughed before Hideo pushed Chieko away and righted the camera.

"*RI-CHU-MAN-SAN!* is talking," Hideo said.

Kent loved the young audio tech for her little kindnesses. He loved the way Chieko looked at him across the *tatami* floor, with the familiar reverb and echo of karaoke music and singing from the other room, her face still that of the high school girl she once was. He loved her tight jeans and clingy T-shirt, her hat sideways on her head, her ponytail undone and spilling around her face. For this drunken minute, he felt as if he were at one of the many parties in which pretty girls had fought to be near him, in which it mattered that he was *RI-CHU-MAN-SAN!*

"I really had something, didn't I? My own TV show, Kumi, money, scripts coming in every day, VIP rooms, endorsements. I'm young. I could have ridden that wave a long time. I know what I had, more than anybody in the world. And that I'll probably never get it back. Don't know why it took me so long to figure that out, but I've realized something else since coming back to Japan: just wanting something is not enough. It's not enough to want to be famous. Just because you want something doesn't mean you have a right to it, doesn't mean you get it. But why shouldn't I?"

Chieko reclined on one elbow. She wouldn't last much longer. Hideo still held the camera, but it now rested on one knee and was pointed at the ground. But Kent wasn't talking to the camera any longer.

"Why did you do it?" Chieko finally asked. "Why did you cheat on Kumi?"

"You won't believe me," Kent said.

"Right now, Kent Richman, I'll believe anything you say," Chieko said and smiled, her eyes closing and opening again slowly.

"The whole damned thing was an accident. Not just the shooting, that was Ozman, still an accident though. But Monique wasn't supposed to happen. I just wanted Ozman to see her with me, get his back up a bit. But one minute she's leaning into me, hand on my shoulder, the next we're in a love hotel in Shibuya. After that, I—*we*—couldn't stop. Guess that star charm was hard to resist."

"Uh hum," Chieko said.

"Then Kumi found the video tape and the whole mess went viral," Kent said.

"Bad, bad, *RI-CHU-MAN-SAN!*" Chieko said. "Poor Kumi."

"Yep, bad, bad *RI-CHU-MAN-SAN!* and poor Kumi. All she had to do was jump around in kid's underwear. Everybody loved her. They still do. She is, was, whatever, beautiful. I was married to the most beautiful girl in Japan." Kent took a long, dramatic drink of *sake*.

Kent felt a surge, as if his story, his whole path to this mountain retreat, made more sense now. Here before Chieko and Hideo, his audience of two, as if he were chasing the dragon again. "There were some busted up parts of my life I didn't know how to fix, a whole other story I'm done with, that made me behave like an ass, I suppose." He'd read an article in the weekly *Asahi Geino* about the actor Mickey Rourke. Rourke had been popular in Japan and a regular in Japanese commercials, shilling for many of the same brands Kent had once represented: Suntory whiskey and Lark cigarettes. Rourke's own impressive comeback was widely chronicled in magazines and on entertainment programs and seemed to get much more press in *Shukan Gendai,* on Star-Gazer.com, and other media outlets these days than Kent. So he borrowed the line about "busted up parts." And a few others. Rourke was staging a comeback and the Japanese loved it. Kent thought a couple of moves from Rourke's playbook might help. He'd risen from the bottom, from obscurity, poverty, and drug abuse to win awards and get meaty movie roles once again. "I didn't know who I was when I got here and then I had this persona imposed on me. Hey, hey *RI-CHU-MAN-SAN!* Pretty stupid name." Kent put his face up to the camera lens. "No offense to your Japanese sensibilities, but it's a pretty stupid name."

Hideo and Chieko both nodded. He shouldn't be talking like this, he knew—Renzo would whip him good for such recklessness. But this night, this moment, left him carefree. He wanted to make an impression, tell the truth for a change.

"And it was mine. I didn't know enough to understand or want to accept the fact that television was a business. I thought it was about acting, about acting and looking like John Lennon. I could do that. Better than anyone else. At least looking like John Lennon. How's that for talent? Looking like someone else who happens to be famous. But that was supposed to just be a stepping-stone, a way to get in and show myself. It wasn't supposed to be the best I had to offer."

Hideo's camera now pointed just left of Kent's head. Later, when Kent borrowed the camera to shoot his own YouTube shout out to Kumi, he caught a replay of the interview to discover that only half of his face was visible in the frame. It made him look schizophrenic, as if some closeted version existed off camera. Worse: it appeared as if the camera did so deliberately, choosing not to show that side of its subject. Not only was Kent Richman cut in two, but he was also out of focus. Chieko had closed her eyes, hardly listening any longer. Midori poked her head in around the door, but Kent didn't stop. He had a few more things to say.

"I've been doing bad things for a long time. You've no idea what I've done."

"Sure, we do, man. The whole country knows," Hideo set the camera on the floor. Kent wasn't sure it was even on any longer.

"Not Monique, not Ozman. I mean back home, before I came to Japan. You have no idea how famous I've been—the notorious Kent Richman. Poster child for Television Violence."

"What the hell are you talking about?" Hideo said.

Kent didn't care. He felt like talking. "I wish I knew differently, because I put myself and other people through a lot of hell. I've had a whole life to regret it. Who wouldn't?" Kent leaned forward, grabbed the camera with both hands, and spoke directly into the lens again. "You hear me, Allan, you hear that, Kumiko Sato, Green Apple girl, wherever the hell you are: I'm sorry. Stupid, stupid, stupid Kent Richman is sorry. I should have killed Ozman when I had the chance."

Hideo clumsily pulled the camera away from him, nearly falling backwards when Kent let go. "Hey, man. Don't mess with my camera." Midori had already stepped away without a word when Kent looked to her for validation, some indication that he wasn't playing the fool again.

Chieko rose with a clumsy jerk. "What's that mean— killed Ozman?" Hideo put his eye to the eyepiece again and refocused the camera on Kent's face. Kent went on as if he'd said nothing.

"I didn't think anything was wrong with me. I thought it was everybody else. And there was a lot wrong with me, but it had to do with, I don't know, stuff, Allan stuff I hadn't come to terms with. Like who cares if you look like John Lennon. And I realized that when I lost everything. I mean, *everything*. Not just my television career. Then you're alone." Kent hardly breathed. "I'm finally starting to understand the wreck I've made. My life has been on fast-forward for two years. I just want to get off." Kent began to channel Rourke. "Because there's a little guy with a sword that still lives inside of me, and he keeps hacking away at every thing good." Kent made chopping motions in the air. "Just mindless chopping away. And I don't know how to stop him."

YouTube Video – Recorded and Posted By Kent Richman

1:23 AM, Cedars Temple, Japan
41 seconds
Viewed 11 times
(Bob Dylan's "Tangled Up in Blue" plays in the background)

This is a message to Kumi, wherever you are, wherever you might see this, preferably early in the morning, when the sun is shining and it's still too early to wake up but, you know, whatever you dream, whatever you hear, whatever you feel there beside you will affect you for the rest of the day. I'll wake you up early to tell you: If I ever leave this world behind, I'll come back and thank you, for the things you did, for leaving me. I'll never get used to it and I'll never forget. But you'll tell me you're all right.

From *Star-Gazer.com*

PHOTO HERE
JAPANESE WOMAN AS SHE
ESCORTS FOREIGN MAN
ON TO AIRPLANE
(TAKEN FROM BEHIND)

HAS KUMI FORGIVEN KENT?

iReporter Haruka Moriyama believes she has captured the celebrity couple *Kent & Kumi* in the Narita Airport. Could this be our elusive couple? On the run from Ozman? And reunited? Has Kumi taken Kent back after everything he did?

Moriyama states she spotted the pair when she noticed a tall foreigner resembling Kent Richman boarding an airplane bound for the United States. With him, a Japanese woman. *Kumi—is that you?* Moriyama managed to get this photograph with her cell phone before the pair disappeared down the ramp way.

"They looked very cozy together. When I realized it was *RI-CHU-MAN-SAN!,* I just assumed it must be Kumi—but she wore a baseball cap and big sunglasses and I couldn't see her face clearly. When I called out their names, he turned but she pulled him through the gate before I could catch up with them."

This marks the first time that the couple have been spotted together. Reports have placed Mr. Richman variously in Tokyo, where he had been living in a capsule hotel, and in the mountains of central Japan, where it was previously confirmed by his agent, Renzo Royama, of Creaxion Artists, that Mr. Richman was on a Zen meditation retreat. Mr. Royama also confirmed that Richman had sworn off all contact with society and was existing on a limited diet of rice and tea. He claimed Richman's retreat had nothing to do with Ozman's escape. "He has nothing to fear from this man."

Mr. Royama released this public statement:

"Kent has devoted his time and energy to simplifying his life. He believes, and I concur, that, following the Ozman Incident, he returned to his career obligations too soon. With this simplification and recentering, however, he hopes to relocate his artistic axis and, before the end of the year, return to his career in television, while also pursuing film opportunities and a host of other endeavors. Kent appreciates the support and affection he has received from all of his fans. And he hopes to give back the love when he returns to Tokyo and his profession. To quote *RI-CHU-MAN-SAN!*: "'A dream you dream alone is only a dream. A dream you dream together is reality.'""

Dream on, *RI-CHU-MAN-SAN!*

Attempts to verify the couple's status as passengers on the US-bound flight were unconfirmed. Additional messages left with Mr. Royama have gone unanswered.

Have you seen *Kent & Kumi*? If so, send us your photos and tell us where you spotted the happy(?) couple. You'll receive a free Satr-Gazer.com T-shirt and a chance to enter our "Vacation with the Stars" contest.

To send your iCU reports visit:

www.Star-Gazer.com/iCU.html and click on the iCU! link.

CHAPTER TWENTY-TWO

—

LIKE NATUREBOY RIC FLAIR

Kent sat on a cushion emblazoned with the Sanrio character My Melody, a simply drawn white rabbit in a pink hood. He'd been in Japan for so long the adolescent furnishings in Midori's room—the Hello Kitty clock radio and telephone, comforter and bed set, the Cinnamoroll bead purse and matching belt, the My Melody jewelry chest and cushions—hadn't seemed at odds with the twenty-three-year-old woman. After Hideo and Chieko returned to the party, Hideo chatting up the lovely "Yoko," Chieko last seen making out with the cross-dressing Tomoyo, Kent found Midori's small room at the back of the residence. The *sake* and the talking had left him exhausted. The cosplay club members continued to drink and sing, their affection for karaoke seemingly boundless. Kent, trying to find Midori, instead found Oji-san and his cosplay partner, his Sephiroth, in a room with several large *taiko* drums. She kneeled before one of the giant drums as Oji-san held his arms around her. Mrs. Kaneda held two wooden mallets. Oji-san guided the mallets to the drum, rocking his hips to the rhythm. Mrs. Kaneda swayed in harmony, eyes closed.

Kent pulled a blanket around his shoulders and read random pages from a book by Kobo Abe he'd found on one of Oji-san's bookshelves. The title reminded him of a trip he and Kumi had taken to Bali, of Kumi covered in sand one playful afternoon. He felt wretched and settled into the fantasy of Abe's shadowy story about a man trapped in a community of sand dunes, deep holes in the earth, like honeycombs. The man was held captive in one of the dune basins with a woman who had lived there by herself for years. Kent sympathized with Niki Jumpei, thinking as he always did that there was some of him in this other's story, some of his life written down there.

"There you are." Midori appeared in the doorway, still in her costume, animal ears silhouetted in the hall light; she spoke from behind Hideo's camera.

Kent looked up from Abe's book. "What are you doing?"

She pulled the camera away and leaned against the doorframe, drunk. "I'm making a movie about the famous *RI-CHU-MAN-SAN!* It's a fascinating documentary."

"When you say it, it almost doesn't sound ridiculous. Anyway, you're wasting your time. Nothing to see here— unless you like disaster movies. Go home, love your family, and forget about what you've seen here tonight, young lady. You'll be happier. The world will be happier."

Midori put the camera down and slipped in beside him. "Are you okay?"

The smells of leather and *Rain* washed over him. "Dizzy, nothing unusual." He held up *The Woman in the Dunes.* "Doing a little reading."

"Where are Hideo and Chieko?" she said.

"No clue. You're the one with their camera." Kent turned to the book. "Listen to this: There wasn't a single item of importance. A tower of illusion, all of it, made up of illusory bricks and full of holes. If life were made up only of important things, it really would be a dangerous house of glass, scarcely to be handled carelessly. But everyday life was exactly like the headlines. And so everybody, knowing the meaninglessness of existence, sets the center of his compass at his own home.'"

"*Daijoubu desu ka?*" She took the book from him and put her hand to his forehead. "You're hot."

"I'm all right. A little drunk—I don't know. But what's new?" Kent took her hand, her palm sweaty and warm like his head. "What do you think he means by 'home'?"

Oji-san and Mrs. Kaneda beat the *taiko* drums, sounds like thunder.

Midori cocked her head to listen. "My uncle's drunk." Then turned back to Kent. "Home? I don't know—where you feel at home."

"He's got himself a lady friend," Kent said.

"Mrs. Kaneda? They've been friends for years. I suppose she's his girlfriend." Midori pulled a corner of Kent's blanket over her knees. "May I?"

He let her lean into him. "I feel weird. This place, the rain and my head. You, in this suit, I can't get over it. Is this home for you?"

"It is—I'm never more comfortable, more myself than when I'm here," she said.

They watched the rain run off the roof and into a large French drain, a river of it from above. She pulled the blanket up to her chest. "Thinking about me?"

"Actually, I was thinking about Kumi. Is that terrible?"

"No." The warmth in her voice chilled. "But I'll leave you alone if you want."

"Because of you, though, and because she's gone. But you're here. And you've been so nice to me. Honestly, for reasons I can't quite fathom. This is the craziest temple I've ever been to."

"What? I'm the consolation prize?" She made to stand.

"Who said anything about a prize." Kent pulled Midori back to the floor. "Don't go."

"So you cheated on her and she left you," Midori said. "What's the big mystery? You act like you're the only person that's ever happened to."

"I failed her. But it wasn't the cheating. She might have been able to forgive that," Kent said.

"Then what? You did something worse than that? I'm not sure I want to know much more about Kent Richman," Midori said.

"No, it's more about what I should have done."

"What does that mean? You know, you talk in more riddles than a Buddhist monk."

"I can rewind and replay again and again, but I still get: Why did she leave me? Why did she leave me? Why did she leave me?"

"Why keep asking then?"

"Because maybe I know and don't want to know."

"And is that really all it is? *Why did she leave me?* That seems pretty obvious? You want to talk about strange, what about the urn?"

Kent unfolded a worn photograph from his wallet. "Sure, I'll talk about strange."

Two boys stand on a beach inside a sand castle. They wear bathing suits in matching flower patterns, the younger one in red and white, the older in yellow and green, little surfers. Their bare, adolescent chests sparkle with wet sand. They squint into the afternoon sun.

Midori picked up the camera again and fixed the lens on him, pressed record, and Kent began to talk like he'd never talked before.

⸺

"Everyone said they understood how it happened, acted as if they sympathized—just two brothers roughhousing. Could happen to anybody, right? But it didn't. It happened to me. I remember everything about that week. And I knew people always doubted. The way they looked at me. Poor, stupid boy, born bad. Some said I was unstable, maybe even psychopathic, should be in an institution and pay for what I did. But they didn't know. They didn't know it had been happening the entire week we were at the beach.

"Allan spent most mornings crushing the shells of horseshoe crabs. He poked me with the sharp tail of one until it broke off in his hand and cut him, so that every time he went swimming for the next few days the saltwater stung, but he blamed it on me.

"Because I wasn't a strong swimmer, my mother insisted I stay close to shore. So, I made up a game called *Look Out!*, where I waded in the surf until a wave rolled in, then I ran to dry sand. I played *Look Out!* while Allan swam. He called to me—*Hey! Landlubber, come on out!* But I just watched, the Atlantic Ocean the biggest thing I could imagine.

"My parents invited some old college friends from Elizabeth City for a bridge party at the rented beach house. They had two girls, one four, one twelve like Allan. He told the older girl how he'd body surfed the big waves and how all I ever did was run from them like a *scared little girl.* She laughed and said she wasn't afraid of the ocean. He told her he was either going to be a professional surfer or an NWA wrestler like "Nature Boy" Ric Flair. He had the long blond hair already and flipped it with his hand. For a second, he looked like Ric Flair, like a superstar. Allan told me to stay inside and watch the four-year-old. They were going down to the beach, and I was not to say anything or he'd crush me like Ric Flair crushed Dusty Rhodes.

"One day while I was playing *Look Out!*, I found a pirate knife in the surf. I called Allan out of the water and told him what I'd found, but Allan said it wasn't, it was a fisherman's knife, probably somebody fishing right then who'd be looking for it. I wanted to keep the knife, a big blade with a deer horn handle—a pirate knife. Allan snatched it from me and took it to our dad, telling him I was too little to handle it. My dad held the knife in the air, squinting at writing on the blade. He weighed it in his hand then looked at me, turned to Allan, frowned and shook his head. *Lot of shipwrecks out there,* he said, *so this definitely could've washed up from one of them, and maybe one of those was a pirate ship. Hard to say. Blackbeard was all over these waters.*

"I had ten dollars to spend on anything I wanted. I considered a shell necklace like the one Allan had bought, a ship wheel clock, and a rubber shark. I found what I wanted at Pirate's Cove Putt Putt: a revolver made of real wood and a pair of mirrored sunglasses. As I walked out of the gift shop to play putt-putt with my family, gun tucked into my shorts, sunglasses on, Allan shouted, *Argghh, matey! It's Captain Dork!*

"My parents fought much of that summer. They never really stopped, even at the beach. They were both drinking a lot

"Dad drank beers from the cooler and Mom made drinks in a blender, like slushies.

"One night after Allan and I went to bed, we heard them screaming at each other. Mom kept saying we were supposed to be on vacation and why did he have to keep bringing it up. We were supposed to be relaxing. I asked Allan what Dad kept bringing up that was making Mom so mad. At first he didn't answer, then he said it was nothing for me to worry about, grown-ups fought just like kids, and I should go to sleep.

"Mom broke a glass lamp filled with shells. It was the first time I'd ever heard her curse. That made Dad laugh and then Mom and then me and Allan. She said we could keep the shells since we were paying for the stupid things anyway.

"Mom was constantly cracking ice from the ice trays. I hated the sound, still do: the crack of the handle, the ice, like teeth on teeth, like Allan's grinding at night.

"I got up early one morning to watch cartoons and found my dad asleep on the sofa. He was in his clothes from the night before, blue Bermuda shorts and a yellow Izod. Beside the sofa, a cigarette had burned a black spot into the orange shag.

"Allan carved his initials into the upper deck railing outside our room with my pirate knife. He carved them into the boardwalk hand rail, a piece of driftwood I'd found and planned to take home to put on my book shelf, and a souvenir of our vacation where I would've carved *Nags Head / August 1989*.

"Allan and I were supposed to go crabbing with my dad, but Allan said he didn't want to stand in stinking muck and throw fish heads into the water. Anyway, he had his Stephen King book to finish. Dad made a mocking frowny face and turned to me. *How 'bout you, kiddo? How are you with muck and fish heads?*

"In muddy water up to my knees, my sneakers making sucking sounds as I struggled to walk, I thought I'd drown in the shallow, weedy marsh. I cried and said I didn't want to go crabbing anymore. I knew my dad was disappointed or sad or something by his eyes, which looked heavy, like if he closed them it would be real hard to open them again. He stood in waders and bit at his lip. *I know, kiddo.* He reached behind his back, under his fishing vest, and pulled out the pirate knife. *This help?*

"My mom cut her hand with the pirate knife trying to open an oyster. My dad screamed why hadn't she used the oyster knife, never use an ordinary knife to open oysters and this was exactly the reason. She screamed back not to yell at her, she was bleeding. And she was, a lot, into the sink, over the counter, and on to the kitchen floor. Dad said he was sorry but— He helped her wash the cut under the kitchen faucet, his arms wrapped around her from behind, said it was pretty deep, and she was going to need stitches. Mom started to cry, and Dad said it wasn't that bad and kissed her bleeding hand. He poured her a drink and checked the info sheet on the refrigerator for the closest hospital. On their way out the door, my dad had blood above his lip in the space where his moustache used to be, like he'd been kissed.

"That afternoon while my parents were away, Allan watched NWA but the reception was bad. When he gave up on the TV, he turned to me.

"Allan said he'd give me the advantage by lying on the floor so I could try and pin him. I climbed up on the back of the couch, stood like a champion, and jumped, took a dive and landed a knee drop right across Allan's chest. Ka-*boom*!

"I heard the dull thud of my knee against his chest, the air rush out of him like a balloon untied, Allan's cry turn into a moan, then nothing but this horrible wheezing. Then quiet, the sound of waves breaking over the sand.

"Allan didn't move, his face deeper and darker blue. I ran to the beach and kept running, but it was dark and I got scared. When I came back, I heard them before I saw them: Mom and Dad sitting on the sofa, Dad holding Allan in his arms. Mom's hand wrapped in a puffy white bandage. Allan's face was no longer blue but pale. Dad looked up, his eyes bugged out, his mouth twisted. He tried to speak but couldn't.

"Wrestling's fake, everybody knows that, my best friend Roman had told me. I thought he was lying.

"My mother ran to me like she was going to tackle me. But she ran her hands over my body, checking for wounds. *Are you all right? Are you hurt?*

"I first I didn't tell them what had happened. My father hadn't let me see Allan like that once I came home and they realized I was okay. *Get out! Out!*

"He didn't let me see: the crater where Allan's chest should've been, as if he'd been deflated.

"He didn't let me see: the blood that trickled from his mouth and pooled in the collar of his shirt.

"He didn't let me see: the great dark bruise blossoming across his chest.

"He didn't let me see: what they later called an interrupted heart.

"Dad blew air into his lungs, which heaved briefly, then collapsed again. He put his hands on Allan's chest, but seemed afraid to press down too hard. He pulled him up by the arms, held his head in his hands, trying to undo what I had done.

"Wrestling's not real, didn't you know that? Mom stood before me, a drink in her hand and already drunk. *Didn't anybody, didn't we ever tell you that?* She tried to light a cigarette with trembling hands but couldn't and threw it unlit to the carpet. *I told your father again and again that violence begets violence. I told him not to let you all watch that goddamn fighting.*

"From the sliding glass doorway, I watched Mom on the deck looking up at the stars—she wouldn't talk to me. When Dad came home from *handling things*, he told me to go to bed, he'd take care of Mom.

"That night, I kept the radio on low listening to a rock station in Norfolk but a coming storm left the station mostly static. It sounded like Allan's wheezing, like breathing through a screen.

"My dad told everyone I hadn't meant to hurt Allan—*He's just a kid, for Christ's sake.* My mom didn't talk to my dad or to me. After that, nobody talked to anybody anymore. After that we pretended like Allan had never been there at all."

Midori set the camera down. "I had no idea."

"You asked me once if I was famous in America? I was. Famous for killing my older brother."

"It was an accident, you said so. Who would blame you for such a thing?" Midori ran her hand over his lips and under his chin, around his neck and the back of his head. "I think you've hurt yourself." She pulled at the ragged ends of his hair and smiled weakly. "And you need a haircut."

"Oh, nobody blamed me out loud, but they all did. When you're *that kid*, you're always *that kid*, the kid who killed his brother. They even have a special name for it: *fratricide*. I haven't felt that kind of hatred since, not until recently, as if the world conspires against me. No matter what I do now, it's what I did *then*, what I did before that matters. I feel like I'm always one step behind, always trying to make sense of the mistakes come and gone. Like I can never live in the present."

There wa s pause, silence.

Then Midori said, "I can do it tomorrow." She scissored the air. "I used to cut Kenji's hair."

"Ah, a strong recommendation," Kent joked. "But why not? Don't think I'm going to the stylist any time soon."

This simple request answered, Midori kissed Kent on the forehead, on the cheek—"You're burning up"—her lips brushing his. "Tell me, Kent Richman, what other secrets do you have?"

Kent scanned Midori's face for some hint of motivation. What drove this woman to want to know so much about him? To care when he was no one to care about? The concentration required all of his energy, the last of which was fading fast, motivation to move replaced by an odd euphoria. A Beatles song came to him. *Close your eyes and I'll kiss you*— Kent had sung the song in a crooner's tempo for an outdoor benefit, the host organization lost on him now. The Beatles song was upbeat but the producers didn't think Kent could pull it off and asked him to slow it way down until it became a ballad. As did most of his live numbers, the song barely rose above karaoke. The producers had even dressed him in a satin blue jacket and black slacks, a white shirt with an open collar. Somewhere along the way Tony Bennett had subverted his association with John Lennon, but he didn't care.

More than the details of his bizarre performance, Kent remembered the way he felt that evening under hot lights on an outdoor stage, rain falling over a festival audience. Nothing in his life compared with the moment he looked across a sea of swaying arms, some wrapped in parkas, others braving the steady drizzle that had fallen all afternoon leaving the sports field a muddy mess. Midway through the song, Kent felt the lyrics rising out of him mechanically, like his feet moving under him across the stage, and his arm wave to the crowd, acknowledging their cheers, their camera flashes and applause. Kent had never felt more like a hero. And he'd been straight for the performance, though afterwards he beelined for the green room and the bottles of whiskey lined up for the talent, the only thing he found that helped him contain his good feeling before it lifted and vanished. Kent watched the rest of the benefit from a corner just off stage, marveling at the life he'd come in to and happy to be alone in his bliss. He found he needed nothing more from the moment. He declined invitations to do drugs and skipped the after party, happy to head home where he hoped Kumi waited for him in bed, a book in her lap, the soft glow of lamplight warming the room. He felt that way again, with Midori, a blissful, painless satisfaction.

Kent had closed his eyes, for how long he didn't know, when Midori kissed him gently on the mouth. Her lips were warm and soft, so soft that Kent felt as if this was the first time they'd ever kissed, then remebered that it was.

Boom boom boom boom, went Oji-san's drums.

"They're at it again?" Kent whispered.

"It's what they do," Midori said.

Boom clackity clackity boom, the drums beat, their tempo increasing.

Kent was dizzy and a little sick, certain that his bees would return. He closed his eyes.

"Are you okay?" She asked so faintly he could hardly hear her.

Clackity clackity boom boom.

"A little dizzy. You're—too much—for me—" He tried a laugh. "I'm sorry." Kent sensed her blushing as she pulled away. Little flashes of yellow had begun to pop before him, eyes open or closed, it didn't matter. His head hurt, stomach spun, and he needed to throw up, but he couldn't move. "Just kidding, I'm—" Kent tried to smile.

"Kent?" Midori held his face in her hands.

"Hmm?"

"You're so pale."

"I'm sorry, I— "

"God, you're really hot." Midori pulled away and knelt beside him, put her hand over his head. "I'll be right back." She stood, wrapped the blanket around his shoulders, and slipped from the room. The sounds of Oji-san's drums echoed *boom boom boom* through the house, the rain splashing away outside. A chill settled over him, the cold rain reminding him that even in the remote mountain temple in the Japanese mountains, he felt the presence, the sting of everything that had come before.

From *Star-Gazer.com*

EXCLUSIVE:
KUMIKO SATO IN
HO CHI MINH CITY HOSPITAL
WITH BABY BUMP

New reports out of Vietnam suggest our favorite daughter Kumiko Sato could be pregnant. Ms. Sato was reported to have reunited with her cheating husband Kent Richman. And where is that two-timing hubby? Still hiding *RI-CHU-MAN-SAN?* *Star-Gazer.com* sees all!

While vacationing in Vietnam, a *Star-Gazer.com* iCU Reporter recently spotted the former top model leaving a Ho Chi Minh City hospital. And *Star-Gazer.com* learned that Kumi may be pregnant. The photo reveals that Kumi, long a favorite in Japan, is five months pregnant. Our iCU reporter said that husband Kent Richman, better known as *RI-CHU-MAN-SAN!* on TV's *The Strange Bonanza,* was nowhere in sight. But who is

this man? Does Kumi-chan have a new lover? Did she drop Richman for good?

Rumors of Kent and Kumi's separation have swirled ever since the Ozman Incident, in which the Australian shock comic terrorized husband and wife in their Shibuya apartment in a jealous rage. Ozman's wife, Monique Martine, of Montreal, Canada, had been having an affair with Richman for some months. Following the incident with Ozman and initial appearances on television, the pair stepped out of the spotlight. Friends suggested that Kent and Kumi had left show business in an attempt to repair their marriage and focus on the "more important aspects of their lives." But others claimed Kumi had had enough of Kent's cheating ways and left him. "She wanted a family and he didn't," a second source, who prefers to remain anonymous, confirms.

Richman has since been spotted in Japan again, without Sato. *Star-Gazer.com* was the first to confirm Richman's residence in an Akihabara capsule hotel. Richman, who has since left the capsule hotel, is rumored to be hiding away in an Aomori monastery.

Ms. Sato was later seen at Joe's Cafe, a popular seaside café in Mui Ne, a coastal resort town in Binh Thuan province along the southeastern Vietnamese coast. While she sipped bottled water, her dinner companion, an unidentified man, downed beer and smoked cigars.

Telephone calls to Cho Ray Hospital in Ho Chi Minh City and Ms. Sato's Tokyo representative were not returned.

Are you a future iCU Reporter?

If you have photographs you would like to share with *Star-Gazer.com,* visit:
www.Star-Gazer.com/iCU. html and click on the iCU! link.

CHAPTER TWENTY-THREE

—

KENT RICHMAN GOES *BOING! BOING!*

Kent was cold, shivering underneath the light sheet that covered him, but his head was wet with sweat. Music thumped from the other side of the temple, and he thought he heard someone crying. It sounded like it might if he heard it from underwater. He was reminded of Kumi's own cries, of their honeymoon in the Greek islands. How the ocean had rolled calmly outside their bungalow and the hush of evening fell over the remote island village, the smell of flowers and garlic and fresh fish. Kumi moved in the kitchen like an angel, a breeze from an open window lifting her skirt. Then blood spread over the front of her shirt when she cut her palm trying to trim a piece of cod, an odd replay of his mother's own accident with a knife. She wailed all the way to the hospital, like a child frightened more by the sight of blood than the wound itself.

And then again as Kent had knelt before Ozman, helpless to stop her cries. He'd wanted to but had been unable to look her in the eyes, couldn't see her there on the floor tied up like a pig to be roasted.

Now, how does it feel to be one of the beautiful people? Ozman said, as he applied lipstick to Kumi's celebrated pouty lips. Her efforts at resistance only smeared the makeup across her cheeks and over her chin, until she looked like an inept clown. She laughed weakly. The defiance that had been there died, fear growing like the dark rose around Kent's eye. Ozman gently lifted Kumi's hair from her eyes, inspected his work, then stood and turned to include Kent, opening his arms. *Now, for my final and most magnificent trick.*

A ghostly Middle Eastern rhythm played on the stereo, its spell maintained by an electronic hum, hand slaps against a drum, and the drone of vaporous voices. Outside, the sun sank beneath dark scattered clouds, as if somewhere in Tokyo an oil fire burned. Sunlight reflected off the skyscrapers' glass. A stormy autumn evening was on its way.

Your husband ruined my marriage. Do you understand that? My one and only. Something you people don't seem to know anything about. Ozman pulled Kumi up by her arms to her knees and bent to kiss her, more a caricature of a kiss than anything. *You think I didn't love her, is that it? That it was just some made-for-TV thing? A part of the act?* Ozman stared at Kumi. His eyes watered and he shook his head. *I loved her, you stupid, stupid people.*

Kent struggled harder against the duct tape but couldn't free himself. Kumi had turned her head up to the ceiling, away from Kent's. He was grateful; he had nothing to offer her but panic and regret.

Ozman stepped away. He touched his hands to his lips, muttered as if in prayer and stared out at the darkening sky. He didn't speak again for at least a minute. Kent thought Ozman might have changed his mind, seen the folly in his revenge scenario. He thought Ozman might forgive him if he asked.

baby, you're a rich man

Ozman dropped his hands to his side, turned, and without a word unbuckled and unzipped his cargo shorts, which fell to the floor with the clank of his belt buckle. Kent saw only his pale white ass—and beyond that Kumi's face, which told him much more. Her skin had gone slack around her eyes and her mouth was pinched shut. Ozman swayed in front of her as she turned away. Then her courage swelled again and she looked up at Ozman. *I don't care what you do to me, but I will take that thing with me.* She tapped her top and bottom teeth together loudly.

I have no intention of giving you such an opportunity. With his right hand Ozman stroked his cock as if a timer had started. *This is how the ancient Japanese used to punish their women when they were caught fucking other men.* Ozman fondled himself in earnest. *All the village men would join in the shower of shame.* He giggled, turned his head to the ceiling, and stepped another foot forward, his penis inches from Kumi's face.

The music, now a trance, played hauntingly slow, a rhythm Kent didn't recall ever hearing on the CD, as if the track played at half-speed. Kumi closed her eyes, refusing to cry.

I've inverted the punishment to suit my aims, Ozman said. *Those aims being degradation and humiliation, which is what you caused me. And I aim—forgive the pun—to please.*

Kent always had trouble remembering exactly how the afternoon had unraveled, questioning his own recall. But now, the scene came to him, Ozman's voice loud and unmistakable.

Also of interest to the student of Japanese—that's you and me, Rich Man—bukkake is the noun form of the verb bukkakeru, to splash, in particular, water. Ozman turned his body to Kent, forcing him to look at his red and swollen penis.

You probably knew that. Kumi's eyes remained closed, her face indifferent, resigned. Ozman turned back to her. *But leave it to the Japanese to twist that into something much more interesting.*

Kent squeezed the raw puncture marks in his arm where Ozman had so efficiently wounded him, needing to feel the pain. A Greek island, a taxi ride, the metallic smell of blood and garlic and antiseptic. Pounding drums and a violin, picking up a steady beat, a guitar lazily behind the tempo. Then Kent heard nothing but wind whining between the towering apartment buildings. The sun set. Halogen spots overhead automatically whisper-clicked on, illuminating the soft, yellow haze of Ozman's cigarette smoke. And Kent soared a hundred meters above the scene, wrapped in clouds of yellow and purple.

i ━━▶

The rain fell harder, the wind was up. The muscles in his neck and back, the joints in his arms, hips and knees all ached with a soreness that suggested he had a bad case of the flu. A dull, unvarying pain thumped at the front of his skull. He was queasy and needed to go to the bathroom. He tried to stand, the blanket wrapped over his shoulders, but wobbled on his good foot and fell back to the floor. As soon as he wondered if his bees would swarm they did. Where had Midori gone?

Standing again, Kent steadied himself against bookshelves, pulling himself higher until he was balanced with the aid of the top one, but his stomach jammed with cramps and his bowels were loosening. He needed ventilation. He let go of the bookshelves and raced—as much as he could on his twisted ankle and bum knee—

past the empty kitchen and into the bathroom, its musty smell and damp floor enough to make him sick. But his need for release elsewhere was greater and he got his shorts down just in time. His body was finally calling a halt to the abuse and shutting itself down, flushing itself of every poison. His stomach cramped again and he felt as if he would throw up, but he had to get out of the stale bathroom. He checked himself in the tiny mirror—pale skin, matted hair, lips skimmed in dried mucus—and he lifted the eyepatch to find his injured eye no longer red. Though he'd grown attached to the eyepatch, he removed it, testing his sight. No pain, but his vision was still blurry, if less so. Kent blinked in an attempt to clear the smear he felt across his eye. But it would take more time.

He replaced the eyepatch and went to look for Midori. No sign of her or the others in the temple's community center. Karaoke music, only the empty music without vocals, played to a vacant room, words for no one scrolling across a screen, accompanied by a video of a young woman through a gauzy white lens walking pensively by a river. He pulled the blanket closer around his shoulders and hobbled away, lost in the compound's warren of buildings and rooms. Wood creaked and popped as if someone walked elsewhere across the temple's aging floors, a door slid open and closed, metal met metal somewhere in the house. Outside the wind blew in great gusts. Kent followed the sounds but found only emptiness and swaying treetops, the pervasive smoke of incense. The funeral arrangement had been cleared and no trace of the deceased remained save for a handful of fresh blue and white flowers. Kent called out in the cavernous temple, "Anybody here? Hello? Midori? Chieko?" Though there was no response Kent sensed company, a presence he couldn't identify.

He didn't like the stillness, the emptied temple leaving him feeling watched, that once again he was the victim of someone's reality show voyeurism. Where *was* everyone? He was so weak, shivering again from the chills, that he only wanted to return to bed, curl up under a sheet, and sleep. His whole body seemed on the verge of mutiny, his stomach swishing emptily as he limped around the quiet temple. He rushed for the bathroom again but realized he wouldn't make it. He tried for the entrance at the front of the temple, throwing up instead on the sliding screen door, his body heaving with spasms.

He tried to open the messy screen door, but tripped over the blanket, which had dropped to his feet. His knee penetrated the thin, fragile mesh, and, off balance, he tumbled through the cheap aluminum frame. The flimsy door separated from its frame as Kent spilled with the door over the meter-high edge of the house to the ground below. He landed on his right side, pain shooting through his elbow as it took the weight of his body against stone pavers. The shock of falling displaced his upset stomach and, despite the pain, Kent felt better lying face up on top of the dislodged screen door, the wet ground underneath, rain cooling his skin. A Halogen motion sensor light popped on above him, illuminating the trees above. He didn't have the strength to care what happened next.

Cedars rose and vanished into the black sky, their impressive trunks like the fat, round legs of giants, their long limbs stretching out over the top of the temple. Kent was oddly buoyant, numbed by his stupor, as if floating in the darkness above and surrounded by mist: fade, dissolve, forget. He wanted to sleep under the trees, to soak up the rain and let his body begin to heal itself. He considered that he might die in this alien forest, a miserable, confused foreigner, sick for home, no apparent path to lead him away from his muddled life. He tried sitting up but nausea returned. He felt better laying there in his underwear. He closed his eyes and summoned comfort: sparrow song, sunshine glistening over choppy water, a futon and a blanket, the scent of cut tangerines, Kumi's wine-stained mouth on his, the surge of *shabu* spreading over his skin and seeping into his bones like warm water through his veins.

With the drone of the wind, the first phase of gentle sleep came over him, a drifting, his body no longer weighted by gravity, his head clearing. Kent wanted so much to give into it all, to slip away and follow easy darkness to a place where he knew nothing, where he could feel spacious flat fields or an ocean with no end in sight, nothing but the horizon before him. What he really wanted, what he'd dared not ask for, what he feared was lost forever, was to be back in his Tokyo apartment, stretched out in his recliner after coming home from a long taping day on Stage 909-B, as Kumi came through the door with an armload of shopping bags.

She'd uncork a bottle of wine, disrobe in the living room, and model her new purchases for him, the stem of her wine glass tilted to the sinking winter sun through the enormous window overlooking their Shibuya airspace. She shimmered in the warm light, her hair, skin, and eyes. She fell on to him in the chair, her slender frame slipping in beside him. She smelled sweet, expensive, like a department store, swaddled in finery. She kissed him, her breath coffee and cigarettes, a hint of mint. *Hello, Kent Richman. Do you love me?* He did, didn't he? This was no fiction, no daydream: this had been his life. He'd loved her, she'd loved him. Wasn't that true? Their lives—television sound stages, photo shoots, VIP gift bags, drivers, assistants, interviews, fan mail, guest appearances, five-figure paychecks, paparazzi, clubs, *shabu, shabu, shabu*—had concealed a private life within, where they found shelter beneath the celebrity sheen.

He wanted to patch together this quilt of home life, but in reality he couldn't recall one concrete moment with his wife. Had he erased or suppressed such moments, a self-protecting amnesia? When he thought of Kumi, he had no link to the *and she was*. All he could conjure up were the details of her absence from his life, the *and she is no more*.

Rain fell, though lighter now, and Kent was colder, a chill wind blowing across his face and bare body. Still, he felt better, his stomach settled, his headache reduced to a dull throb. Gone was the feverish chill. He sat up and surveyed the damaged screen door. Vomit covered much of the torn mesh, some of it underneath him, the middle support bar bent where he'd crashed through to the ground. He stood uneasily, the dizziness and bees gone. He leaned the damaged screen door against the house, a plan to at least spray it clean later, and stepped back in. His back and legs were patched with dirt and he needed a bath. The temple was still and empty, not a sound from inside or from the cemetery behind, save for the endless stream of karaoke music. Until he heard rocks crunch underfoot.

"I'm sorry but *that* was brilliant."

Kent turned to see a drunk Hideo about fifteen feet away on one knee with the Sony on his shoulder. Chieko stood in soaked clothes, an umbrella over Hideo and the camera, unsteady on her feet. The director moved his cap up and down on his head, like an apology.

"Thought you were dead for a moment," Hideo said. "But all's well, *all—is—well*. And, don't worry. We don't even need audio on that one. We'll just let the camera do all the talking."

Chieko looked up with a heavy head and smiled. "Kent Richman goes *boing boing*."

CHAPTER TWENTY-FOUR

—

TOO MUCH NITTY GRITTY

Kent was surprised by how spongy Hideo's flesh felt, how easily he could throttle the man's neck, and how little of anything there was between skin and bone. But he was weak, and Chieko, surprisingly strong, jumped him from behind, wrapped an arm around his throat and pulled.

"Get off, asshole," she cried and pulled tighter against his throat.

Kent gasped as Hideo choked out half-words. He stumbled backwards and fell, landing on the pretty sound tech, her slender frame flattened beneath his. He heard an unhealthy knock of bone on stone and Chieko yelped.

Hideo dropped the camera and back-pedaled on bent legs, one hand struggling to balance while the other shielded his throat. "*A-re*—?" He fell backwards, pushing earth and gravel with his feet as he fought to catch a hold. "*Bakayaro!* You asshole."

Chieko whimpered, "You broke my ass."

Kent rolled off her, his ankle smarting as he tried to stand, and massaged his own throat where she had wrapped her arm around his neck. He choked out: "No right."

Chieko rolled on to her side and rubbed her bottom. Mud stained her T-shirt and jeans. Her lingering wail was like that of a child astonished by the violence of her fall, just waiting to find an ear. Hideo could only cough and sputter what sounded like botched curses.

Kent stood, still rubbing his throat, and offered Chieko his hand. "I didn't mean to hurt you."

Chieko swatted at him and kicked gravel at his feet. "Screw you, *RI-CHU-MAN-SAN!*"

"You were choking me." His arms and bare chest were still speckled with dirt-caked vomit. He offered his cleaner left hand to Hideo as a peace gesture. "Seeing you with the camera trained on me like that—can you blame me?" Kent stepped away from Hideo to show he was no longer a threat.

Hideo picked up the camera, wiping water away with his shirt. "This is a four-thousand dollar camera, man."

"I'm sorry. Let me make it up to you. Drinks are on me," Kent said.

"We're done here, man." Hideo inspected the camera for damage. "You think we're going to stick around for more of the loser show? Look at you."

"You can't leave now. What about all the great footage you got, and the stuff you haven't gotten?"

"What?" Chieko stood, still rubbing her back. "You rambling and whining some more? No, thanks."

"We'll be doing you a favor, man." Hideo brushed dirt and tiny bits of gravel off the camera, and from his pants and shirt. "The Kent Richman Show is *not* pretty. Trust me."

Kent knew what he said was true, but couldn't let go of the image of himself on the big screen, his story compelling and sympathetic, his pain becoming the audience's pain. "I thought you wanted nitty gritty. Cinéma vérité. No makeup. No masks. The *real* Kent Richman."

Hideo waved a hand at him and turned to walk away. "*Too much* nitty gritty, man, *too much*."

Kent dumped the contents of his hockey bag onto the floor: three T-shirts, one dress shirt, too small, a pair of sweats, two pairs of jeans, shorts, underwear and socks, all mostly dirty; Rushdie's tattered and swollen *Midnight's Children*; torn copies of the celebrity magazine *Shukan Gendai*; his dressing room star; the bottle of limited edition *Kame no O sake* and a half-empty bottle of cheap whiskey; seven packs of cigarettes; a pack of matches; a copper hash pipe; a pink Hello Kitty Zippo he lifted from Midori's car; two mushy, brown bananas split open and mashed against the bottom of the bag; and one urn. He turned the clothes inside out. He rummaged through the bag's contents on the floor. He shook the hockey bag. He shook it again and again, until there it was, the miracle he'd hoped for: a plastic mini-baggie he'd either forgotten or never realized existed winking at him through the banana mush.

The mini-baggie held a fingernail of *shabu*, the crystallized rock flattened into an icy powder. Kent knew two things. One: he should toss the baggie into the grimy toilet. And two: he wouldn't. He wiped banana pulp from the baggie and shook it before him. A couple of drags would displace all of his aches and pains, clear his head, help him find Midori and pick up where they'd left off. Forget Hideo and Chieko. He'd do anything to feel better.

Kent went to the kitchen for tinfoil then returned to Midori's room, stepping just outside the back door where he'd imagined a woman crying. He rolled the sheet of tinfoil into a thin tube. On another piece, folded in the middle to create a conduit in which to burn the powdered *shabu* until it became liquid, he tried to light the crystallized rock holding the Hello Kitty lighter underneath. But the air was gusty. He stepped back inside to light it again, the *shabu* bubbling up at him as it heated. With his tinfoil straw he inhaled then repeated the procedure three times until the *shabu* was gone. Within minutes his head cleared, his need for food and sleep vanished, and he didn't care.

CHAPTER TWENTY-FIVE

—

CEMETERY CONTEMPLATIONS

The drizzle felt good on his face and arms as he did a night dance among the grave markers in the cemetery. He walked a lopsided shuffle among the dead, struggling to maintain his balance and hold Allan's urn at the same time. The last of the *shabu* had given Kent new life and he felt up to anything, though he limped on his tender ankle. Having told his story to Midori, he felt a renewed need to put it to rest. And what better place than a cemetery, where he might bury Allan for good. He'd never understood it when the grieving spoke of closure, but Kent believed that's what he was after now. And closure meant getting rid of Allan's urn. How much longer could he hold on to the thing? If he'd seen himself as others saw him, he'd have thought he was nuts, carrying around the dead like that. It wasn't right.

He ran his fingers in and along the grooved characters that marked the gravestones, the names of the dead chiseled into the smooth granite surfaces wet with rain. The cemetery was crowded with austere black and gray monuments. Narrow wooden signs rose up from behind—*o-haka*, Kumi had called them during a visit they made to her grandmother's gravesite. Elegant characters in black ink spanned the length of each wooden spire, a Buddhist message for the afterlife. Some graves were bedecked with fruit and rice cakes that looked months old, picked at by birds and squirrels; *sake* bottles had been tipped over, some broken, some empty; joss sticks had burned out in their containers, ashes turned to mush by the rain.

Kent set Allan's urn on an old tomb, lit a cigarette and sat, the rain so light, his skin so numb, he could hardly feel it anymore. The eerie mist enhanced his view of the cemetery and the dark forest. And he felt good. So much better. Why not just leave Allan here among the other dead? Who'd know the difference? Like Kumi, Allan wasn't coming back nor would he be allowed a do-over. During his brief stint in rehab, they'd told Kent he had to do the most difficult thing first—forgive himself. It had all sounded like so much bullshit then, but now he felt that maybe he could do that. Forgive himself and move on. Allan's urn, a glittering gray, blended in well with the dark granite headstones. Why not here in the mountains of central Japan, amongst the cedars?

The *shabu* surged, and Kent felt good too that Hideo and Chieko had abandoned him, the pressure to perform lifted. What good could've come from such an intimate look at himself anyway? The young pair would edit Kent Richman into a caricature of failure, their only apparent angle on him and his career that of a disillusioned has-been. He'd let himself believe otherwise, for a while. But that was all right. He'd start fresh tomorrow, give himself over to Midori and her uncle when they returned, see what they had to offer. He'd explain what happened with the screen door and repair it—he was good with his hands, he could fix a simple screen door. He could fix anything, everything. He'd call Renzo and end the serial disaster that had been this trip. He'd repent and repair. Kent had even started a letter in his head he planned to send to Ozman when he was returned to prison, which Kent now believed inevitable. How long could a monster like that roam free in Japan? But whenever he got past I'm sorry, he couldn't think what else to say.

Dear Ozman:

I'm sorry for sleeping with Monique—really. But I should have killed you when I had the chance.

Yours forever,

KR

Perhaps he'd visit Ozman in prison, bring Hideo and Chieko along for the ride. He wished he'd thought of the visit before he pissed the pair off good. Such a rich scene might give them something to look forward to. He knew Hideo especially would love the idea. It would also guarantee he saw them again, let him repair any damage he'd done to his image while they filmed at Cedars.

Kent felt good enough to reach out into the mist, through the forest, up the hill and to wherever the mountain climbed. But this grave wasn't the place, not yet. He'd have to find the perfect place. He picked up Allan's urn again, nestling under his arm like a football. He imagined placing it next to one of the grander gravestones, where he'd leave it, in turn leaving Allan and that summer at Nags Head and his nudist mother and stargazing father and his singular notoriety behind with it. He'd ask Oji-san to give his brother a new name so that Allan's death might no longer haunt him. Yes, yes, yes, he'd do that. He'd do it. Just not yet.

The *shabu* surged, enhancing his calm and confidence and compulsion to make things right. He giggled with the bubbling underneath. He had to move before Midori and Oji-san witnessed yet another Kent Richman wrong turn.

Back again at the other side of the temple, he scrubbed at the screen with a towel. But vomit clung to the fine mesh and he had to pick at it with his fingernails. The chipped fingernails of his right hand, at one time a strong set of vitamin enriched, well-groomed fingernails for playing the guitar—fingernails that had perhaps saved Kent and Kumi from Ozman's wrath, that had scratched and torn at the duct tape around his wrists when tied up in his apartment.

How helpless and pathetic Kumi had looked. How ridiculous, with clownish lipstick around her mouth and face. One part desperation and one part inspiration, Kent had begun to pick at the duct tape with his guitar-playing nails. Ozman turned on the video of Kent and Monique, the one Kumi had made viral—Kent at Monique from behind. Ozman circled Kumi in ritualistic hunker as the video played.

Where Ozman had once been composed by his anger, he'd come unhinged, his eyes vacant, lost in his own performance. The ceremony about to begin. He seemed to have forgotten Kent for his dance with Kumi. *How does it feel to be ME!* The nutso Australian comic drew his dialogue from a long list of dramatic crazies, his pokerfaced delivery seemingly sincere. For a distracted minute, as Ozman rifled through his bottomless bag of humiliating and painful acts, Kent became preoccupied by his game of trying to match Ozman's cinematic sentences with actual movies, actual villains. James Cagney as Cody Jarrett. Robert Mitchum as Max Cady. Dennis Hopper as Frank Booth.

 —

Kent's rattled daydreams were kayoed by dopamine. He scrubbed again at the screen. Dirty work was okay. Clean up his own mess for a change. Allan's urn sat on the floor in the open door frame, as if watching him, making sure he settled his accounts properly. Start small, a mangled screen, and work his way up to personal life and then on to career. He'd return downtown tomorrow for another afternoon in the odd coffee shop. Baby steps. Apologize to the café owner, explain that he'd been surprised by the comic book rendering of himself. Who wouldn't be? Pick up a bottle of *sake* to replace the one he'd pilfered and from the cemetery. Turn the day into one of mending, stitch up those torn patches where he'd stormed through unwittingly and caused injury where there had been only kind and generous people.

Once he had the screen reasonably clean, Kent tried to bend the middle piece of aluminum back without tearing the mesh. He balanced it over his knee, forcing it straight. The bar was bent at a funny angle and kept wobbling in and out of one irregular form after another until he put his fist through the mesh just as the karaoke music stopped and the operatic chords of Mrs. Kaneda's earlier Sephiroth performance rang out through the temple.

CHAPTER TWENTY-SIX

—

SON OF BIG SUKAI

Ozman resurfaced much the way Kent had played his own revenge scene in a made-for-television drama that never made it to the television. He starred as the twin brother of a New York English teacher working in Japan who goes missing after a run-in with high-level yakuza. Kent played both twins, the dead one in flashbacks.

The protagonist has come from the United States to get to the bottom of his twin's mysterious disappearance. Upon discovering the yakuza connection, Kent's character tracks down the people responsible for what he discovers is his brother's death and exacts his revenge with violent ferocity. But not before his character meets and subsequently falls in love with his dead twin's Japanese girlfriend. Kent recalled staring down into the camera (or the face of the yakuza baddie), his own face filling the frame, just as Ozman's mug filled the frame as he peered down at Kent in a POV shot: maniacal sneer, rain dripping from his face, eyes wide with zeal, head shaved to a wet sheen. Except for the shaved head, Kent too had sneered and dripped and gone Jack Nicholson in *The Shining* all over the scene. A film critic for *Tokyo Journal* who had been invited to a preproduction rehearsal wrote: "Mr. Richman plays the vengeful brother like community theater on steroids." Soon after the article ran, the movie lost its greenlight status.

Kent suspected he was dreaming again, lost in some series of cause-and-effect fantasy, his paranoia and ill state producing hallucinations bred by his worst fears. He'd thought of little else since he learned of Ozman's escape. Until he noticed the black-handled *chisa katana* in a lacquered scabbard around Ozman's waist, Kent believed he was safe in his reverie, if still on the ground outside Cedars and in a stupor.

"Arrgh, me hearty," Ozman said in English and pressed the heel of his black prison shoes on Kent's outstretched arm. "Shiver me timbers, you look ridiculous. Remember me?" He righted himself and surveyed Kent on the ground. "You seem to be doing well, Richman. Got a little Zen-pirate thing going on here in the mountains. Interesting, if a bit confused. But, hey, you always did it your way, didn't you. Cappin' Kung Fu?"

Kent had abandoned the broken screen door and grabbed Allan's urn, following the music to the temple's community center, where he expected to find Oji-san and Mrs. Kaneda revisiting their performance via some erotic foreplay, or Midori, who had vanished, luring him towards her own cosplay fantasy. But the room had been empty, the music loud. Kent moved to turn down the opera when he was felled by a blow from something flat and hard and pushed out the open doorway to the gravel path outside, once again on his back.

Kent heard himself whimpering yet the sound seemed to come not from his own body but elsewhere.

Ozman followed Kent's eyes. "I met your new girlfriend," he said in English.

Kent turned his head to see Midori on her knees, hair matted to her head and face, her costume torn at the sleeves, and hands bound with the karaoke microphone cable. Ozman turned back to Kent. "How do you do it, Rich Man? Doesn't she know what kind of man you are?"

"How did you find me?" Kent didn't know why the question mattered. Ozman *had* found him. Who the hell in Japan couldn't find Kent Richman?

"Rich Man, you leave a trail like a snail. Seems like every time you fuck up, somebody catches it on camera."

Midori tried to shuffle backwards on her knees.

"Not so fast!" Ozman snapped. "Why don't you just sit still. We're enjoying a bit of déjà vu here, aren't we Rich Man?"

Midori tried to stand.

Kent wiggled beneath Ozman's boot. "*Please*, she's got nothing to do with this."

"Maybe. Though comforting the enemy comes to mind. Then again, how could she know?" He pointed to the ground. "Sit."

Midori looked at the wet, black-pebbled path. "What do you want?"

Ozman, more swiftly than Kent thought possible, pulled the steel sword from the scabbard and waved it at Midori. "Sit!"

Midori jumped to attention and returned to her squat, trembling in the rain.

Kent had again drawn others into his misfortune. It was inevitable, this state of affairs with Ozman always unfinished. Every step he'd taken, no matter how far from Ozman, led inescapably to him, Ozman the only outcome no matter what he did, how far he ran? The *shabu* surged and, with the surge, Kent accepted his lot. This was, after all, his chance to fix what he'd broken, a chance at a do-over. He'd choked at the prospect of killing Ozman and lost Kumi forever. If given a second chance, could he be the hero? He'd always believed life just kept on going. How else could he think of it? Now he understood that life might stop, here and now, and take him with it. Kent Richman, the one *he* knew, would vanish.

He tried to distract Ozman from Midori. "What do you want?"

But Ozman had his eyes elsewhere. "What's this then?" He squinted at Allan's urn, which had shot from Kent's arm when Ozman attacked him and landed on the gravel path.

Kent realized a new horror.

"What's this?" Ozman lifted the urn. "What's inside then?" He held up the urn and read out loud from the label on the side. "*Curtis Allan Richman. Son and brother. 1977 - 1989.* What ho? Who's this? A Rich Man in a bottle? He attempted to open the lid. "Sealed right tight, isn't it."

Kent tried again. "What do you want from me, Ozman. I made a mistake. I'm sorry. If I could do it all over again—"

"But you can't, can you?" Ozman fixated on the lid like a child with a candy jar. "No." He unscrewed it and peered inside.

Kent shuffled on his knees, the gravel cutting into his

skin. He watched as Ozman stuck his nose into Allan's urn. He thought he might upend the urn and pour the contents into his mouth. He'd exposed Kumi and Midori to Ozman, now Allan too.

"You act like you made a little goof, just stumbled a bit, Rich Man?" Ozman looked away from the urn to Kent again. "And look at you: free to fuck up all over Japan while I rot away in Fuchu Prison. You running loose, dropping the Kent Richman scent wherever you roam. You, a talentless ape out here while good talent goes to waste behind bars. And where's Kumi? Decided she'd had enough of the Kent Richman charm? So, come on. Who's in the urn, then?" He held the open urn before him as if Kent needed to look inside before he answered.

Kent had no lies left in him. "My brother. It's my brother Allan."

"And what the fuck are you doing carrying him around?" Ozman seemed genuinely mystified. "Who does that?"

Kent felt oddly calm, as if he, like Oji-san had advised, had let go of the physical world, relinquishing his role in the material one, no longer flapping his giant, troublesome butterfly wings but giving himself to whatever forces were at play. The past no longer dictating the future. No more running, no more seeking answers from the-what-came-before where there seemed to be none. No more fighting the inevitable.

"Did I hit a sore spot, Rich Man? You know, my long six months in prison have allowed me to reflect on what I've done and, more importantly, on what you've done, particularly to me. I don't think my lesson in pain got through to you last time. Not only did you escape relatively unharmed," Ozman glanced at the needle scars along Kent's forearm, "—but you threw me under the bus before you left for sunnier climes. And my beautiful albeit cheating wife with a hole in her face."

"You did that." Kent had trouble focusing. Ozman's face blurred and doubled. "Not me."

"You tell yourself that, do you? Help you sleep at night? Makes me wonder how your brother got in this jar. You do that too?"

Ozman had no idea how right he was. Kent had done that, had put his brother in a jar. "It's the truth."

"The truth? What do you, a pathological liar, know about the truth? Because you didn't pull the trigger doesn't mean it wasn't your fault. Actions have consequences. You touch something, you change it. You left your grimy fingerprints all over my life, you giant egomaniacal asshole."

Ozman was right, and when the mokawked Australian sheathed his sword, lifted Allan's urn in the air, and turned it upside down, Kent could do nothing. He had meddled in this man's life, had taken liberties and caused him pain, he knew that. And now Ozman did the same as Allan's ashes spread like an upended bag of flour over the gravel, quickly turned to a mud-paste in the rain, and began to trickle away as nothing more than storm debris. He'd leave his brother here after all.

When the gun had gone off, the 9mm round splintered Monique's jaw and exited through her left cheek. She lay in a growing puddle of her own blood, a dark red sheen across the granite floor. The Beach Boys sang from the stereo, harmonies upon harmonies, all Kent could hear. Ozman stared at the gun like a man betrayed, tossed it to the floor and bent to Monique, blood pouring from the wound to her face like drink from an upended bottle. As he leaned over his wife, Ozman slipped on the wet marble and landed on his face in a puddle of Monique's blood. Kent recovered the 9mm and waved it before Ozman with a new sense of hope.

Oh shit. Ozman looked up at Kent with a grim smile. *I killed her.*

Still on the floor, Kumi sobbed, rocking herself as best she could with her hands still bound behind her back. The gun shook in Kent's hands.

Go ahead. Ozman strained to look up from where he lay. *Thing's got a hairy trigger.*

Monique didn't move, the white of her shattered jaw and teeth shining through the blood. Kent felt certain Ozman was right—he had killed her.

Kumi broke the silence. *Shoot him.*

Kent didn't turn, afraid Ozman would surprise him. *What?*

Shoot him! Kumi screamed.

What are you made of, John Lennon? Ozman said, his eyes wide.

Kent pressed the gun to Ozman's forehead. All he had to do was pull the trigger and *Bang!* a neat little hole right through the back of his head.

Was this thing over? Police sirens would likely kick in behind Beach Boy harmonies any minute. Could he hold Ozman there until they arrived? And then what? It was his gun.

Shoot him! Kumi screamed again.

The gun slid from Ozman's sweaty forehead, a slip Kent believed would cost him his life. But Ozman didn't move. The gun barrel had left a red mark above his left eye.

You can't do it, can you? Ozman smiled.

Kent wondered if Ozman was disappointed in him. He placed the gun to Ozman's mouth. He wanted to shred Ozman's lips and push his teeth into the back of his brain. But once Ozman realized Kent wasn't going to shoot him, he opened his mouth and put his lips around the gun barrel, simulating fellatio.

The Beach Boys (*I know perfectly well / I'm not where I should be*—), police sirens, and Kumi's crying had left Kent nostalgic for their Greek islands and the ocean breeze that once upon a time had lifted his wife's skirt above her knees.

Kent should have pulled the trigger, but he hadn't.

Yet, he'd suffered. "You think I haven't paid. I have *paid*." Kent pulled the eyepatch away from his face and let it snap back in place. "Look at me." He pointed to the pile of cream-colored ash that caught up in the wind like desert sand. "And now look at what you've done. What more do you want? I've paid."

Ozman grinned at Kent, the eyepatch, Band-Aid, shirtless and in his underwear, pale and thin with his long, greasy hair and patchy beard. At the vanishing contents of Allan's urn. "Perhaps you have suffered a bit," he said and dropped the emptied urn. He moved to Kent again. "But you've had the free will to fuck up your own life. You had *choices*. What did I have, mate? What the fuck did I have? You get one life and when someone else tries to ruin it—you get pissed. It ain't right. I prepare goddamn cupcake doilies all day. A man like me preparing cupcake doilies. Even the words sound wrong. Sound like a good time to you? And what have you been up to? Some down time in the Gulf of Thailand. Hanging out in Buddhist temples with your new girlfriend, making movies. Yeah, I read the tabloids and, yeah, you've really paid, haven't you? Oh, and don't kid yourself, Rich Man, Kumi would have left you no matter what you did. That was written in the cards long before you loused up your marriage. She was always destined for better things. Now me, I've been locked in solitary, and that does some crazy shit to your mind. I saw things quite clearly. You and I, we started on a path together. And here we are, just as we should be, on that path again. Because we got to walk it together. We have to find out where it ends." Ozman pulled the sword from its scabbard again and waved it in the air. "And I can't do that without you."

"Where does it end, then?" Kent said as the *shabu* surged again. He felt at peace. He had nothing left in this world, nothing to lose, not even Allan's stupid ashes. He turned his head up, certain that Ozman would swing for his neck. His face frozen in a stoic grimace, Kent would feel nothing. Blackout. End of story. End of Kent Richman. Switch off. Nothing would bother him ever again. No Allan. No Kumi. No Ozman or Monique. Photos would circulate over the web within days. Kent Richman would be a hero, his fate to die on Japanese soil at the hands of a villain, his lot in life to lose his head for his sins. This is how he'd pay, this is how he'd die. Then he heard Midori whimpering nearby and remembered that he wasn't alone.

Ozman bent over and grabbed Kent's hand, yanking him upright on his knees. "We're going to find out, just like in a good thriller. Think of this moment as that key scene where the villain—and that's you, by the way, not me—hangs from a precipice, a deep ravine far below."

Ozman wouldn't make Kent's heroism easy. And just as easily as he'd accepted his death, Midori's cries reminded him that he could instead kill Ozman. This time he could do it, this time he could pull the trigger, if he only knew what the trigger was. Last time all he had to do was pull the fucking trigger. This time it would take more.

"I dragged this whole drama out last time and paid for my pleasure, which it was, *it was*, watching you suffer, enjoying myself all over your pretty wife's face. But I'm tired of messing around." Ozman began to swing the *katana,* both hands gripping the handle, cutting slow, even arcs in the air, practicing a form of martial arts Kent couldn't name. "We have come to our end, you and me."

The *chisa katana* had always been a component of Ozman's act, the slicing open of his forearm and the slow cut across his own neck that left him running with blood. An illusion, everyone explained, even if they reeled in genuine horror. "Shock schlock," the Tokyo Shock Boys had declared when their own brand of shock comedy suffered in the shadow of Ozman's extreme stunts. But he swung the curved blade with practice, as if carving up the falling rain.

Midori wept, rocking on her knees.

Kent turned his face up to the cedars that swayed again, violently now—*trees bend*—as black clouds rolled, with monster Typhoon Jude marching in. Kent no longer felt pain. His ankle, his eye, his head ceased to be a part of him. His fingertips tingled and his throat was so dry he could hardly swallow. The only other sensations were the sting of rain on his face and water streaming from his hair over his eyes, nose, and mouth. There was no sound but the rain, and he wondered if Ozman had already taken his head, if the feel and sound of rain were all that remained. So many had talked of heaven where he'd found only horror.

Ozman floated before him in a trance of motion, unhurried and so balanced it seemed he hung just inches above the ground. As he swung, the blade whispered its passage, flashing wet before him. Kent closed his eyes and enjoyed the last sensations of his life.

With a great clanging, Kent went down hard, as if a tree had fallen over him. A coppery smell rose as blood dripped and ran down his face, running into his good eye and mouth. He opened his eye to see but it stung shut again. He tried to sit up but something held him fast to the ground. Death had come at him with more blunt, physical force than he'd imagined.

"Kent! Can you hear me?"

Kent thought of angels, *I can*, but no words came. *Shabu* surged, the weight was removed, his body lightened, and Kent was lifted from the ground.

"Kent? It's me. Are you all right?"

I am, he thought, *I am*, but again no words. He stood, unsteadily held up by someone beside him. He squinted through the blur and found Oji-san supporting him. Midori leaned over him. On the ground before him Ozman lay in a puddle with a long, red gash from just below his neck and diagonally across his back, his shirt stained pink and growing more red. Beside him lay Oji-san's giant sword, the one he'd used to reenact the fight scene with Mrs. Kaneda. Cloud's sword. Enough to put a foot-long tear across Ozman's back.

Kent stared at the bloody figure on the ground. "Is he dead?"

Oji-san squatted and placed a hand on Ozman's head. "I doubt it." He looked up at Kent, smiled, and somehow lit a cigarette in the rain.

He just caught it, but Kent made out two figures huddled under an umbrella near the hedgerow some thirty feet away. The glass eye of a video camera peeked out. Below that, he saw two pairs of legs. He recognized the red Chuck Taylor's and the smooth, slender legs that rose from sockless feet.

PART THREE

THIS HAVING LEARNT

CHAPTER TWENTY-SEVEN

—

THE STRANGE BONANZA

B OY WASABI, SON OF KING YELLOW MUSTARD
Kent shivered from chills despite the cup of hot
tea in his hands. His headache and fever had returned. He
had to hobble to the bathroom every fifteen minutes to let
go of whatever poisons continued to cling to his insides.
He couldn't keep anything down save for the mild green
tea that Midori prepared for him. A nurse secured a blanket
over him even as he sweated out all of the tea and water
Midori encouraged him to drink. Kent simultaneously
shivered and sweat, his head on fire and thick with pain
at the front of his skull. He had shit his pants once, its
cleanup a messy endeavor Midori had supervised, against
his nurse's protests. He was entirely dependent upon her,
his legs too rubbery and weak to walk much farther than
the bathroom, his body threatening to shut down. Police
had come and gone. Somewhere in the same hospital
Ozman was under heavy guard in his own room.

Kent didn't see how he could be so sick. He was
certain his mind was at least partly responsible, his spirit
of good health chased away by Ozman's return. He'd
driven himself right into malady. No soap opera could

do it better. Oji-san had come in several times to ask how he felt. During one visit, he shook a small bell over Kent and recited a short Buddhist prayer. "For the bad blood," he mumbled.

He smelled incense burning but hardly trusted his senses anymore. He thought he heard the old man touching his toes and dropping to the floor to top off his regimen of exercise. He heard Hideo and Chieko bickering like Tweedledee and Tweedledum, karaoke music playing, his mother screaming, *Wrestling's fake, everybody knows that, everybody.* Rain poured. Lights periodically flickered as thunder boomed and lightning flashed more regularly. The fever kept him in and out of heated sleep, the chills shaking him silly. He recalled an ambulance. Motley dreams blinked before him like his dream movie projector, flickering images of all that had preceded his term in this sickbed, a warehouse of stories, stacked one upon the other and melting into a collage of colors and faces.

He dreamt the telephone rang and rang and rang.

He dreamt of Kumi. He dreamt of Allan.

He dreamt of Kumi on the telephone, her voice so low he couldn't hear a word of what she said.

He dreamt of Ric Flair diving from the ropes, his glistening, muscular arms like wings suspended over the ring.

It's Cappin' Dork!

He dreamt he was Boy Wasabi, son of King Yellow Mustard. Trademark: green mask with a shock of green hair; fiery wasabi shoots from his nose like a green harpoon; soy sauce bombs rolled from his mouth like squishy pinballs. His side-kick Plummo, a walking plum with deep red skin and yellow-green plumage, known for his Satsuma Flesh Fronds, rolled along beside him.

He dreamt of a long, silent drive, a short hike, and lunch on a volcanic hillside. Sitting in the outdoor pool of a natural hot spring with Kumi's father, Kumi and her mother on the other side of a wooden wall. Mr. Sato on a stool by a spigot, washing himself. His body thin and hairless yet still firm against his bones; a scar across his stomach and his penis a fleshy head wrapped in a wrinkled pouch.

He dreamt of stabbing horseshoe crabs with a pirate knife, of a rogue wave—*Look out!*—rolling over him, pushing him to the bottom of the ocean, his skin peeled away by rock and sand and shell.

He dreamt of the messy screen door, its frame bent and broken in his hands. Repeatedly he tried to bend it back into shape, the mesh coming loose and scratching at his skin, tearing from the frame, flying away into the sky like a magic carpet.

This one he dreamt again and again, his mission always unsuccessful: he couldn't fix the screen door, leaving him to toss and turn with frustration. *Zip!* Kent was back at it again, trying to bend it straight but nothing, only broken aluminum pieces and the mesh screen zinging up into the cedar tops.

T HE STRANGE BONANZA
Whether dreaming or not, he recognized the theme song from *The Strange Bonanza*. He'd kept up with his old show, hoping it would fail without him. But it maintained its top-two ranking in the 8 to 9 p.m. slot. He recognized a few of his old cast mates.

Petite Plum screamed at the camera, a string of absurdities Kent couldn't follow.

Joe Three-toe with his pencil-thin moustache and his famous foot was there.

Reina Morioka, the elder matron of Japanese soap opera, who he believed had come on to him in his dressing room one evening after a shoot.

Nami Panda sat smiling, her white-white teeth gleaming against the J-pop star's carroty makeup.

Kokoro Kodo's magnificent tits nearly popped from her shiny satin top, squeezed into a rising bubble of soft flesh.

On each end of the talent console a young woman in bloated blue satin dress, oversized bloomers underneath, and colossal blue bow atop her head roosted like a sexy Alice blown up while high on magic mushrooms. Around them set designers had created a wonderland of giant monitors with images to satisfy any ADHD audience: blinking lights, and varieties of Styrofoam *kanji* and patterned shapes, all in vivid colors as if Alice had fallen not into a rabbit hole but a Tokyo department store display window. The console girls beamed and giggled on cue.

Kent watched the show, but spent most of the episode thinking of Midori in her red leather cosplay suit. He'd seen her in a new way, the glistening fabric, wide-eyed mask, pale yellow cups, and magnificent leather V. The plumping tummy. Just as Ozman had gone trance with his *katana*, Midori had disappeared inside an interior terrain, a place where Kent Richman didn't exist or matter. And he wanted in, wanted to peek inside, find out what the big deal was. For Midori, Oji-san and his friends, their costumed life was home. Kent Richman could be happy with that.

*P*LASMODIUM FALCIPARUM
        "The mosquito, more than most other living things,

is completely self-serving. She thinks only of herself. She does not worry about what happens elsewhere." A doctor with boyishly long hair and crooked teeth stood over Kent smiling. "And to do the one thing she desires, she must have blood. Unfortunately, we are one of her best resources. This is where our world meets hers. And we lose this battle, Mr. Richman."

The smiling doctor told Kent he suffered from exhaustion, malnutrition, dehydration, post-traumatic stress, and malaria. The result of a parasite that had incubated in his liver for over six months, a rare period of dormancy. He guessed the parasite must've been strong to survive six months in his liver. With his body weakened, the organism had finally slipped into his bloodstream, thus causing the further decline. The doctors told him that a bad lady mosquito (the female *anopheles*) stuck him, almost certainly while he was in Thailand, and exchanged his blood for a dose of the *Plasmodium falciparum* parasite. The doctors guessed the strain was already highly resistant to the most common malaria therapies such as chloroquine. Not to worry, they stressed, they had alternative therapies and, therefore, would keep him for a couple of weeks.

Midori was there when Kent woke again from restless sleep and more of his mundane dreams. His joints, at the elbow and knees, ached, his back was stiff and sore, but the doctors would not give him painkillers. *No narcotics,* they said, but didn't elaborate. Occasionally, his body would shake with convulsions and he'd heave dryly into a steel pan. Midori slipped in and out of the room, bringing with her the smell of cigarette smoke and noodles, as if she'd spent the evening in a restaurant. She told him over and over how lucky he was.

Kent didn't feel lucky, but he felt better knowing Midori thought so. When his fever spiked again and his body was rocked one way by cruel chills then another by bone-rattling shivers, he understood Midori was no longer there, the room empty. Darkness was fractured by lamplight from the window. Splashes against the pane, silver streaks before the light. Kent was at the end of something, what he didn't know. Ozman's pale face with gaping mouth and wild, staring eyes flashed in the window. Kent wanted to jump from the bed, rise up and run, but he couldn't move his aching limbs, couldn't raise his head. And where would he go?

In the early morning hours of his second night in the hospital, he became delirious with a fever that kept him fitful and dreaming again. He dreamt he and Midori were back at her uncle's temple where she swept up pale ashes from the *tatami* floor. She was on her knees with a hand broom, digging at the remains between the cracks like a paleontologist carefully extracting dinosaur bones. Kent watched her in silence as she swept a handful of ash onto a piece of paper, which she set on one of the classroom desks. She turned to him, biting her lip, her eyes still flushed with tears, and down again at the pathetic pile.

Kent awoke to Midori standing over him, a pleading look in her eyes. Outside, the sky remained gray, the windows still spotted with rain. The room was bright with florescence and the hall buzzed with activity. A Japanese samurai drama was on the television, but the sound was muted. Allan's urn sat on the floor in a corner.

"Do you want tea?" Midori asked.

"Tea?"

"I don't know what else to do, so I made tea."

From *Star-Gazer.com*

HAS *RI-CHU-MAN-SAN!* GONE CUCKOO ZEN UP IN THE MOUNTAINS?

Has the playboy American gone Commando Zen? Kent Richman, known as much for his onscreen role as *RI-CHU-MAN-SAN!* as his off-screen life of love triangles, abductions, and violent showdowns, appears to be settling down and, let's say, cleaning up his act. That's right.

Local residents believe Mr. Richman had been in town for a week or so before our favorite lunatic Denis Ozman tracked him down. And just what sent Ozman to the hospital? iCU reports suggest one big sword. But who did the cutting? Hard to say, as police are not responding to inquiries at this time.

Wet, blurry video posted just yesterday on YouTube by Thrill Thrill claims to be THE showdown between Kent Richman and Denis Ozman.

Others confirm that Richman has spent the past two weeks recovering in the hospital for an undisclosed illness. Is that a euphemism for rehab? If so, what's the big deal, *RI-CHU-MAN-SAN!* Embrace your inner addict. We'll forgive you. Cheating we won't abide, but kicking Ozman's ass and a minor "dependence concern" we'll understand. Good luck to you!

AND WHO'S THAT GIRL IN A TIGHT LEATHER SUIT?

Mr. Richman was also spotted with a young Japanese girl dressed from head to toe in red leather and pointy cat ears, aka Asuka Langley Soryu. Sources say she was seen, in costume, in the hospital garden, drinking tea and smoking. Our source, a hospital insider, offers that the woman is a regular visitor to Mr. Richman's room. Has *RI-CHU-MAN-SAN!* settled down with another?

WHAT'S NEXT FOR KR? ANIME CONVENTIONS!

Shall we stop by your table at Comiket or Dragon Con? Sources hint that we'll be at least hearing from Mr. Richman soon. Hope you're not planning a covers album. Do we really need another version of "Knocking on Heaven's Door?"

Whatever you're up to *RI-CHU-MAN-SAN!*, we at Star-Gazer.com have your back.

To send your iCU reports visit: www.Star-Gazer.com/iCU.html and click on the iCU! link.

EPILOGUE

—

BABY, YOU'RE A RICH MAN

ERE AND NOW
Kent and Midori stood on the Kisen Ferry platform waiting to return home: an island in the Sea of Japan off the coast of Niigata Prefecture, a former penal colony and a place of exile. They were returning from Tokyo where during the week Kent had done voiceover work for a new anime series and on the weekend hung out in Harajuku with other *reyazu,* or players. At Midori's urging, Kent had embraced the cosplay world, taking up his own character and costume, which he'd become quite proud of—*Supaiku Supigeru,* Spike Spiegel, the protagonist and tragic hero from *Cowboy Bebop.*

A bounty hunter and former member of the Red Dragon Crime Syndicate, Spike was obsessed with the memory of his time in the Red Dragon organization and his romantic relationship with a strange woman named Julia, as well as his former syndicate partner and villain, Vicious. Spike was a rebel in an electric blue leisure suit, with wild, dark-green hair, and mahogany eyes.

Kent had let his hair grow out longer, even darkened and moussed it for cosplay events. Midori had taught him how to sew and make his own costumes. He won an award for Best Solo Costume at Comiket 2010. He justified his continued cigarette smoking because Spike often had one in his mouth, regardless of rain and *No Smoking* signs. He even enrolled in and stuck with a martial arts class so he could imitate Spike's skill with *Jeet Kun Do*, the form developed by Bruce Lee. Whether at local cosplay parties, in Harajuku's Yoyogi Park, or at the larger cosplay conventions, Kent Richman *was* Spike Spiegel. Rumors of a *Cowboy Bebop* movie left Kent curious enough to mention it to Renzo. But Keanu Reeves had also been mentioned for the part.

The video Hideo and Chieko had captured, including Ozman's attack at Cedars, had gone viral, viewed over one million times on YouTube, launching the young documentarians to temporary celebrity. Hideo was trying to piece together what video he had to complete a full documentary. And when the amateur documentarians and others had asked Kent for more interviews, he declined, despite Renzo's pleas to seize the moment.

"This is the kind of opportunity you were working towards. I've got producers, directors, you name it, calling me every day. Everybody wants a piece of Kent Richman now," Renzo told him one day on the phone.

Ozman's escape and subsequent attack on Kent had put him back on the map, made him the hero he longed to be. *The Strange Bonanza* and other shows wanted him on TV again. Requests for interviews came in weekly, as Renzo continued to point out. But for the moment, Kent was content to take only work behind the scenes:

voiceover work, a few commercial gigs, but nothing in public or on a sound stage. He wasn't sure he'd ever go back, as much as he'd wanted to before. He realized his story would be told, some truth, some rumor, some utter fantasy and lies, no matter what he gave the media. Kent Richman had stopped wanting, for now.

He hadn't forgotten Kumi had left him. The newspapers and tabloids seemed endlessly interested in her whereabouts, especially since she seemed absent, vanished from the print and screen and Tokyo scene. One magazine claimed she'd been tricked into being a mule for drug runners, that because of her Japanese nationality and her celebrity status she could fly under the radar of customs' agents and security personnel more easily than others. Kent hadn't heard from Kumi or anyone representing her, though dozens of media outlets continued to pester him about her. He only knew what he read in the papers and heard on the television news. He had nothing more to give. Kumi was gone from his life, perhaps for good. He could find no other emotion for her but sadness, even if it was only a quiet sadness, a gentle throb under his ribs that evoked the scent of jasmine and the last days of their marriage when he believed in the possibility of its renewal.

Perhaps Kumi had always been a mystery. Perhaps he'd rendered a scrubbed-clean young girl that never existed. Bought into the apple-scented version of Kumiko Sato that the rest of the nation so eagerly embraced. Filled an open vessel with everything he'd wanted her to be, pouring the ashes of his own life into hers. Or perhaps she'd have left him anyway, like Ozman said, vanished without his participation in the drama, his role a simple pawn in a much larger game.

Kumi's battered Saint Christopher, the chain long gone, went into what was left of the ashes of Allan's urn, buried but not so, a lingering sense that she might need it again, his own reliance upon it finished. Kent stored Allan's mostly empty urn in the top of a closet with an old hot plate, a box of Midori's photographs, a sewing kit and light bulbs, an outmoded telephone, and a Hello Kitty cassette player, hidden from sight in the same way that Kumi remained underground. One story did emerge: a minor web-only anime hit called *The Prisoner*, which imagined Kumi as a prison leader named Stella. Kent generally avoided the internet now, but he actually liked *The Prisoner*.

Ozman was back in jail, paralyzed from the waist down after the blow from Oji-san's heavy sword—made from stainless steel, it turned out—fractured one of his cervical vertebra and damaged his spinal cord.

An Osaka theater group was producing a musical of Kent's life. *Big in Japan: The Musical.*

Kent had trouble recalling much of his career. He'd hoped to remember more so he could pen a memoir, tell his story, which he believed to be a good one. And wasn't it? But whenever he sat to write, he managed only a few pages. He thought of his career as he thought of life: he flashed on this earth before he was either extinguished or he flamed out. If he started looking too closely, considering all the possible damage the world could do, he might never step outside the small, seaside house he shared with Midori and never give himself to anything or anyone again. In this way, the past killed, and kept on killing. Who would take that risk? Did he dare? Who would willingly accept the known outcome? His only hope was to be lost in the flash, lucky he looked the other way when the past came back to haunt him.

A FTERSHOCK

Kent and Midori watched the news for hours. A catastrophic earthquake had shaken the eastern coast. They'd suffered only rattling dishes and a photograph knocked off the wall. But tsunamis followed, destroying entire cities and leaving the country in near-nuclear meltdown. Already they were calling it the Great East Japan Earthquake, the largest to hit the nation in recorded history.

Midori finally slept with her head in Kent's lap after a fitful two days during which she'd been unable to reach her parents or her uncle. Oji-san had gotten through earlier in the afternoon to tell her everyone was safe, though the temple had suffered some damage. CNN, BBC, NHK, NTV all maintained a twenty-four-hour vigil over the ruined cities, the extent of the destruction still impossible to accept, footage of water washing cars and houses away like toys in a bathtub. Kent sat in front of the television, unable to move, smoking cigarettes, drinking tea, and watching the same clips over and over.

Kent watched as fire fighters, police, volunteers, and Red Cross workers pulled survivors from the rubble and the burning houses, plucked them from rooftops and floating debris. And they found missing persons, buried but alive, exhausted but strengthened by the miracle of their survival. The camera aimed its lens on the husbands, wives, parents, children, friends, lovers, the curious and horrified bystanders who'd been standing by hoping some divine shaft of light would shine down from the heavens and find their loved ones. *Here they are,* they'd shout in disbelief, hope and joy—and pull them from the rubble, bruised and bloody but alive, ready to tell their story. And the media—the faithful, tireless deliverers of tragedy, the generous syntho-link to human drama—categorized it immediately, distinguishing the saved from the damned, the lucky from the dead.

Kent waited for the telephone to ring with a miracle, for the call that said it was just a mistake, that's all, an accident, but he's all right and she's coming home. And then. That divine shaft of light would illuminate his loss, when that bullet of good fortune struck—struck with all the mystery and extravagance of *Oh my God!* The reported dead and missing called. *Hey, I'm alive.* It *was* a mistake, it really was. *Thank you, God, thank you.*

Would it save him from the future if he just accepted there was nothing he could do to change the past? They either lived or they died. *We were there, just there,* was all he could think. And that he should've been there in the middle of the Great East Japan Earthquake. He should've been amidst the rubble and dust, the toxic wreckage caught between water and fire that brought the cities down. Maybe he would be. Maybe he'd call his mother and father, and tell them, *Yeah it's me, I'm here, yep, right here in the middle of disaster central, buried under a pile of rubble in the dark, air running out, cell phone battery fading, legs crushed, sipping water that drips from the ruins of concrete and steel: The Tohoku Earthquake. What do you think about that? Are we even now? Are we good?*

But he was safe and warm with a woman he'd come to love asleep in his lap. And he wouldn't call.

Midori stirred, barely opening her eyes, a sleepy smile for him.

"What time is it?" she asked.

"I don't know, late," he said. And she returned to sleep, and he returned to the news, the fires of distant tragedy burning burning burning.

ACKNOWLEDGEMENTS

No book is the work of one person. Therefore, I would like to acknowledge and thank the following for their help in making its completion possible:

To Eric Davis, my first reader.

To Kieran Michael Brown who recognized adventure when he saw it.

To Todd Robinson, "Big Daddy" editor at *Thug Lit*, for publishing the story that became the novel, "Big in Japan," and to Katrina Gray, editor at *Atticus Review*, for publishing the short story "Deep Blue Sea," an altered portion of which appears in the novel.

To Sheri Joseph and Josh Russell for always tolerating and answering my many, many questions.

To Patricia Richmond and Andrew Hill for their friendship and their empathy.

To Chad Prevost and Ryan Van Cleave at C&R Press for taking a chance on a story that others didn't know "how to market."

To Andre Dubus, III, for showing me the beauty of the craft and helping me understand the discipline necessary to pursue it.

To Max Currie, for visualizing so beautifully what I saw in my head.

To my brother David who has never been in it for the money.

My love and gratitude to Jack and Myrna Bundy for telling me stories and having books in the house.

Very special thanks to my friend, reader and writer Man Martin for always shining a light into the darkness.

And, of course, to Jamie Iredell, whose friendship and dedication to the craft inspire me daily, who never stopped championing this book, and who told me to "stop revising already."

Finally, my love and deepest gratitude to Jennie and Harper—for without you I would never even make it to the desk.